PRAISE FOR *LET M*

"A wild ride that kept me turning ... ...
are richly drawn with Davis's deft wit, as is the fascinating cast that
populates this astute debut."

—C. J. Washington, author of *Imperfect Lives*

"A fun and timely lens on contemporary Barbados."

—Stephanie Black, filmmaker, *Life and Debt*

LET ME LIBERATE YOU

LET ME LIBERATE YOU

a novel

ANDIE DAVIS

Little
a

Published by Little A, New York

www.apub.com

Amazon, the Amazon logo, and Little A are trademarks of Amazon.com, Inc., or its affiliates.

ISBN-13: 9781662515644 (hardcover)
ISBN-13: 9781662518416 (paperback)
ISBN-13: 9781662515651 (digital)

Cover design by Sarah Congdon
Cover images: © isaxar / Shutterstock; © Kellis / Shutterstock; © good_mood / Shutterstock

Printed in the United States of America
First edition

For Joan and Kortright, my original storytellers

AUTHOR'S NOTE

Over the course of this book's journey to publication, several real-life similarities to the book's fictional events have occurred. I have tried wherever possible to refictionalize. If I've missed anything, dear reader, please take it as coincidence rather than clairvoyance.

Chapter 1

At the far end of a Brooklyn industrial lot, closer than anyone should get to the Gowanus Canal, Sabre Cumberbatch was starting to itch.

Here she was, trapped with three other artists and a *New York Times* reporter in a shipping container turned speakeasy, dreading the moment when it would be her turn to speak.

The leather pants she had foolishly put on for the first time that morning were already stuck to the grime on the bar's couch, which meant she could not move without either ripping the upholstery or adding a sound effect to the interview going on beside her.

The guy being interviewed at the moment, a graffiti artist from Nepal who had not paused for breath in a good five minutes, was claiming with a straight face to be related to the Dalai Lama.

Sabre reached for her drink, a cranberry seltzer. The paper's photographer swooped in to capture the act. She waited until he had finished snapping to glance at the others, putting faces to names that, like those of the graffiti artist and Sabre herself, had been darting around art circles like fireflies the past few seasons.

An African American sculptor who spoke not in sentences but in chips of stone that had to be swept into a pile and decoded. Her index fingers, large, knobby, and callused, had tattoos—a claw on the left one and a beak on the right. Something about a sanctuary for rescued poultry that she planned to open upstate.

A Mexican Korean collagist who worked in found objects. Famous for reproducing the US Constitution in Korean using only pennies from the tip jars of Koreatown nail salons. He had been raised in Provo but spoke fluent Bushwick, and Sabre had been doing her best to avoid eye contact with the gold codpiece winking at her from his open fly.

The reporter wanted them each to reveal something personal. For the fans.

At first Sabre thought that the reporter might be a fan herself, from the way she leaned in. But then she noticed how the reporter nodded hard and narrowed her eyes before someone could finish a point, how she continually flicked her hair even when it wasn't in her face.

The reporter was saving Sabre for last.

~

Something personal? OK, what if she said:

"Jean-Michel Basquiat is not me. Jean-Michel Basquiat is not me and I am not him."

"And you are sure about this?"

"I looked it up."

"Intriguing. Elaborate."

"He was a painter. I am a photographer."

"A painterly photographer. That's the key. Works out better for you, doesn't it? These days anybody with a phone can be a photographer."

"The work is different. His colors and figures are all jumbled up like a riot. Have you seen the stuff I do? Look at the pieces in this bar. Grey and streaky, almost sliding off the walls. You can't compare. He's fighting. I'm running away."

"Ah yes. Let's talk about your anger. Another commonality."

"Anger?"

"Well. Your hair."

"What? Basquiat had big thick dreadlocks, and I'm—"

"Bald! An act of resistance? A postfeminist blah of male hegewhat?"
"It's alopecia."
"A bold choice."

Stuck to a couch, unable to scratch her knees, Sabre could hear her mother now:

Fix your face. Stop this nonsense before you bite the hand that feeding you.

Also:

Flattery leads to flatulence.

That second one had been her mother's mantra since the thesis show at the end of art school, inspired by pieces that did not match their titles, by titles that did not match their backstories, by artists who got on her nerves. Accountants were not built for thesis shows. Unreconciled statements right and left.

At the thesis show, her mother had picked up a spring roll from the refreshment table and found it speared to a cord that brought a flush of confetti down on her head. Suddenly there had been game-show music and a spotlight. The artist had rushed over wearing a toupee. He'd put his arm around her mother and announced through an oversized mic that the work was a meditation on gluttony. He had ended up winning first prize, and the kitchen had run out of spring rolls.

Flattery leads to flatulence. Yet here was Sabre, all of twenty-nine, unable to lift a leg from a decrepit couch.

And why not?

She shifted. The couch protested. There was a scuffle between leather and chintz. A peeved rip. Then the faint but distinct *boi-oi-oing* of a coil springing to freedom from inside the foam.

Everyone snickered, except the sculptor. The reporter moved on to the collagist, whose codpiece sent Sabre a wink from the opposite couch.

Who wouldn't come running when the *New York Times* called? It was surely an upgrade from the kind of coverage she usually got:

headlines that were actual lines about her head, complete with stock photos of her bare scalp or brow. One influencer had taken to calling her "Sabre the Sylph" for being five eight and gangly. Her complexion got a "midnight," or "cocoa," once even a "midnight cocoa," as if cocoa looked any different midnight from midday. Designers she had heard of were sending leather pants to her agent's office. Invitations had begun to pour in from strangers who later claimed she showed up, whether or not she did. She was becoming someone whom certain New Yorkers staked their credibility on appearing to ignore.

The posts, the pants, and the invitations had been as jarring as sunlight to a mole. But when her agent had assured her that this was to be a group interview, Sabre's anxiety had ebbed. A piece on "analogs in the digital age" had seemed comfortably obscure. She had pictured the article nestled in a mossy corner of the paper, deep in the Arts section where few bothered to tread, to which she could retreat now and then for a tangy hit of *New York Times* validation.

Wrong!

A paper with a whole arts section sticking four artists in the Style pages? Really? Of all the times to try out these leather pants. The others were probably thinking she'd worn them to look the part of "badass artist on the rise," when in fact she'd only just realized that this interview was to be one of those "A Night Out with . . ." stories, where they follow some public person around a club, recording everything that comes out of their mouth and everything that goes in. Except now Sabre knew that those, too, were staged, since here they were on a Tuesday morning, door barred and shades drawn against the January glare.

The reporter shot Sabre an anticipatory smile. The itch crept up her legs.

The first time someone had called Sabre "the Basquiat of her generation," it had sounded important, so she'd looked it up. But the only similarities she could find were that they were both Black, and they both got stared at a lot.

Even that comparison was sketchy. For one thing, as far as she could tell, Basquiat had enjoyed the staring. Had lived for it. He had come up from the underground, desperate for the world to know him.

Whereas she had hidden herself down in a darkroom, desperate for the world to forget her.

And not only that.

Basquiat had clearly been born to scribble and paint. To be loud. It jumped out from every square inch of his work: the layers of ideas, references, colors, figures, words, scratches, noise. *Passion.* Something different to notice every time. He had it: true genius. Genius in the wise way. Not in the way people meant it when they talked about her.

All right, then, hissed the hives snaking up her thighs. *Come clean and get this over with.*

The only reason she had started taking pictures was to escape.

At school, the darkest place she could find to hide had been the darkroom in the basement. If that basement had had a coal mine under it, she'd probably have become a coal miner instead.

Yet for all the years she'd spent hiding out in darkrooms since the ninth grade, she had never learned the proper concentration for developer or how much to dilute the fixer. She still could barely tell them apart.

This comparison to Basquiat was as embarrassing as it was ludicrous. It underscored her fraudulence. The only bigger frauds were the people who kept insisting on her genius. Starting with the nuns back in high school, who had encouraged her interest in photography partly to help her cope, true, but mostly as an excuse to inflate the darkroom budget.

In those days, Sabre had been prepared to do anything to get away from the other kids. To disappear. Balding, she had quickly discovered, was the worst move a ninth grader could possibly make. The taunts stuck: Mange Monkey, Bald Pigeon of Bed-Stuy. On the rare occasion she opened her mouth, someone was always there to mock her hot-potato accent. The cold, cracked, grassless playground of Transfiguration High became a prison yard.

She would hide away and cry. Tears from the inside, hair from the outside. Shed till there was almost nothing left of either. Some of the splotches on her early prints had surely come not from the saline solution among the darkroom's chemicals but from the salt of her own tears.

And then those splotches had ended up as her salvation, because from the moment Sabre won her first photo contest at fourteen, nobody cared if she knew a darkroom chemical from a double-glazed doughnut. The streakier and splotchier her work, the more trophies—and the more cash. The judges, reading her slurry abstractions as sophisticated creative choices, declared her a prodigy, mainly because they couldn't make out what the pictures were supposed to be.

From then on, if she wanted to stay a prodigy and keep winning, all she had to do was keep making the same chemical mistake.

Most of the people name-dropping Basquiat couldn't name a single piece of his work. What they liked was his name, the weight of it, on their tongue.

Also—she barely dared think the thought—hadn't Basquiat been a bit of a fraud himself? Sure, he'd acted all tormented by exposure, but he still preened around town, obsessing over whom to be seen with at Studio 54 or wherever. Never met a limelight he hadn't wanted to low-key outline.

All that posturing. All that feeding of people's egos. How draining it must have been.

But that was New York. Shit, that was America.

And here was Sabre Cumberbatch. Bald Pigeon of Bed-Stuy. Teen prodigy. The Basquiat of her generation. Posing in leather pants for the Style section, thighs pickled in hives.

Did people realize that she hadn't just sprung from the concrete? The Bald Pigeon of Bed-Stuy, hatched in the basement of Transfiguration High with a Pentax in her hand?

She'd come from somewhere. She had a trail. Roots.

Roots beyond Brooklyn. Roots that busted through the splotches riding up her legs, not to mention the ones passing for genius on the walls of this bar.

Roots that busted through brick and glass, through the darkroom floor, through the mud underneath it. Roots that shot off, tunneling through the earth, through the sea, all the way to the place where her father had snatched the hairs from her head, one by one, and dragged them with him into a grave:

Barbados.

Lately she'd been thinking about it more and more. As if the harder this city tried to gas her up with its hot air, the harder those Bajan roots were working to hold her down.

How long had she been away? Nineteen years? No, wait—twenty. Damn.

Solid Barbados, grounded and unpuffed. No nonsense. A place where they thought nothing of flunking kindergarteners. It had happened to this one kid she remembered. Year after year, he'd been made to squeeze into a tiny kindergarten desk until he could get his articles right: *a* star, *the* moon, *some* quicksand. The teacher used to rap his knuckles with a ruler whenever he messed up. Harsh, yes. But he'd probably graduated by now. And without anyone pretending that "*a* quicksand" was some genius reimagining of grammar.

Tight desks and rulers were the Bajan love language. Exhibit A: her mother. Exhibit A-plus: her aunt Aggie, her mother's sister, back home in Barbados. The pair of them like two rolls of barbed wire, winding around everything of value and in need of being kept straight. As children, whenever Sabre or her cousin Lisette, Auntie Aggie's daughter, weren't getting lectured about something, all it meant was that they were between barbs, due for the next.

The wire was smooth. The barbs were well spaced. But not so far apart as to allow anyone to forget they were there.

Suppose she'd stayed?

She'd probably be better now. Grounded, unpuffed. She couldn't have bobbed along as she'd been doing here in New York, and even if her whole life had never brought her the kind of money she had made in just one day last fall—when Topsheet, "preferred purveyor of fine linens and bedding for the Netherlands and Netherlands Antilles," lost their Dutch minds and paid $739,000 to use Sabre's photos on their first product line in the States—she'd at least have to know what she was doing.

In Barbados, she'd have to be real. A real *something*. Instead of a fraud, a blimp, filling up on hot New York air, unpopped by Bajan barbed wire.

"Sabre? You with us?"

"Huh?"

Everybody went quiet. The reporter's chin was pointing at her. The photographer slid to her left and began to shoot over her shoulder.

"Your turn." The reporter flicked and smiled. Her head started bobbing.

"I'm sorry," Sabre sputtered. "I can't."

"Are you all right?"

"I—I think I'm getting a rash."

"Humph. Hormones . . . chicken," the sculptor mumbled to the floor. Everyone's eyes converged on the untouched pile of complimentary buffalo wings congealing on the table.

Sabre peeled up from the couch, her bottom ripping off a patch of frayed chintz. "I have to go. Sorry."

"Go! But we haven't—"

"It's all right," said the photographer. "We got a lot of her we can use."

Sabre scrambled for the door, stumbling over the others' feet.

"I'll call you to finish up!" the reporter shouted after her.

The moment she was back outside, lo and behold, the pants started to behave. The rash faded. Even the chintz detached itself and blew away.

Sabre stood in the alley with her coat open to the cold, staring into the peat sky that felt six inches from her face, letting the Gowanus Canal wind wash over her. She took in a deep, cleansing breath of oxygen. And heating oil. And drain cleaner. And rat remains.

And when she breathed out again, she knew.

Knew that she had roots to water. Desks to squeeze into. Rulers and barbed wire to be knuckled and tightened by. To find out for real if she was any good . . . and if so, what for.

Knew, above all, that it was time to get out of this head-bobbing, hair-flicking, leather-panting blimp of a city.

To choose solid over air. Truth over flatulence.

Chapter 2

One thing for sure, thought Isilda Devonish, *the sea makes everything near it a little better.* Like the pinch of salt you added to boiling cassava, or the fresh aloe you rubbed in after washing your hair. Kept the old folks nimble and the young ones strong and lean. Bathed you, fed you, even sang you to sleep. Living this close was real privilege. Like now. Here she was, cooling out on the back veranda with her afternoon scotch and a Cuban cigar, serenaded by invisible waves from South Coast Bay below. Their lullaby lapped along the sloping path, over the hibiscus hedge and the golden-apple trees, across the lawn, and into her ears, a lullaby so sweet and serene that not even the antics of the hyperactive Bastet could ruffle her. Isilda looked on through drooping eyelids at this tuft of fur, who had begun life as Fluffy but been renamed following the family's Egyptian holiday, as he attacked the fringe of a bedspread she had just hung out to dry.

"Shoo, get away," she mumbled, flailing a ringed hand without purpose or effect. Keeping up with that cat was a full-time job in itself, and she—midscotch, post-Ian—was not up to it just now.

She took another unrewarding gnaw on the cigar. *This* was what had had everybody so worked up at last night's party? What with Mr. Toppin producing the humidor from his safe like a deacon at High Mass, looking ready to chant Psalms and sacrifice a ram-goat while he was at it. Justice DaCosta and the other dinner guests taking turns inhaling as the case was passed from nose to nose. What choice had they left her? She had to give it a try, see what the fuss was about. Now it all seemed like some sort of joke, either on her or on them. She dashed the soggy stick away with a suck of her teeth.

This was the time of day that Isilda loved. Ripe afternoon, when Mr. Toppin had returned to the printery, drum-tight with the lunch of ten men. Mrs. Toppin, with her own elastic appetite for the drama of other people's affairs, gone a few blessed hours more. And the twins she could set her watch by. Four twenty-five sharp, they would burst in like wild boars to plant themselves in front of the video-game console in the informal parlor. Their favorite game was nothing but one explosion after another, though sometimes she would get absorbed in it while bringing them their snack. Then one of them—Cedric or Russell, whichever was closer—would catch her and say, *Ready to kill some aliens?* For that he would get a *You hush!* and a flick of her towel to the back of his head.

But all of that was hours away. In the meantime, she had the place to herself. Ian had already come around, and today, for variety, they had tried out the antique love seat in the drawing room. By the end of Ian's lunch hour, as far as she was concerned, that love seat had failed to justify its name. On first inspection it was sturdy, well built, full of promise; but once in action, it was awkward and rickety. Like Ian himself. Isilda overheard her lover now, grunting happily over a cement hill on the construction site next door, and shook her head at how fully his passion for mortar and limestone eclipsed his desire for her. Once again she sucked her teeth hard. Stamina-bodied workmen right and left all over this island but trust her to find the lone specimen who actually turned up at work . . . to *work*. No, talent like hers needed not be wasted on the unworthy. Pearls before swine.

The clock chimed two. She swirled the last scotch drops over her tongue and thought abstractedly of the day's remaining tasks. On her way out this morning, Mrs. Toppin had been babbling about getting the house ready for some relative from overseas, someone important whom she hadn't heard from in years but was now coming to visit, a famous dignitary, some sort of cousin or a niece, but she had been so excitable that only a mind reader could have found instructions in all the babble, and Isilda was not paid to read minds. So nothing to do there. The dinner wares, now those were another story. A mine's worth of party silver she had polished last night and still a mountain of china to put away. Napkins to press and fold and then, though the fridge was crammed with leftovers, lamb chops to season and breadfruit to pickle for lunch tomorrow, because the Toppins would lie down in their graves if ever confronted with the same meal twice. All of it would have to wait until after her manicure.

She swung upright, groaning like a woman twice her forty-one years. As she perched on the edge of the lounge chair to feel for her slippers, something soft tickled her heel. She leaped up, startled, and the crystal goblet she had been drinking from slipped and crashed to the floor.

"Rasshole!"

Bastet scampered from under the chair with a guilty yowl. Isilda's heart began to race. The goblet lay shattered in four. Four gaping, mocking, unglueable shards, one for each dismissal slip she had collected before this job. One for each point of the compass she would have to search for the next. "Christ in Heaven," she wailed. "It done, I done!"

With tears in her eyes, she sat back down, staring into the shards like an obeah woman studying tea leaves. Not hard to predict this one! The Toppins' previous helper, a woman from Isilda's own district, had been shown the door for putting one of Mrs. Toppin's silk tops through the spin cycle one day. Though it had come through in one piece, Mrs. Toppin had insisted that the fabric's weft was ruined. Over this mysterious "weft," she had fired a woman who had been with the family nearly five years, even seen fit to take the cost of the blouse out of her last wages. That had left less than the bus fare home. Luckily Mr. Toppin had intervened in time to send her off like a human being, slipping an envelope into her bag with a finger to his lips. Then again, that was over a piece of cloth, not crystal or an overrated Cuban cigar. It was easy to be generous with other people's treasures. But this time?

On that, the shards had nothing to say. Isilda swept them into a paper bag and mopped down the place as she had never mopped before.

She needed to think. She reached into her skirt pocket and pulled out a pen and the small notebook where she kept her recipe ideas. Flipping past pages of test-kitchen notes, she found a blank page.

Glass, she scribbled at the top.

She drew a couple of lines down the page and stopped. The pen hovered expectantly. Finally, she wrote:

A. beg pardon

B. put back

C. (And here the pen seemed to finish it for her.) *OUT*

Beg? Beg who? Mrs. Toppin was no sweetbread! No matter how she coaxed Isilda to "call her Aggie" whenever the spirit took her, Isilda always considered that invitation as solid as the breath it had taken to utter it. People didn't call Mrs. Toppin "the Terror" for nothing. As for Mr. Toppin, round and jolly like a Father Christmas and always up for second and third helpings of Isilda's dessert recipes when his wife wasn't about, she could no easier explain to him why she had been using that goblet in the first place. It might only make him curious as to what else she had been dipping into around here—and then see how quick his sweet would sour.

She scratched out *A.* On to *B*, and the crystal cabinet in the dining room. Already the missing goblet was throwing off the display's symmetry. Isilda solved this problem by removing a glass from the other side, leaving only six. She looked at the bottom of the stem. *Lotus by Lalique,* it read. *Made in France.* Crap.

She decided to phone Heron's, the department store in town, to see if they had any in stock. While she waited for the salesman to return, her mind ran ruefully to the forty dollars in her pocket, and the Double Draw lottery tickets she might have to forgo this week.

"Right," said the salesman finally. "That's $250 Barbadian, $122.95 US, or duty-free US $97.95."

"Hummuch?"

Moments later she was picking her way across the construction site, to the very man whose days atop her belly she had just decided to number.

~

Ian felt the hair on his neck stand up even before he saw her.

"Come for a little more, eh?" he joked, but his voice cracked on the "eh."

"What? Man, I got real problems, hear? Listen."

Ian listened, with a sinking feeling. He was beginning to sense that this woman did not share his work ethic. Isilda had the wrong idea about him. He wasn't some pickup artist in a hard hat. When it came to idling on a job, he trailed industry standards. That rarely stopped women from rising to bait he hadn't thrown, but most of the time he was too deep in his own zone to notice.

Isilda, however, was an exception. On his first day at the site, he had spotted her, conspicuously picking limes from the Toppins' tree with her skirt billowing up around her thighs. At the first good gust, she had flashed him in full and shot him such a brazen smile that by the end of the week, she had become a major distraction. Yet soon enough Ian discovered that, like the antique mahogany love seat on which they had not long ago made love, Isilda was gorgeous, practical, and sparklingly unique—but also creaky and in constant need of waxing. Her appetite was not for the faint-hearted. She would suck her teeth if she caught him checking his watch, or curse under her breath if he gingerly floated the idea of returning to work. And now, just as he was about to pour a foundation, here she was with this "emergency."

"All right," he said at last. "Hold on a minute."

He went to find the contractor and came back after a brief discussion. "Come."

"Dropping me in town?"

"You come."

~

They got into his truck, Isilda still clutching the goblet and the bag of crystal shards.

They rode along without saying much, Isilda studying Ian's profile. *So he good for something after all,* she thought. Her mind raced ahead to the little scene at the cash register when she'd reach for her wallet, but in his mannishness he would insist on paying for the glass himself.

To break the silence, she remarked, "But look how you does be catchin' ya ass just for lil' bread, nuh."

"I ain't know who tell you to trouble the people things."

"When I get back, I goin' give that blasted cat *one* kick—"

"The cat? You know you ain't had no right with the glass. If you was Miss Toppin, I sure you wouldn't like it."

"Wait, you is a parson now?" Isilda snapped. "I does go church 'pon a Sundy, I ain't want no sermon from you."

"Easy, sweetness."

"*If* I was Miss Toppin? If I was she, I woulda pay people decent, that is what! Giddem ways an' means. Think that big house easy to clean?" She sucked her teeth. "Look, so long as they paying me short, don't blame me for making up the balance, hear?"

Ian shut his mouth. He swung off the highway down a palm-fringed drive.

"Where we going?" asked Isilda nervously. "A shortcut?"

"Heron's you want, right? Well, I think they have a branch at this hotel. Might save the trip to town."

"Oh, thank you, Jesus!" She snatched up his free hand from the gearstick and bathed it in kisses. "You ain't so bad, you know."

"Oho? Cussin' done now?"

"Hush, baby. Don't take me on. Give ya a proper thanking when we reach back." She cupped his hand to her breast, and Ian squirmed.

~

The hotel was one of Barbados's oldest landmarks, a structure as unduly arrogant as the second-string English gentry it had been built for a hundred years earlier. A sprawling horseshoe with its back to the road and its Spanish-style balconies bracing the wind, it rose six stories on a network of deep stone arches, like a troll with too many eyes and a grotesque grin. Each interior archway encased a flight of stairs leading to the upper suites, and scattered across the courtyard were a few shops and offices.

Ian and Isilda found the place all but deserted. As they crossed the courtyard on the way to Heron's, they heard a woman giggle out from one of the archways, "Ooh, your Honor! Hold me, hold me in contempt—right *there*!"

When they reached the archway, they saw the back of a pear-shaped, middle-aged man groping a slim woman whose face was hidden by the man's flab. "All rise!" The woman was giggling. The man let out a strange growl and shoved his hand down the woman's bikini bottom. "Enter the verdict, my lord!" cried the woman in a rasp. "Enter your ver-*dict*!"

The voice. I know that voice, thought Isilda.

The couple shifted forward. Isilda leaned in to look. Sure enough, there before her eyes was none other than Justice DaCosta, last night's dinner guest, with one hand firmly burrowed in the crotch of her own boss, Mrs. Toppin.

"Mistress!"

In shock Isilda dropped the other glass on the tile.

The couple leaped apart at the noise like two atoms rebounding from collision. Seeing Isilda, Mrs. Toppin gave a little squeal, and both she and the judge dissolved into spasms.

"Isilda! What are you . . . why aren't you . . . where you think . . ."

"Mistress . . ."

"I . . . but . . . Answer me, girl! Wh-what is going on here?"

"Mistress . . ."

They trailed off dismally. To fill the dead air, Ian piped up. "Um, one of your glasses broke at the house, and we were just looking to replace it, ma'am."

Mrs. Toppin shot a hard glance at this stranger, at the broken goblet on the tile, then back at Isilda. She tugged at her swimsuit and looked as if she were seriously considering ducking behind the dripping judge, who by this time had backed deep into the arch and turned his face, as though hoping the white walls would somehow camouflage him.

For a moment everyone stood gaping, listening to each other's nervous breathing. Isilda stared at her boss, whom she scarcely recognized without her dark suit and frown, and took in the green-and-gold bikini, the nearly two-dimensional physique, the tiny liposuction scar under her navel, and the bright orange polish on her toes, which Isilda herself might have sampled had she known it was in the house. Then she looked at the judge, whose trunks still clung to his groin beneath the swell of his paunch. A gut to be rivaled only, as these things go, by that of Mr. Toppin. For such a spindly thing, Mrs. Toppin certainly liked them large.

At this Isilda burst out laughing and could not make herself stop. She shrieked and howled and sputtered and doubled over, so long and hard that, out of awkwardness, the others half-heartedly joined in. Still wiping her tears, Isilda bent over and began to add the shards of glass to the bag she was carrying.

Mrs. Toppin stepped forward. "Is that—that wasn't one of the Laliques, I hope?"

"Yes, mistress—two of them. One that break in the house, and the next one that drop just now when I . . . er, just now."

"Two!" winced Mrs. Toppin. She glared at the top of Isilda's bent head, and then again at Ian. Her mouth opened and closed and opened again.

"Two!" she repeated. "Well! Let's look on the bright side, eh? At least there's an even number left."

Isilda gawked up at her.

"Might find them over at Heron's," suggested Ian.

"Yes, we . . . I was just going to look, mistress."

Mrs. Toppin tittered. "Oh! Don't be silly," she cried. "It's just a glass, after all. Glasses break, don't they? It's not your job to replace them. You and this young man"—she paused for an introduction, but none came—"you and your friend didn't have to trouble yourself like this. Imagine!"

She gave that strange little laugh again and glanced behind her, but by this time the judge had managed to slink away up the stairs. She spun back around.

Isilda stood upright. "All right, then, mistress," she said. "Sorry 'bout . . . you know, the glasses and—"

"Ah! You don't worry, dear," cried Mrs. Toppin. "Off you go. I'll be . . . um . . . well, drive safely, hear?"

"Yes, mistress."

"'Mistress, mistress!' Now, Isilda, how many times must I remind you to call me Aggie?"

Chapter 3

As soon as things were quiet, all the composure Aggie thought she had been maintaining unraveled. Wheeling around, she flew back across the yard and took the stairs three by three to the top floor of the hotel. She barged into the suite to find Justice DaCosta lounging on the bed in a giant terry-cloth robe, watching CNN. She sank down breathless beside him.

"Hubert, how are we going to handle this?"

He lay there as though it were the wind addressing him. His handsome face, which must have put the swing to many a hip in its day, now had a way of shutting down completely. Still, neither age nor stubbornness nor the extra upholstery about the jawline could dull its appeal. Eyes that danced. Broad, smooth lips, quick to crescent into a smile. The reddish dent in his once-pierced earlobe. Ruddy olive skin, from presumed Persian ancestors who in fact had drifted up from Venezuela. All of these sat dumbly gnawing at Aggie's patience, until finally the eyebrows twitched.

"Shouldn't be too bad, though, right?" he said.

"Not too bad? Not too *bad*! That girl goin' rake me over the coals!"

"No need to exaggerate."

"Oh. I see! Think you going be so calm when it's all over the blooming island that Clive Toppin wife horn him with his best friend? Eh? Eh?"

"Look, just consider—"

"*You!* Consider *this!* That *I!* Could be in *debt!* To dah rasshole *maid!* For the *rest!* Of *my! Life!*" Aggie karate-chopped each line, her language forsaking the high road for the comfort of Bajan dialect. "Lord know what it goin' take to keep dah trap shut now. Shoulda never follow you down here! I knew it was too risky. I told you. I *warned* you!"

"In debt to the maid now? Aggie, Aggie, Aggie." He pulled her down on top of him and began to rock. "Come. Analyze this thing properly. Who is this woman?"

Aggie shook her head in exasperation.

"The maid, Aggie. A *maid*—"

"Who goin' be livin' like a raja when she get through with the two of us."

"But how, sweetheart? Who besides her and that scruffy chap saw anything? So long as it's her word against yours, you clear. Right?"

He planted a gentle kiss at the top of her head. Aggie raised herself up from his paunch and glared.

"That's your grand solution? That my maid can run 'bout the place licking her mouth and nobody goin' listen? You're a case!" She sprang up. "You don't seem to realize we got serious problems. And I mean *we!* Don't tell me you don't care if this get back to Nancy?"

Hearing his wife's name, Hubert raised the TV volume and let out a dramatic sigh. "Agatha, how old are you?"

"What?"

"I am fifty-eight years old," he said, his voice suddenly magisterial. "My wife is fifty-six. We have been married for over thirty years. So I know how to keep my house in order. Now, however it may be with you and Clive, my advice to you is this: if you are not up to this kind of thing, then it is time for you to find some other source of amusement."

"Source of amusement! What the hell you think this is at all?" She shoved her quivering face within a half inch of his. "*Now* you goin' see! I ain't nobody's little play toy, hear? If that is all the respect you can find for me, you can forget it! Forget it!"

She stalked around the bed into the bathroom and slammed the door behind her.

~

Hubert continued to stare at the screen, or into it, and took himself summarily through the old paces.

The maid and the maid's man, for Pete's sake. Took an amateur like Aggie to lose it like this. Too much reality TV. In real life these types rarely thought that far, and those who did usually had poor leverage.

Of course there'd be talk; the help always blabbed. It was practically in their job description. The amount of scandals his own name had been put to—real and imagined. But when all was said and done, was he any poorer for it?

In any event, Nancy could be guaranteed to be deaf to yet another rumor.

Good. He fluffed the pillow and switched to ESPN.

~

In the gleaming marble bathroom, Aggie locked eyes with her own reflection.

So much for the intricate plotting and timing: who would book this room in whose name, who would park where when, who would sneak in from the beach . . . All now down the drain.

What was Isilda capable of, exactly? Aggie had never had reason to test her claws.

Seriously, what was she in for, with Isilda in the catbird seat?

An anonymous note to Clive? A demand for a 300 percent raise? Leftovers at the next dinner party?

Horrid scenarios continued to lunge from the shadows until vanity rescued Aggie with a distraction: Did Hubert just let slip that Nancy was fifty-six?

Aggie's eyes traveled the length of her body, by any standard ravishing in its new swimsuit. Slim, angular, and freshly taut, a pair of ribs and some stubborn belly fat having been resettled on a rubbish heap behind a clinic in Buenos Aires. That surgeon had been worth every cent. The trainer, the colorist, and the aesthetician were earning their keep, and good genes took care of the rest.

In other words: at fifty-two, with the right lighting and a custom support bra, Aggie could easily pass for Nancy DaCosta's daughter!

This sunbeam burst through her despair and warmed her to the tips of her burnt-orange toenails.

Yes, she was beautiful, her prime indefinite, and despite her age, this fact still mattered to Aggie as much as it did when she was just a little cygnet trailing behind her three sisters, the coveted Ifill swans of Comfort Seat. People used to go to their windows to watch them pass on their way to school, their backs straight as cane stalks, pressed grosgrain ribbons at the ends of their long plaits, careful to lift their feet off the gravel to avoid the dragging sound their father said was "common." To Conrad Ifill, common was what you were until proven uncommon, and in the meantime the punishment was his own lethal contempt. And everyone in Comfort Seat came in for a dose.

His favorite pastime had been to send suitors flying, all the impudent guttersnipes who dared to come calling for Madge or Evelyn or Priscilla. He had a whole science to it. Those with the gall to knock at the front door got run off by the dogs, while the ones who knew to appear meekly at the side door simply came in for a well-rehearsed earful.

"Boy, look here," he would say to the fool in question, pointing out the fowl pen, the pigpen, and the endless rows of ground provisions. "See what my girls accustom to? Who can't give them better ain't got no right at me. You young fellows' foot too hot and yuh pocket always bruck—clear out!"

Aggie grew up watching her ironmonger father smelt every budding romance down to nothing, her sisters' hearts tinkered and pounded like alloys. But in the end it was Aggie herself who stood longest by the fire. By the time her turn was up, field-workers, tradesmen, their sons, and the sons of their sons all knew better than to try. Her own father would not have made the cut.

Throughout her adolescence, as others were taking their first taste of love deep in the moonlit cane fields, Aggie's knees were glued tight. And tight they stayed, until through the front door one evening strolled Clive Toppin, an affable young man of whom little more was known than that he worked at his family's printing press in Hastings and had taken a liking to the twenty-four-year-old Aggie, then a shop clerk in town.

After the wedding Aggie lost no time in producing a daughter and naming her Lisette, after the mother-in-law whom she considered the summit of human kindness for smiling occasionally and seldom forgetting her name. Then, armed with the right props—an heir and an air—she took to the stage for the role she had been preparing her whole dreamlife long.

That it came so naturally, right from the start, surprised even her. Ingenue though she was, she seemed to sense, as if by instinct, just how to raise her eyebrows in greeting the gardener: high enough to suggest *Fine day, isn't it,* but too low to be mistaken for *How lovely to see you!* The trick was to work in a little frown at the bridge of the nose, rather than arching the brows from the center, since an arch might convey warmth, and who wanted to convey that. She knew how familiarity could breed, quicker than fruit flies on a rotten soursop.

Her innate sense of the order of things held up at teas and cock-tails, too. At first she had a grateful smile for whoever would bother to mash her toe. But in time she recognized the game, and her mingling and consorting began to take on a poker-like shade. Bishop trumped deacon, cabinet member trumped Member of Parliament, surgeon trumped dermatologist, unattached high rollers wild . . .

And when the night came and Clive rolled on top of her, how quickly she learned to regard his earnest puffs and grunts as the small price of all this *ha . . . ha . . . hap*-piness!

It was not until around Lisette's twelfth birthday that the first fissures of discontent began to appear. By that time a veteran of the leisure class, Aggie found herself growing restless despite the lull of comfort. Her daughter had breezed into the most prestigious secondary school in Barbados, having been tutored for her entrance exam by that school's own teachers. The family's printing business had expanded and absorbed more of her husband's attention. She was riding the social carousel more or less on autopilot, as others' prospects of outclassing her faded in proportion to her fortune. And so, to ease the boredom, she announced to Clive one day that she wanted another child. He was so delighted that, with his typical exuberance, he gave her two.

The mommy to whom Cedric and Russell were born was not the same shy newlywed of the first go-round. This one wore the comfort of a matriarch. No more fretting over unkempt hair or whose child might score higher in arithmetic. This time Aggie flung herself headlong into motherhood, unburdened by the vanity and insecurity she had felt in the past. She accepted their warm, grubby-faced hugs with glee, laughed as they tried in vain to repair a dissected lizard before giving up and leaving another mess for the housekeeper to clean. She planned elaborate birthday parties, picked out songs for them on the piano, and made it her mission to feed their bottomless appetite for books and games. And gradually, the voices in her head fell silent.

When the twins began to shine at school, Aggie was not surprised. Back in her own schooldays at Comfort Seat Primary, she had rarely missed the top ten in any subject. She spent her days watching Lisette blossom into young adulthood and the twins grow more independent, and she glowed with maternal pride. These were her fruit, *her* progeny, born to all that she scarcely had known to dream of as a girl. Young, beautiful, moneyed, and bright, with the glittering path of their futures stretching infinitely skyward before them. *Her* children . . .

When did the cloud finally steal across her heart? Aggie could not say. But gradually, the same sense of dissatisfaction that had led to the birth of her twins calcified into a vague, undirected resentment. Though lacking nothing, she began to fancy herself a victim of life's caprices, condemned to underachieve by the timing and circumstances of her own birth. The petty contests to which she and her friends subjected each other grew boring, although she made sure to remain at the head of the pack all the same. She craved novelty, passion, a sense of completeness, and she felt that some implacable force was holding her back. She began to take competitive interest in Lisette's homework, looking over her daughter's shoulder and secretly racing her to the solutions. At parties she strayed from the usual polite, vacant patter to political debates, where even those closest to her would not be spared a public duel.

And that was why nobody blinked when Aggie, all forty-eight years and mother-of-three of her, chased her adrenaline addiction all the way to its logical extreme: law school. After graduation she set up an office in plush Sandringham, where clients happily paid top dollar for the histrionics she was selling in place of experience. Week after week they streamed in to watch her lay waste to opposing counsel, no account too trivial for a pageant.

"Sir, am I to understand that your client, whose 'restaurant'— loosely speaking, of course—negligently poisoned my client with a cockroach-laden soup, now proposes to make my client whole by serving him a *second* course of roach soup? Poison for poison, that's your idea of a settlement? Don't call here again until you're ready to talk business!"

Each time she annihilated the enemy, Aggie could feel the power building inside her. High on herself she would charge down the highway, confident at last that her life was hitting every mark. In this new spirit of conquest, she began to take the family on holidays to places like Egypt and Borneo and Machu Picchu, to collect imperial furniture and leather-bound first editions of anything she could.

And she did not stop there. At night when she climbed in beside her husband, it was not unusual for her to mount him, to make it worth his while and leave him spent and flagging in a corner, all without uttering a word. Clive mistook these episodes for evidence of long-overdue passion, which he was only too glad to indulge. It was true he had never stopped thanking the stars for the gift of this extraordinary woman. As he drifted off in blissful stupor, Aggie would lie awake, turning him over and over in her head, like a beloved pair of old shoes that had grown too tight and did not quite match the new bag. Flat and comfortable, they might well come back in style one day, but . . .

Once again, the familiar rumblings of discontent began to stir. Aggie tried to quiet them with the logical reasoning she had mastered in law school:

Happiness equals success.

Success equals doting husband, cheerful children, bright career, cellulite-free thighs.

Ergo . . .

Happiness equals husband, children, career, thighs.

Conclusion: happiness, *c'est moi.*

Logical reasoning had its limits, so over time she learned to find distractions whenever the pangs surged: buying something extravagant for Clive, redecorating a guest room, planning the next holiday, having the fat sucked from her something, or terrorizing the household staff.

And so Aggie was overripe for the plucking on the morning that Justice Hubert DaCosta accidentally brushed his leg against hers, once, twice, then seven times, as they sat across from each other during a motion hearing. Prior to that moment, Aggie had never dreamed of an affair, seduction having always been, to her, a game in which the winning mattered more than the prize. Besides, Clive and Hubert had been thick as thieves since childhood.

How uncouth even to contemplate such a thing.

How uncouth and savage.

And wanton, and deviant. *And* vulgar.

And now, four months in, here she was sniffling in a bathroom mirror.

How could she have let him drag her down to this? One wink from an aging playboy and she was ready to abandon her dignity? Then try to reason with him, and what? Dismissing her like a common mosquito. No one, from the president of the republic back down, treated Agatha Toppin so. If any dismissing were going on around here, it would be done by her! But she would show him, oh yes, him and that flouncy maid, too. She would show them both.

Aggie pulled herself together, dabbed at the waterproof mascara racing down her cheeks, and got dressed. Chin in the air, she swung open the bathroom door and went straight for her bag on the table beside the TV. Out of the corner of her eye, she could see Hubert preparing to roll what should have been a postcoital joint.

"You good now, darling?" he asked sweetly.

Aggie could not resist. She swung around to face him. "Hubert, lovie, I think this has gone far enough," she trilled. "Let's call it a day. Don't want things getting too serious. But, you know, I enjoyed myself, I did. Just now we'll be laughing at this whole mess. OK? Well, I'm off. Take care."

She made for the door and was almost home free when a voice that turned her knees to pap growled, "Aggie, come here to me."

She dared not face him. "What now?"

The next instant she was enveloped in terry cloth, a tongue tip in her ear, one hand caressing her nipple and the other riding up her miniskirt. Aggie's breath caught in her throat.

Teasing her earlobe between his teeth, Hubert muttered, "If you really want to go, then go. But make sure you call me when you ready. Hear? Anytime you ready . . ."

On the drive home an hour later, she commended herself that at least she had resisted that joint. After all, she needed her wits about her to figure out what to do next.

～

The next morning, Isilda begged off sick for the first time in her employ. Aggie was tremendously relieved. And yet a part of her worried whether this could be the beginning of Isilda's impertinence. Afraid to launch an offensive lest she offend, she accepted the sickout, kept busy, and braced herself for she knew not what.

Chapter 4

But Isilda, for her part, had no plans. No sail rigged to ride an unexpected tailwind. Instead, she spent the day sucking on the episode like a juicy marrowbone, the crunchy-salty sweetness of the scandal at turns mortifying and tickling her.

These rich people. What could have possessed Mrs. Toppin to look twice at the likes of Hubert DaCosta? You want to step out, fine, but at least step *up*!

There was nothing Hubert could offer that Mrs. Toppin wasn't already getting at home, and without putting up with his demeanor to get it. His voice had one of those low gurgles that always sounded like he was about to hack and spit. He had a way of tilting back as if to see you better, only to look right through you like you were not there. He even looked at his wife like that—when he looked at her at all.

Why God didn't give out taste the same time he was sharing out money and brains, who could say. Isilda felt downright embarrassed for Mrs. Toppin and, for that matter, Mrs. DaCosta, too.

She returned to work the next day, determined to keep her head even lower than usual. Ian was already on the job when she reached the construction site. As she passed, he looked up from his paperwork and dashed her a devious smirk that nearly made her pee her pants.

"Behave, yuh clown," she hissed. Of all the mornings for Mr. Stickback to get slack. Ian rearranged his face and turned his back. As she entered the house through the side door, Isilda cleared her throat and strained to compose herself with sober thoughts:

Unemployment. Diabetes. And of course, her longtime nemesis: aspartame, foulest sugar substitute ever belched from the innards of hell. Aspartame was proof that people with no cane-cutting in their blood had no business making bold to come up with replacements for sugar. Leave that to the likes of Isilda, whose own parents cut cane until their wrists knotted up like mammee apples. Her father had died of diabetes, and her mother, like many from that generation, was living with diabetes now, yet still didn't think twice to put three sugars in her Ovaltine and four biscuits around the saucer. Isilda was determined to find a substitute they could take to; she'd been experimenting with all kinds of things. The answer was right around the corner.

Sounds of movement inside the kitchen brought her back to the present. Taking a deep breath, she pushed open the swing door.

"Morning, Isilda."

It was Mrs. Toppin's daughter, Lisette. Isilda relaxed in her bones.

Lisette was tottering about the kitchen searching for something, which could have been anything, as she was a rare visitor to these parts.

"Morning," Isilda replied. "Need help?"

"Have you seen my Versace coffee mug?"

"Coffee? Not too sure," Isilda answered, taking in for the first time the idea that anyone in the house drank the stuff. Then again, Lisette had studied overseas, in a coffee-drinking place, and seemed never to have fully planted all ten toes back on Bajan soil.

"I need it for this Friday when I go to the airport," Lisette said, as she crossed to a cupboard on the other side. "I'm the one picking up Sabre." She had on a multipocketed khaki suit that made her look like an animal trainer, and her dolly feet—size seven, as Isilda's investigations had long ago determined—were stuffed inside a pair of shiny, black, red-bottomed heels.

"Oh yes. The cousin from New York."

"Mm-hmm. Mummy left that for you." Lisette pointed to a sealed envelope on the counter. "She had to take off early today."

Isilda's heart quickened. So this was how it was going to be! Out of a job for doing the right thing, all over a stupid glass. Meanwhile, that unmannerly cat, the true culprit when you really got to the bottom of it, would continue getting fat on meals he didn't do a thing to deserve. The injustice of this world sickened the soul.

Lisette's mumblings—cousin this, coffee that—fell away as Isilda opened the envelope with a quivering finger and peeked inside.

Dear Isilda, the printed note began, *I do hope you are feeling better. Please pardon the urgency of this request, but as my niece will be arriving this weekend, there are a number of tasks, which I respectfully ask you to prioritize today . . .*

So . . . she *wasn't* being fired? Isilda drew the paper out of the envelope, and two one-hundred-dollar bills fell out. She caught them to her chest before they could get far. Lisette didn't notice.

Isilda scanned the to-do list, undaunted by the fact that it ran onto a second page. Of course she would do them all, or at least the ones that could be easily checked: she had a job to keep!

The note ended: *Given that the above workload may prove inordinately arduous, kindly accept the enclosed bonus in appreciation of your dedication and discretion. With thanks, A. Toppin.*

No wonder people paid this woman to talk. She had the gift. Isilda gave the note and envelope another shake to check for stray bills, then tucked them into her apron pocket. Exhaling with relief, she went over to the fridge and helped herself to a big glass of cool water. Once the house was all hers, dedicatedly and discreetly, she and Ian were for sure going to celebrate today.

"There it is. Finally." Lisette pulled out a black travel mug with a bejeweled lion-looking face on the front, the perfect accessory for her circus-tamer outfit.

Isilda tried not to laugh. "Oh, goody," she muttered politely, hoping Lisette would soon be on her way. The Toppins' esteem for their drinkware was really something.

"I needed this, see?" Lisette said. "With my fancy cousin coming. Got to make sure I come correct when she sees me. It looks good in my hand, right?"

She posed with the mug and laughed a little ashamedly at herself, an echo of Mrs. Toppin's nervous titter at the hotel two days before. Then she lingered, as though expecting a response, so Isilda asked if she and the cousin were close and prayed for a one-word reply.

"Like sisters. Ever since. I really hope she likes it here. I wonder what's bringing her home. If she even thinks of it as home! That grand piano in the parlor? She and I used to play together. Make sure and polish it good. She's an artist, you know, she would have an eye for these things. Famous in New York. Just poof, out of nowhere. Well, not nowhere. You know how I mean. New York is big-time. The biggest. You know how many people dream of . . ."

On and on she went, while Isilda nodded and fondled the bills in her pocket, picturing herself astride Ian on top of the piano, wearing nothing but this apron and some too-tight heels, just as soon as Lisette would shut her mouth and be off with her lion-face cup.

∼

Grantley Adams International Airport was the usual hive of inertia it became whenever a large jet was due in. People sauntered into the arrivals area like cowboys entering a saloon, exchanging terse nods and angling for the best positions to stand and wait for passengers. Jingling keys, scrolling phones, checking watches by the half minute and shifting from flip to flop, they took in the scene around them, a scene rewarding to the well-trained eye.

For those who live in a big place, an airport holds limited thrill. But in a small place, it is the downbeat of a pulse, the reassuring prelude to one's blip on the radar screen. Small-place people tend to keep their antennae raised to catch the signal, convinced that the world is happening somewhere else.

A single sweeping gaze is as good as an hour's observation if one knows what to look for, as Bajans do. A simple technique allows them to calibrate with molecular precision the general decency of a crowd, and their own place within it. This is key to determining how one should behave, how one should stand, which muscles to clench and which ones to relax, the appropriate range of swivel in one's neck, where and on whom to let one's gaze fall. In any setting this technique is second nature to a Bajan, though anyone with enough will and perseverance can master it, too.

Survey the landscape using a "melanometer." (Those not issued a melanometer at birth, as most Bajans are, have to develop one through practice.) Like a photographer's light meter, which calculates the ratio of light to shadow, the melanometer measures the collective melanin content of a crowd and calculates the average tonal factor (ATF). This ATF can be any point along the spectrum of complexion from barley-water white to coal-cinder black, a spectrum encompassing such permutations as light, fair, clear, clammy cherry, gooseberry, ginger, spoil yam, sapodilla, olive, yellow, red, weak tea, high brown, musky, dusky, Milo, and brown. Though the melanometer can be thrown off in the presence of British tourists, who tend to overexpose in the heat, it is essential that its first reading be trusted, before the eyes have a chance to adjust. This will serve as the baseline.

Now, if the ATF reads gooseberry or darker, adjust it according to the presence of the following: late-model phones, lighter; raffia baskets, darker; loud conversations with much gesticulation (in European-sounding languages, lighter; in local dialect, darker); eating from a greasy paper bag (with visible napkin, lighter; without, darker); gold (rings, lighter; teeth, darker). Lastly, fine-tune the reading based on the following criteria: recognition of faces, accuracy of past readings, gut reaction, appraisal of own decency, faith in value of exercise.

With practice all this occurs in a fraction of a second, down in the folds of the subconscious, resulting in a final crowd-decency rating on, say, a scale of one (darkest, lowest) to ten (lightest, highest). It is wondrous in its subtlety, like breathing or swallowing, a complex exercise one learns to perform without thinking.

Standing there with her arms folded, Lisette did not realize that the figure she had assigned her surroundings upon arrival was a 7.2. The ATF had come in at a respectable enough weak tea, but on the way in from the car park, she had seen a woman with a raffia basket slapping a little boy who seemed to have spilled something down his shirt, and this had put her off enough to send the decency factor tumbling. Oblivious to the workings of her melanometer, Lisette stiffened her upper back and hoped—as her eyes wafted over the tour guides laminated like the placards they held aloft; the clumps of taxi drivers ready to pounce; and the wide, empty gangway through which their prey would soon pour—that the new Sabre would not find the place too provincial.

After all, she could never have become what she was had she stayed. It had not been in the cards for her.

~

Their first exchange in nearly twenty years had been a surprise.

Sabre had found Lisette on Instagram. Lisette had at first been delighted to hear from the cousin whom she had had to train herself over time to forget. Then she'd been awed that the training had been so successful that it had never occurred to her to try to look Sabre up. And finally, she was gobsmacked to discover that her geeky, implacable cousin now had thirty times the followers Lisette did, and with about a third as many posts.

Sabre was *famous*-famous. Yet just as awkward and anachronistic as Lisette remembered.

Liz! Are you here? Sabre had written, as though yoo-hooing through a kitchen window instead of an activity-tracking app that could have answered the question for her. Dazed by the follower count, Lisette had tried to sound casual. *Say! Waddup girl?* Heart-eyes emoji. *Been a while.*

Coming home. Need to! Medicinal. Crying emoji.

"Home"? The word felt . . . unright. Lisette's long-lost, big "twin sister." The living departed. First callus on her heart. One moment they were together, girls in matching dresses bellowing and banging on the piano, trying to bump each other off the stool; the next Sabre was watching her father being lowered into the ground, and then she was spirited away to the States with Aunt Cil, never to return.

Never, until now. Coming "home," with a bald head and a stardust tail. And an ailment?

Oh wow. You OK? Lisette had typed. Worried emoji, gleaming-heart emoji.

Sabre replied with a thumbs-up emoji. *Hope to be. Auntie Aggie says I can stay.*

Lisette sent a thumbs-up and a prayer-hands emoji and scrolled Sabre's page for clues.

When? she asked.

Next week. Nervous emoji. *Cray ZAYYY.*

One of the more recent posts showed Sabre smiling at a podium, shaking hands with a woman who appeared to be the head of a corporate team. Captioned in another language as well as in English, it seemed to have been reposted from a PR firm. *Proud to partner with the incomparable Sabre Cumberbatch . . .* the English caption began.

Incomparable. Well, that she had always been. Some people are incomparable because they are peerless, and some are so overlookable as not to warrant comparison in the first place.

And despite the hand she had been dealt, Sabre had always ended up in the first camp.

Wonderful! Can't wait, Lisette had typed back.
Double-kiss emoji, triple-clap emoji.

⁓

Sabre had left Barbados at the age of nine, right before things got real
for kids at school. Back then, anyone who hadn't found a way to secure
their future by age ten was better off running away to America.

It started with preparations for the high school entrance exam,
known as the "Eleven Plus" for the age at which all Barbadian children
had to compete for places in the island's high schools. Beginning in the
previous year, those who could afford it would hire teachers from elite
schools as exam tutors, the same teachers who would soon welcome
them into their classrooms if the applicants were successful. Those who
couldn't hire tutors fell back on whatever resources they had: work-
books, class prep, genetics. The entrance exam was given on a single
day, with no special accommodations or provisions for makeup tests.
Woe to the sick, the maladjusted, the panic-stricken, the fainting-prone,
the incontinent. A single test set the arc of one's destiny from eleven
to eternity.

Then, once set, the arc had to be followed. The brightest kids studied medicine and became doctors. Those who were bright and aimed
for medicine but missed, they landed in the catch bin below with the
general scientists. Those who were almost as bright as the scientists
but were bad with numbers studied letters and eventually went to law
school or became teachers. Those who showed particles of brightness
but didn't speak up in class ended up studying arts or became hair-
dressers or architects, and probably not famous ones, either. Those who
were more obedient than bright hopped on the vast conveyor belt to
an assortment of desk jobs, jobs behind counters, jobs with clipboards,
jobs in uniforms and nice shoes.

The work-around to all that was to study accounts or computers,
the shortcut to true status and security.

~

Lisette was bright, so she joined the other bright ones and floated like plankton toward her ordained future. She had reached as far as her second semester in Montreal before ever thinking to ask herself why she wanted to become a doctor. All the other students seemed to be having an obscene amount of fun in their interpretive dance and psychology classes, while she hustled to the lab to dissect a gallbladder. They were kayaking at dawn, singing in talent shows, and running for student office, and she was behind a pair of goggles measuring foul-smelling powders on a scale. Their reward was a spot right next to her on the dean's list, profiles in the student weekly, and regular sex with partners of choice, whereas Lisette had to contend with the furtive fumblings of Jean-Louis from applied physics, with the tufty unibrow that he hadn't yet worked out how to put into play. But the cruelest blow came at the end of that semester, when her roommate in the international dorm, a bubbly anthropology student from Seoul, won a summer internship to do research on Easter Island. All Lisette had to look forward to was summer credit as a lab assistant to her nearsighted biochem professor, whose beakers seemed to be in constant need of sterilizing.

That was when, to the anguish of no one but poor Jean-Louis, she dropped the beakers and defected to the other side. There, free of her bright-girl shackles, she underwent a transformation so profound it was a pity few took notice. One drunken evening she chopped her long black hair and dyed it white down the middle. And because she couldn't take the smell of weed, she developed a continental cigarette habit instead, continental in that she used a cigarette holder, like Holly Golightly in *Breakfast at Tiffany's*. Coiffed and propped, Lisette donned a persona worthy of a thousand Instagram posts, before Instagram was invented to enthrone her.

At the end of school, she rinsed out the skunk patch and came along home to a less than glorious reception: some claimed the post she took at the National Tourism Association was invented to curry favor with her daddy's empire. They pointed to the long-serving employees and the list of aspiring marketers begging to intern for free, plus the fact that, from the dawn of time until the moment Lisette had returned to Barbados, the VP of marketing had managed just fine without any Assistant VP.

Others dismissed these claims as standard Bajan bad-mouthing. Lisette, they observed, was just one of several new AVPs, full of fresh ideas to get bottoms back on beaches for the flagging tourism sector. No perks, just a foot in the door for a bright young lady eager to serve her country. Or something like that.

Lisette had badly wanted to believe she'd come this far on her own. She interrogated her parents, who swore up and down that they had not intervened to get her the job. This was enough to see her across the office threshold with her head high, but no sooner had she settled into her ergonomic chair and been issued her phone than she began to yearn for a little specialness after all. For she was surrounded by clones: shiny boys and girls, everybody so clever, oh so witty, so scrubbed-down and speakey-spokey! All fresh from university, the ink still damp on their diplomas, speaking fluent jargon. On top of this, they were pleasant and approachable, which meant that no one perceived in Lisette the slightest threat whatsoever. It was peace, love, and efficiency from first light to last back-slap every Friday at team-building happy hour at the bar up the road. However glamorous a figure she cut on her hotel visits, clacking through lobbies in her patent-leather Louboutins, back at the office Lisette was nothing more than a "valued member of a dynamic team striving to take Barbados to a higher level."

Some days it roiled her to the core.

~

The arrival doors parted, and the first passengers trickled out. The tour guides and taxi drivers refreshed their poses. Lisette checked the Sabre Cumberbatch feed on her phone.

How must it feel to be a famous artist? Not rich, probably, or why would she need to stay with them, and besides, artists mostly had to die to get rich. When she scrolled through Sabre's artwork, the black-and-white blurs and blandness made her feel superior to the rubes who would neither understand this as high art, nor know, like Lisette did, to at least pretend. Her fingers stroked the handle of her Versace mug.

"Lizzie?"

The soft voice startled her. She looked up from Sabre the meme and beheld Sabre in the flesh. The living, gleaming flesh, smiling and radiant in full saturated midnight cocoa.

"Say!" Lisette threw her arms around her cousin, and they dissolved into breathless, laughing tears, barely noticing when the Versace mug fell to the floor.

Chapter 5

Two hours after stepping off the JetBlue flight from JFK onto Barbadian soil, Sabre was already feeling herself restored to factory settings. Grounded, unpuffed, a blimp no more.

Here, whizzing along the highway, joining the cavalcade of vehicles filtering into and out of roundabouts unadjudicated by traffic lights or legible signage, was an atmosphere of sanity and collective order.

Here, through the open window and sunroof of Lisette's gargantuan SUV, was a wash of breeze, instead of hot air.

OK, hot breeze, yes. But *sea* breeze. Organic.

Sabre looked over at her cousin, to whom she was barely pretending to listen as Lisette pointed out this and that along the way. She was feeling the shift of time.

This was how they might have been if she hadn't left, the pair of them off together on some morning errand, close and conspiratorial, at ease in each other's company, taking the long way home, as Lisette was doing now. She was all grown up, Lisette was, and she smelled the way she looked in her Instagram posts—the way Sabre imagined ylang-ylang to smell. A tamed and sensible smell.

She leaned out the window as they passed an elderly man riding a bicycle on the edge of the highway. He had on a cream shirt and brown pants, both pristine and perfectly pressed, brown shoes, and a leather bag across his body. When she studied his face in the side mirror, his expression was serious and dignified. He felt like a sign.

Like *Welcome home, child, to the land of the sensible and serious.*

~

"Sabre! Oh, my S*abreeee!*"

Auntie Aggie hugged her with a purple squeal. Or so Sabre imagined it, since her aunt was clad in an identical shade of eggplant from headband to heel.

"Oh dear, can hardly find anything to hold on to! So lovely and slim!"

"Don't comment on people's body shape, Mummy," chided Lisette.

The whole family was gathered on the terrace: Auntie Aggie, effervescent and purposeful and purple. Uncle Clive, ever his jokey, sweet self. Lisette, whose cheerful demeanor at the airport had now been overlaid with a touch of sullenness. The twins, Cedric and Russell, who Sabre realized had only recently learned of her existence, just as she had learned of theirs, and who seemed to be secretly mimicking anything she said. Bastet the cat, fluffier and cuter than his name, rubbing up against her ankle. Everybody chattering and purring at once.

The house tour was about to start.

In scale, decor, and architectural ambition, the Toppin mansion was the landed equivalent of a cruise ship. Curve here, nook there, cathedral windows, baroque patios, Ionic columns, a motley collection of roofs, all the way up to a big balcony at the top, jutting over the cliff as though daring the sea.

On the ground floor, it was the tropics: royal palms in a massive atrium, the sound of the waves rolling in from all sides. Then, powder rooms like jewel boxes from an Ottoman palace. The thick carpet and dim lighting in the library called to mind New England. And the art—so much art!—on walls and pedestals, in corners. Old masters, new masters, sculptures, prints. Some of the frames possibly more expensive than the paintings inside. Taking in the variety of genres, Sabre reassured herself that the grey, streaky piece she planned to offer as a gift should fit right in to the mix.

"Getting your bearings, love?" Uncle Clive asked as they ascended the stairs.

"My groundings," she replied.

The twins glanced at each other and stifled giggles.

"And now, my darling Sabre," said Auntie Aggie, turning to face her on the landing, "our humble offering to you, for as long as you'll grant us the pleasure."

Before them was a set of heavy white double doors, which Auntie Aggie pushed open with a flourish. They entered a cool, airy, white-furnished, white-tiled semicircle of a bedroom, straight off the side of a Grecian urn. In the middle stood a large white bed on a raised circular platform, surrounded by four fluted columns. Beyond the bed, a wide, half-moon balcony overlooked the sea.

Sabre gasped. The twins giggled.

Auntie Aggie swept inside with a full twirl. "Ta-da—oh!"

"Oh!"

There was someone inside. A woman with a young face, curly wig, and liquid skin. Wearing an apron over leggings and holding a lumpy paper bag.

"Are those the cherries from downstairs?" Auntie Aggie asked the woman, her energy noticeably shifting. "But I was—you didn't have to—I left a—"

The woman said, "I saw the note to put them in the—"

"The white bowls, yes! That was just a reminder to myself. I know you have enough to do. No, no!" Auntie Aggie rushed forward and swiped the bag from the woman's hands. "That note was for me, I . . . Anyhow. Meet my niece Sabre from New York. The one this is all for. Sabre, this is Isilda, our . . . well . . . practically a family member, you could say, right?"

Auntie Aggie seemed skittish around the woman, presumably the housekeeper. Was her aunt being shy? Sabre melted a little at the thought.

"Hi, Isilda. It's nice to meet you. You have a beautiful name."

"Thank you," Isilda replied, barely making eye contact as she wiped her hands on her apron. She headed for the door as Auntie Aggie jaggedly began to shake the fruit into the bowls.

"Watch out, Mummy," Russell called. "You're spilling them."

Isilda bent down to gather the scattered cherries from the floor. Sabre bent with her, picking up one that had rolled close to her foot.

"Ah, now you really getting reacquainted," said Uncle Clive, as Sabre examined the cherry. "You used to put away so many of those you almost started bearing cherries yourself."

"Really?" Sabre replied. She popped the fruit into her mouth.

"Nasty!" Cedric cackled. "She ain't even wash it!"

Sabre shrugged and laughed, but Auntie Aggie snapped.

"Listen to me," she scolded. "Isilda has this floor clean enough for a queen's dinner."

"Ooh, it's tart," said Sabre.

"You got to dip them in sugar, Yankee girl," said Lisette. "Let Isilda do some for you."

"Or carob syrup. Nutmeg and cinnamon good, too," Isilda added.

"Now that sounds incredible," said Sabre, glad to see Isilda warming up.

"I never heard of putting them in nutmeg and cinnamon," said Lisette.

"And that's why none of us can match this one in the kitchen!" Auntie Aggie burst out, a little loud. "Cinnamon. Nutmeg. Eh? Pure genius!"

"Genius is right," Uncle Clive chimed in. "People still talking 'bout the party from couple weeks back. You believe Hubert call me today, say he still licking his fingers from the dessert?"

"OK, all!" Auntie Aggie sang out, balling up the empty bag. "Let's let Sabre rest now. She must be tired."

"I'm fine," Sabre protested, but Isilda was already hustling down the stairs. Auntie Aggie bundled everybody out of the room.

"Dinner at six thirty!" she trilled, closing the door behind her.

~

The pumpkin soup is warm, creamy with dinner talk, and dream-flecked with nutmeg and cinnamon. And so she dives in.

Below the surface of the viscous pumpkin sea, she can hear laughter, the sound of spoons against bowls, the gentle slap of a slipper.

She comes up from the depths. The soup flows warm down her scalp and drips from her ears.

A wave is forming. She climbs onto her surfboard to catch it.

In surround sound, the barrel of the wave says, "Old girl, you come to see me at last."

She holds still, determined to keep her gaze straight ahead.

"So long you don't bother to visit. Like you block me."

She steadies her feet.

"Say-Say. This is how you treat your father after so long? Look what I've done for you."

"Done for me? You left us without a pot to cry in. I mean piss in. Whatever. You never even visited my dreams."

"Your mother banned me. I couldn't get near either one of you, my love. I tried."

"You ruined her life."

"She was better off. So were you. Look what you've become."

"Yeah, look. The Bald Pigeon of Bed-Stuy."

"The bald, beautiful, exotic genius. Suits you. Serves you well. Think I

can allow myself a little credit. Leather pants and all. Nice."

"Do you have any idea what I've been through?"

"And come out a champ on the other side. You're an artful one. My own child."

"Shut up. I'm nothing like you."

"Say. Sugar dumpling. I've given you a way to ease your path. Just take it. Keep going. Feast on the bounty of our pain. You've earned it."

"No, I haven't. But that stops now. I'm not you. I'm not going to coast through life on luck and smiles."

"You're coasting now. Why else have you come to me?"

"I'm here to make sure I don't become Basquiat."

"Basquiat rejected his father, too, love beet. Too far east is west."

"You wasted your life and came to nothing and destroyed everyone you were supposed to love, and everything you touched turned to shit!"

"Cursing. A real American. I know your mother didn't teach you that."

"And get this shit through your surround sound. You stood for nothing, and now I'm going to stand for something. For everything!"

"Swim in my soup, pumpkin angel. For you, it will never get cold."

~

Sabre woke with a sputter. Beyond the open balcony door, a wave crashed ashore.

An annoying intrusion.

Of course there hadn't been time to think about him. Either that, or she'd been thinking of nothing else. The dead take up residence in your sinus, in your chest cavity, in the force of your breath. You stop noticing that you notice.

Pumpkin angel.

The cherry bowl sat on her nightstand. She picked it up and went out onto the balcony. From one corner she could see the edge of the driveway, its flickering lamps glowing, soft like moonlight. And before her, spread like a peacock fan of boundless possibility, the sea.

She stuffed three cherries into her mouth at once, teased off the tart flesh, and rolled the soft, yielding, star-shaped pits over her tongue.

Chapter 6

"To go and eat cherries? That's what you're throwing away your future for?"

The echo on the line doubled the sarcasm.

"What's your problem?"

"My problem? Honey, I don't have a problem."

Sabre could hear her mother's keyboard clacking away.

"You know what I have?" Priscilla continued, in her office voice. "I have two condos and a pension, and a plot in Parklawn for when I really get sick of you. OK? The question today is *your* problem."

"My problem is a mother who's afraid to go back to her roots."

"You stay there looking for roots while the branches dry-rotting."

Sabre sighed. As her mother clacked and clacked, sunshine streamed through the balcony doors and spilled across the white silk bedding of her bed, where she had been served brunch on a rolling tray with linen tablecloth and embroidered napkins, presumably by Isilda, since it had been there when she first opened her eyes at 11:40 that morning. She took a spoonful of cherry stew and willed herself to leave her mother's metaphors untouched in their flammable packaging.

"Meaning?" she sighed at last.

"Roots. You realize who sold Kunta Kinte to the white people, right?"

"Huh?"

"His own flesh and blood. Own flesh and blood."

"Oh, and I had a dream about Dad. A first."

"Really."

"Do you ever dream about him?"

"Look at that. Even in death he can't get a visa. Had to wait for you to go down there."

"Do you?"

"Sabre, I live my life awake, in the present, among the living. You should try it."

"He wasn't himself, though. He came as a bowl of pumpkin soup."

"Surprised it wasn't a bottle of gin. The afterlife must have dried him out."

"Everybody here is amazing. Auntie Aggie has twin boys you didn't even know about."

"Who says I didn't know about them?"

The suggestion panged her heart. Was her mother serious? How damaged did a person have to be to keep such a thing to herself? She decided against opening a new front in the ongoing battle against Priscilla's stubbornness.

"Auntie Aggie's throwing me a huge welcome party next weekend," she said. "Talking about putting me on some radio talk show about current affairs. Super nice."

"*Soo-per* nice." Priscilla smarmed, the echo drawing out the mockery.

"Do you just get off on being toxic? I don't get you."

"And I don't get you. Your timing is atrocious. All kinds of things could be happening for you now with this paper out. Front page of the Style section that everybody reads. You realize people here in the office are asking for *my* autograph? Bernice even got her hands on a print copy and had it laminated. Just when things heating up here—"

"The world's gonna end if I leave New York for six months?"

"You down there eating cherries and digging up roots like a monkey."

"A *monkey*?"

Her mother clacked on, oblivious.

How many years had she gone without being called that?

She waited for her mother to catch herself. To recall the tears, the taunts at the school gate, the suggested clapbacks that never quite seemed to land. Could she really have forgotten?

But in the lull, prolonged to extract an apology that was not to come, Sabre realized that the insult had lost its sting.

Maybe she really was safe now. Home, reset. Sitting high on a Grecian urn–type bed with her Bajan cherries. If only her mother could reset, too.

"Mom. It's nice here. Come visit. Please?"

"Sweet child, I gone. Give my regards."

"Give them yourself."

"Bye."

~

The next morning, too early, came a call from her agent.

"Hello?"

"Wakey-wakey!"

"Katya?"

"You guess, darling! It's like we're halves of a whole, the way I miss you!"

Katya's Russian intonation, accompanied by a violin concerto that Sabre could hear in the background, settled over her like a chilled duvet. Although she was barely awake—was Katya really calling her before nine, had they met?—Sabre instinctively found the surly-teen mode in which she tended to engage her agent.

Perhaps it was because she was still a teenager when Katya Alekseevna had first approached her, late in a photography show at city hall featuring the work of high school seniors. Sabre had been stationed as instructed by the nuns before her prizewinning pieces, in hopes of drawing a photo-op handshake from the mayor or one of his high officials. Instead, she had been set upon by a stranger in metallic boots and matte lipstick, who had wandered away from her nephew's varsity-wrestler series in search of more inspired work.

"You catches the eye, darling," Katya had declared, so enthused over the shy girl's every utterance that neither of them noticed when the mayor swept by in a phalanx of handlers.

At the end of Sabre's freshman year of art school, Katya had signed her as a client. Stunned to discover there might be an audience for her work beyond diocesan glad-handers, Sabre had not been surly in those days. That had come later, a posture that had taken time to develop, her reticence degrading into petulance as Katya's faith in her talent ripened into indulgence. All the sass she knew not to throw her mother's way was left for Katya to catch.

"How did you get this number?" she whimpered to Katya.

"Ooh, bad girl, run away, forget agent who misses you, eh, I love it . . . ! Don't be angry. Your mother gave to me. It was emergency, darling, don't get upset. First of all, now. How is the vacation going?"

"It's—"

"Good, good. So listen. I have good news, and I have better news. Which do you want?"

"Whichever one ends this call faster."

"Darling! Such humor, this is why they love you. First of all. The *Times* story is out. Did you see? Talking about how you got up all of sudden in the interview and walked away from the others, even walked away from New York, even from America, it is so wild, so shocking! You are big hit, my darling, they love you till loss of consciousness!"

"What?"

"Yes! The phone, it is all the time ringing now, everybody is wanting you! But guess what, this is not the best part! Best part, Topsheet is again calling, requesting you for their launch campaign this summer!"

"Wait, what? We already have the deal with them."

"No, not your pieces, darling. *You!*"

"Me? As in—"

"As in, yes, exactly, as in!"

"Ugh. Katya, no way."

"Sabre. It is golden opportunity. The face, eh? The body. You can do however you like. Darling, they want you can name your price, any price. We negotiate, of course. Any price!"

"Katya, no. No price. This is what I was trying to explain before. Don't you get it? I've got nothing to do with Dutch duvets. I'm not a mascot."

"Again with this 'mascot.' Darling, I don't understand. It is just image, an idea, it is real, it is not real, who cares? The Dutch, they have good taste. You don't have to feel ashamed. You are not these people on box of cereal, I don't know, bottle of water, whatever. It is a high product, elegant."

Sabre sighed. Katya could be hard to argue with, which was why Sabre so often found refuge in obstinacy. For better or worse, she couldn't point to a single instance of misdirection on Katya's part.

But this was not about options and their relative merits. It was about . . .

What, exactly?

She sat up in bed and looked through the balcony doorway toward the sea.

"Well," she said, "I do care."

"Darling. Do you forget that it is Topsheet who is paying for Barbados holiday?"

Sabre had no pushback for that one.

"Listen. You do this deal, you pose for Topsheet, with wild bad-girl pose, whatever, they put you for the launch campaign, in the publications of best taste, very discreet, you name the price, you take holiday to Barbados for next twenty years I promise you, my darling. It is win-win. Win-win-win-win."

The violins in the background matched Katya's staccato cadence.

"Hmm. I don't know . . . I'm not in this headspace right now, Katya."

"*Sooo* . . . you think about, yes?"

"I don't know."

"Yes?"

"No."

"You think, just think about it?"

"OK, I'll think about it."

"Darling! You make me happy. I tell Topsheet you think. Now. You relax, you think, take all the time you need! We discuss in one week, yes?"

Chapter 7

People don't come to paradise to ruminate on bed skirts.

Camera strapped across her sundress, Sabre spent the first few days wandering the grounds of the Toppins' estate in a trancelike state, ambling amid the colorful hedgerows that lined the lawn like a tropical Versailles. At the bottom of the garden, she lingered by the pool, dipping one foot, stirring it this way then that, taking it out, dipping the other, twiddling her toes, shaking them off; contemplating the planters of red, yellow, and magenta bougainvillea along the sides, stroking the petals with the back of her hand, bending to inhale their scent of nothing; rising again with deep, shrugging breaths and long, open-jawed exhales as she gazed beyond the swooping drapery of the gazebo to the sea. Then, with sunlight dappling the sweat beads on her scalp, she sauntered down to the garden wall and paused at the top of the steps leading down to the beach, spreading her arms and legs, lifting her chin to the sky, and standing there, motionless, like that old-time sketch of the naked man, for so long that if Isilda didn't know better, watching all this through the kitchen window, she might mistake Sabre for some new statue Mrs. Toppin must have added to the already plentiful outdoor collection.

This Bajan Yankee was more idle than the cat, Isilda thought, and she certainly was doing no favors for the afternoon program with Ian. But her presence was turning out to be a blessing. So long as Sabre—apple of Mrs. Toppin's eye, dumpling of her soup, salt meat of her rice—was there to be fed and pampered, with the extra room to tidy and cherries galore to stew, Isilda could relax in the knowledge that her job was safe. All she had to do was lie low and keep the niece happy.

～

Upstairs in the master bedroom, Aggie looked out at her niece as she basked in the sunshine and sea air at the foot of the garden. Even from this distance, she could read in Sabre's body language the eagerness with which she was absorbing the therapeutic properties of home. Aggie could almost observe the cartilage decompressing between her joints. Being a famous New York artist was a splendid achievement, but it came with the drawback of having to live in New York. What a blessing to be able to flee that cramped, malodorous mayhem for the largesse of an aunt who adored her and was overjoyed to welcome her home.

Yes, Sabre's welcome party would be the answer to it all. The perfectly timed distraction for Aggie's ruffled nerves, while she waited to see how this messiness with Isilda would play out. An affair for the ages, worthy of the niece who, despite checkered origins, had risen to the heights of international art stardom. Worthy of the sister whose self-imposed exile Aggie still could not help but take personally. Perhaps this display of honor could finally bridge the gulf between them.

This distraction justified hiring caterers, so as not to lean too hard on Isilda. In fact, Aggie planned to give Isilda a special uniform for the night, more impressive than the others, maybe something with epaulettes and gold trim, to mark her authority over the hired help.

That week, ignoring Sabre's pleas to scale back, Aggie sent out 240 invitations. In the end, about 80 RSVP'd, which meant that a further 70 to 90 could be expected, including the extended family, those Ifills and Toppins remaining in Barbados, many of whom would scarcely recognize Sabre as the little wallflower who left all those years ago. Some murmured what a fine redemption this must be for poor Priscilla, to see her only child amount to something after her own fall from grace. Others wondered what on Aggie's menu they would be able to pronounce. There would be business associates of both Aggie's and Clive's, the partners, colleagues, clients, and clients-to-be; Lisette's friends and workmates, provided they dressed properly and behaved themselves; members of the island's small arts elite, over whose swelled heads Aggie looked forward to vaulting; and a scattering of acquaintances and friends.

Of course, there would be no getting around inviting Hubert and Nancy. But given the grandeur of the occasion and the generosity of spirit she was displaying, Aggie could only hope the fates would reward her goodwill.

~

The gulls circling overhead weren't sure what to make of the bashment on the Toppin lawn. Hindu wedding? Minor coronation? White table-cloths fluttered over the green, and every few yards, citronella torches blazed, even with the sun still high on duty. The place was more than its usual riot of flowers, the center of each table an eruption of pink, yellow, and cream anthuriums, crimson ginger lilies, violet orchids, and gold-tipped Pride of Barbados. The crowd, which approached young sapodilla on the melanometer, was circulating with a stiffness not fully explained by the freshness of the hour nor the women's heels sinking into the earth with each step.

There were men in navy blazers and khaki trousers, good cologne, and that Caribbean perennial, the shirt-jac. There were women in florals to the knee, windproof hairdos, and another Caribbean perennial, the fishtail skirt. A quartet was stationed at the entrance to the garden path, within earshot but out of the way, ticking through their repertoire of jazz standards and the Caribbean mainstays of classical music played as soca and soca music played as classical. Food was piled high on a grand, sweeping semicircular table, some of it steaming and some on ice, some apparently still alive, some arranged on trays or under tagines, but every morsel manned by a sharp-eyed servant in full livery and, therefore, none of it available to be picked at or shat on.

~

Floating among the mortals in a long peach toga, her curls spilling from a gold hair band that matched the slim belt about her waist, Aggie was struggling to contain herself. This party was already an unequivocal success. She flitted from cluster to cluster, laughing, kissing, fielding compliments, posing for photos, encouraging gluttony, and pointing out the guest of honor. Each time she moved off again, the envious stares she could feel at her back lifted her like a kite in a warm wind.

As usual, her instinct for showmanship had been bang on. How right she had been to channel the goddess in her look. Charitable though she was, she could not help but notice how, with their collapsed chests, middle-age spread, and unsuitable footwear, her guests seemed to be sinking into the earth even as she soared above it. Prostrate at the altar of her beauty! Didn't they realize gravity was a thing to be constrained?

Like Hera beaming down from Mount Olympus, Aggie bathed one and all in smiles of compassion as she looked about for her Zeus. There he was, perched on an elbow at the edge of the bar, chatting with one of the junior bartenders. His shirttail was starting to creep out of his trousers, and she hoped he didn't plan to install himself there all night. Catching her gaze, Clive blew her a kiss.

~

From the corner of her eye, Isilda saw Mr. Toppin's lips pucker as she swept past on her way to the house, and a flash of panic bolted through her. Quickly she came to her senses: either he was picking something from between his teeth, or Mrs. Toppin must be around somewhere. The man had eyes for no other; of that much at least Isilda could be sure, even if she couldn't say the same for his wife.

She wove briskly, absently through the crowd, an empty tray balanced on her shoulder. The din of the party had lulled her into the autopilot she had mastered in her last job, lunchtime waitress at the Sun Dragon Snackette in town. There, with the constant babble of Chinese from the kitchen behind and the equally opaque talk of the office workers up front, she had learned to arrange fried pork on lettuce beds, to water down soft drinks, to add up large orders in her head, and to flirt for tips, all while miles away.

For such a big party, the workload felt too light. She stopped in front of the buffet with her empty tray. Despite all the fanciness Mrs. Toppin had put out, in the end only the rice and peas seemed to have been dug into with enthusiasm. Before Isilda could reach for the nearly empty bowl, a designated rice-and-peas attendant appeared at her side, scooped it up, and replaced it with a fresh one.

"Let me take that to the kitchen for you," Isilda said to the attendant.

"No, no, it's aah-right, ma'am," said the attendant in a small-island accent. "They comin' around to cle-ah de wares now-now."

Pretending not to hear, Isilda swiped the empty bowl from the rice-and-peas attendant's hands, loaded it onto her tray, and made for the kitchen. *Ma'am.* Why? Because her uniform had scratchy gold piping and theirs didn't? When she entered the kitchen, the buzz died down. Someone whisked away her tray without a word. She went over to the large window by the sink, a position that was second home to her during the week, and stood between the plate clearers and the cake icers, who were busy decorating miniature mousses. They looked up expectantly.

"Getting through?" she asked.

"Yes, yes, ma'am," came the mumbles.

One of the women set a tray of dessert cutlery clattering onto the island counter in the middle of the kitchen, causing everyone to jump. She dipped down to rescue some spoons from the floor and came up again with a sheepish look.

"Don't hurt your head, darling," said Isilda, as the cutlery minder approached the sink to wash the spoons. She nodded toward the window. "Some o' them mouth so nasty already, these spoons ain't even bound to clean."

The plate clearer and the cutlery minder giggled. Isilda took out a towel and began to polish the spoons as they were rinsed.

Framed by the cool white of the window and the fluorescent kitchen light, the party looked to be picking up speed. The sun was just starting to disappear, taking with it over the horizon the top layer of people's best manners. Over by the pool, some couples were dancing. Guests were rearranging themselves from tidy tables of ten into spontaneous clumps around the lawn. She could hear a hacking laugh rising above the general noise from the bar area. Of course . . . Justice DaCosta again, clinking glasses with Mr. Toppin and splashing out the man's good Barbancourt with not a jot of shame.

Isilda sucked her teeth. "But looka that dutty dog, though."

"Hmm?" said the plate clearer.

"That one, that no good one across there," said Isilda, jerking her chin.

They looked. "He all right, ma'am, just enjoying himself," said the cutlery minder.

"Humph! Y'all ain't know," grumbled Isilda. "Some people wutless, hear? And got a nerve to boot. You ain't to number-two where you eat—I learn that from small. Wutless!"

The plate clearer and the cutlery minder glanced at each other across Isilda's thrashing towel.

~

Out in the garden, the citronella flames swayed like khus-khus sheaves in the gathering breeze, thickening the haze through which Sabre was taking in the night. She could not have felt any farther from New York if she had landed on the far side of Neptune. Each hand that clasped hers, each name that evaporated before she could catch it like the lobster meringue on Auntie Aggie's table, sank her deeper into the soil.

"Well, well, well. Look at Priscilla, eh?"

"Bit of Ronnie, too, round the eyes."

"Check them long fingers! Young lady, I hope you kept up the piano?"

"Tell your aunt send you to me. Got some nice wigs to sort you out, love."

They had known her, really known her, these people. Known her when she was only nine. And they knew her now, at twenty-nine, without the aid of a media profile. No one was asking to rub her head or pose with her. People were taking her in stride. It felt good to be normal.

"Girl, come here," a man called as she passed the bar. It was Uncle Kenroy, Aunt Evelyn's husband. "You doing this thing backward. The hand light and the head heavy. Take this." He thrust a full glass into her hand.

"What you over here doing?" Aunt Evelyn loomed up behind her husband. "Child now come and you trying to drunk she already. Mind they don't ban the two o' we before the big food start serving."

"Big food what," sneered Uncle Kenroy. "Evelyn, you ain't know you sister by now? Why you think I got the chicken home thawing out?"

Aunt Evelyn emptied her glass in a gulp and turned to Sabre. "Darling, you back on the rock at last. When you coming by us to get some good country air in them lungs?"

"We could pose for you and all," said her uncle, cupping his chin and striking a pout.

"No naked pictures, though," her aunt added, winking. "Have to charge you for those."

Four of the servers were easing down the steps toward the buffet, hoisting a palanquin on which sat a giant red flamingo crafted out of speckled gelatin. Passing a tableful of gawking guests, Sabre overheard

Auntie Aggie's trill: "Of course it's real flamingo. Never had? Come, try it. Very lean, Marjorie."

Sabre slipped past them into the house. Making her way across the parlor, she heard Lisette call from the other side: "Hey, rock star! Come out here with us!"

A VIP lounge was taking shape on the balcony. Lisette and about a dozen others, clocking a solid ginger 8.8, were sprawled out around an assortment of bottles, ashtrays, and finger food. Sabre plunked onto the free half of a lounge chair.

"Did we miss your speech?" Lisette asked.

"What speech? I'm supposed to make a speech?"

"Relax, I'm joking. You know who taking the stage if any speechifying going on." Lisette rolled her eyes. "Any excuse to show off."

"How can you say that? Your mom is awesome," said a woman beside Lisette, in a vaguely secondhand American accent. "Puts her heart and soul into everything."

"Cathy, you're a fine one to talk," Lisette replied. "You forget how she behaved at your wedding? You had to wonder who was the bride."

"Me, I was glad enough for the help," Cathy drawled. "If it was up to you, my shower would have been some rock cakes and a piñata. Of your mother."

The woman sharing Sabre's lounge chair was talking to a guy dressed in linen pajamas. "It dread," he was saying, shaking a head of limp brown ringlets. "Dread. Them want me to create, but them don't want me to enter the cipher."

"Mmm," nodded the woman, solemnly topping up her vodka. "When you say 'cipher,' though, what you mean exactly?"

"I ready to fire the work," the man said, ignoring the question. He took a drag on his cigarette. "Them old-school architects I work for don't appreciate the creative process. Like the House of Akan say, Jah dissipate when man aggravate."

"Akan?" The woman wrinkled her highlighted nose. "You mean the Rasta commune out East Coast side?"

"Correct. I does go out there once a week to reason with the bredren."

"But what you would do if you left that job?"

"Just sell piece of my family land and build some condos."

"Ahh. Right." The woman studied him studying his beer bottle.

Sabre leaned over to Lisette. "So, which one's your man?"

"Not here yet," Lisette said. "Who knows if he's coming at all. He usually doesn't do these types of events."

"What's he like?"

"Oh, stubborn and scrawny. And white."

"Really? From where?"

"From right here on this rock," she said, with a meaningful, slow-spreading smirk.

"And don't forget, *pisssing* rich," said a husky female voice from behind a cloud of smoke. "Which I suppose is redundant if you're a stubborn, scrawny, white Bajan."

"Lord, Paloma," Lisette scolded. "You got to be so backward?"

"I just noting the obvious," Paloma replied. "The man does pick he nose with a roll-up hundred. And I woulda still take it from he when he finish. That is legal tender."

"Sabre, your cousin is going out with a *Gibbons*," Cathy explained, enunciating the name.

"Gibbons," Sabre repeated. "Is that some sort of . . ."

Paloma chortled. "The only sort."

"Oh, stop it!" Lisette threw an olive at Paloma, laughing. She turned to Sabre. "His people own a few businesses. Big deal."

A sudden commotion on the lawn below drew everyone's attention. The red flamingo stood in the middle of the buffet table, tailless and beakless. One server was rescuing fragments of the black beak from the grass between the guests' legs, while Aggie was loudly berating another for miscarving the bird's behind. The enormous beak had been too dense for the body structure.

"Pure flamingo-liver pâté!" Aggie wailed. From where they sat, they could see a guest tipping his plate of red gelatin into a flowerpot. Chunks of flamingo floated among the lotus flowers in the pool.

"Serves her right," grunted Lisette. "It was probably endangered or something."

The linen Rasta gazed at her blankly.

"So what do you plan to do while you're here?" a woman near the balustrade asked Sabre. "Do you have a project in mind?"

"Must be amazing to be a real working artist," said Cathy dreamily.

"I used to go out with a artist," said Paloma. "Apples and asses, that's all he could draw. Same shape, different direction."

From the balcony on the opposite side of the parlor, Sabre watched the workers cluster around the tray of black flamingo glop like medical students inspecting a cadaver. One pinched off a piece to taste. When she failed to drop dead, a few others began to follow, picking at the beak as they passed by the counter.

What *was* she doing here? What was her plan?

To get away.

Done. Now what?

To find herself. To be real.

Look, here she was, on this lounge chair. Real.

Was it enough?

"Look who's here!"

Auntie Aggie appeared on the patio with a skinny blond man in a splattered T-shirt and work boots. Her headband was off-center, and she seemed breathless behind a wide grin.

"Evening, all," said the man.

"Bumpkin!" Lisette got up. "You reach at last. And look, you even put on a shirt."

"Leave the boy," Auntie Aggie shushed her. "You don't see he's coming straight from work? Where they had you today?"

"Same place, up North Point side. I goin' dead o' boredom up dey if de wind don't carry me 'way first."

"Well, before that, come meet my cousin," Lisette said, hooking his arm. "Sabre, Damian."

"Hey!" said Sabre. "I've been waiting for you. You look exhausted."

"Don't mind him, he just vex he had to spend a Saturday on the job instead of on a surfboard," teased Lisette, tugging at Damian's shirt.

"Sun too blasted hot, man." Damian gave his head a lengthy scratch.

"As if you don't own the damn company," Paloma muttered.

"Good evening to you, too, Paloma."

"Leave my darling alone," Lisette cooed.

"Lisette, get them to fix him a plate," trilled Auntie Aggie. "Make yourself at home, dear. Now, Say, let me borrow you." She took Sabre by the hand—"Just for a minute"—and led her back through the living room.

"Wow, Auntie Aggie," Sabre gushed.

"Enjoying it, darling?" replied her aunt. "All for you. I'm so—"

Auntie Aggie stopped short in front of two servers standing in the kitchen doorway.

"What you still doing in my house?" she snapped. "I sent you home twenty minutes ago. What you waiting for?"

All activity froze behind the two servers' backs. The elder woman straightened hers and said in a low voice, "The wages plus the gratuity, Mrs. Toppin. It's twenty percent for a full day on the weekend."

"Gratuity!" Auntie Aggie exclaimed. "You expect me to be *grateful* to you for ruining my specialty course, getting flamingo stains all over my guests' clothes and making me look like a fool?"

"It really wasn't that bad," Sabre offered.

"No, Sabre. It was completely unacceptable," retorted Auntie Aggie, turning to Sabre with an exaggerated toss of her head, a loose curl whipping the two servers' faces. "This is not New York. You don't understand the hell we go through in this country trying to find workers who know to use their damned brains when they handling delicate things."

"Mrs. Toppin," said the elder server, her voice strained, "we apologize again. But as I explain to you, the dish needed to set longer in order to—"

"So now it's my fault for insisting that you serve the food on time?" Auntie Aggie shot back. "Who you think you talking to, girl?"

"I didn't—"

"Not one red cent for such incompetence. You lucky I don't charge the lot of you for destroying my property." Auntie Aggie was hissing now, to keep from shouting. "Eh? You want that? You have any idea how much that flamingo cost? Worth more than all of you put together, I can assure you. Wages and gratuity my backside."

"But we done work the hours already, mistress," quavered the other server. "Is in we contract. Mr. Sobers say—"

"Mr. Sobers!" Auntie Aggie gave a bitter chortle. "You tell your boss to call me if he has a problem. I guarantee you it's the last time you'll be working for him. Now take off those uniforms and get out. Don't let me pass back and find you here."

Auntie Aggie flounced off. Sabre watched, mouth agape. She turned to the two servers, who continued to stare after her aunt.

The younger woman began to hyperventilate and blink back tears. But the elder's face had gone mineral. Her lips were clenched, her eyes hardened into igneous rocks of rage, cut through with a silt of resignation.

The woman turned her stony gaze on Sabre, nearly knocking her off balance.

Sabre gawped. "I . . ."

The word thinned to a wisp. Both women looked at her expectantly.

"Sabre?" Auntie Aggie called from the doorway. "Come, sweetheart."

She was smiling, her arm outstretched, her face bright, as if nothing had happened. As if the servers were not still standing there, within her line of sight, waiting, expecting. Sabre's head began to swim. She opened her mouth again, her gaze darting between her aunt and the women.

"This way, love," said Auntie Aggie, beckoning. "Quickly."

The older server sucked her teeth and turned back to the kitchen, unbuttoning her collar. The younger woman followed. Sabre felt a fleeting compunction to go after them. But she rushed over to her aunt instead.

"Auntie Aggie," she pleaded. "Was that necessary?"

"What, dear?" her aunt replied, so placidly that Sabre wondered for a moment if she had imagined it all. "You mean those nincompoops?" She flicked a gold-cuffed wrist. "Small thing. Forget them. Let's enjoy this fabulous night."

She had fully reset to charming-hostess mode. When they reached the top of the steps down to the lawn, a server was waiting with champagne. Auntie Aggie took two glasses and handed one to Sabre. Right away the band struck up "For He's a Jolly Good Fellow," and all the guests joined in. There was a suspiciously hearty hip-hip-hooray. Then, projecting effortlessly without a mic, Auntie Aggie addressed the crowd.

"Ladies and gentlemen, thank you for joining me in welcoming home my beloved niece, who is as dear to my heart as my own children. Tonight has been a humble expression of my joy. As you know, Sabre has done wonders in America, making not only us, her family, proud, but also, dare I say, her country. Now that our national treasure has been restored, let us bask in her glory and continue to be inspired by her brilliance. To Sabre!"

"To Sabre!" bellowed the crowd.

Sabre cleared her throat. Before she could get out a syllable, a terrific boom sounded over her head, and the sky exploded in fireworks. The crowd gasped. Two photographers rushed to the foot of the steps. Aggie straightened her headband and pulled Sabre closer. "Surprise, darling," she muttered through clenched teeth.

The fireworks began to cascade without interruption. Boom! And there was Aunt Evelyn, screaming with laughter as Uncle Kenroy fished her shoe out of the pool. Boom! Lisette draped over the balustrade with Damian, shaking her head. Ba-boom! A kiss on the cheek from Auntie

Aggie at the photographers' cue. Bada-boom! A toast and a wink from Hubert DaCosta.

Boom-boom-boom-boom-boom-bada-boom!

In that fractional silence between finale and cheer, Sabre heard the lonely scrape of fork against plate. Looking back in through the kitchen window, she saw Isilda leaning with her hip against the sink, mashing into a dish of rice and peas the remnants of the black flamingo beak. She scraped and mashed, mashed and ate, registering nothing at all.

Chapter 8

In the middle of that night, her throat feels sore. Sabre goes down from the balcony and in through the kitchen window for some water.

The water dispenser lights up when she places her glass under it, casting pink light over the still, dark kitchen.

"The champ is thirsty."

She turns toward her father's voice. The gelatin flamingo stands on its plate on the counter, intact except for its black beak and tail lying on the lettuce bed.

"Enjoyed the feast, Say-Say?"

"It was wonderful, actually. The perfect cure for New York. Could have done without the fireworks, though. Auntie Aggie puts her heart and soul into everything."

"What heart?"

"The heart she had to save us with every time you messed up."

"Butter lily, I was a mess, and I will maintain to eternity that I have been more use to you dead than alive. But the same aunt that saved you also boils flamingoes. Think about that."

"I'm sure it's legal. She's a lawyer. Hasn't kept you from harassing me."

"Anyway. Drink up, so you don't lose your voice again."

The water in the glass glows grainy with silt.

"What are you talking about?"

"You could have interfered. Convinced your aunt not to fire those workers."

"It happened too fast. You weren't there."

"So it was fireworks for you and firings for them. You could have paid them yourself with your Topsheet money."

"I didn't have a chance. Besides, they work for a company, so it's probably fine. Auntie Aggie has her own housekeeper, and she wasn't fired."

"No. She scurries around like a little mouse. As invisible as possible. Always behind a door, never at the table. You don't notice how you can't hear her footsteps when she walks? How she never makes eye contact? Always eats her meals in the kitchen?"

"What's your point? You never liked Auntie Aggie anyway. You resented her because she saw through you."

"I wouldn't say that. We had our bouts, but I will always love her for loving you. She did for you and your mother when I couldn't."

Sabre looks at the glass of silty water and puts it to her lips. The flamingo says:

"Apples and asses, that's all he could draw."

"Who?"

"There are those who walk with no sound, and there are those who boil flamingoes. Same shape, different direction."

"Dad, I can't understand your flamingo talk."

"You get me, tigerpaw. Swallow that water. Swallow."

Chapter 9

Three days later, Sabre stood barefoot under a grove of casuarina trees outside a radio station, digging her toes into the earth. The casuarina needles tickled, and the prickly cones massaged the soles. An underfoot spa.

She was minutes away from being interviewed live on the air. Closing her eyes, she wended through the trees, guided by the trunks' wispy bark, feeling the grounding of the cones pressing into her heels, her arches, her metatarsals.

Since her arrival in Barbados, Auntie Aggie had been pitching this radio show in terms that seemed to hover between honor, favor, and obligation, explaining that as *Open Mic* was the most popular call-in show in Barbados, it would be the ideal way for Sabre to get her "name out there."

Name out there for what? she had wondered, as her aunt trilled on about the "unmissability" of such an opportunity.

She opened her eyes to find the security guard staring. For the thousandth time, she nodded hello. The guard raised a brow and went back to his paper. His demeanor had shifted from wan to alert the moment she took off her shoes.

Did she look crazy? Or was it only that he recognized her from that morning's paper? In the center pages, there had been a shot of her with Auntie Aggie amid the fireworks. The caption read NATIONAL TREASURE RESTORED.

Vonda, a producer from the show, came running over. "Sabre, your segment is next," she announced. "You ready?"

Something about the warmth with which Vonda looked her in the eye put Sabre at ease.

"Ready," she replied.

Vonda looked down. "Would you prefer to go in barefoot? That's fine, too."

"Oops! One sec."

Sabre ran back through the trees to where she had kicked off her flip-flops. And as she bent to retrieve them, she scooped into her pocket a fistful of cones, for pluck.

∿

The interior of the recording studio was what Katya would have called "Soviet kitsch." Everything from the stained walls and chipping paint to the bullet-sized dings in the plaster bespoke grim times. The only respite for the eye was the large window facing the casuarinas in the courtyard. On a table in the far corner, an empty water jug and four downturned tumblers collected dust. At the center of the room was a round desk with two microphones, a half-empty pint of Smirnoff, and no glasses.

Vonda ushered her in and disappeared into the producer's booth. Two men were seated at the mic table. One of them, a salt-and-pepper head who looked to be in his early forties, turned to face her.

"Miss Cumberbatch, welcome. I'm Keith Everton." He gave her a weary, resigned smile, the corners of his mouth drooping like a mule dragging the weight of the world uphill. "Sit anywhere you like while we finish up this segment with Muddy Pickering here."

The other man greeted her with a nod. *Muddy Pickering?* Yes, confirmed Google, that was his real name. An environmental engineer. His papers were bunched up on the desk, and his glasses looked as though he used them to collect soil samples.

Sabre took a seat against the wall as a curtain of tension, which had momentarily lifted to greet her, closed again around the two men. Turning back to his mic, Keith frowned his eyes shut and began to massage the black off his temples. Muddy continued to shuffle papers around like a mad professor. Both seemed to have already forgotten she was there.

The source of the tension was soon revealed. Muddy was there to speak out against overdevelopment along the island's shoreline. It had to do with Barbados being composed of coral, the water table, the coastline shrinking, and the reefs disappearing. Muddy passed Keith a report drenched in yellow highlighter and scrawled up in red. Keith read a part about beach erosion, climate change, something about the sea urchin population.

As soon as he finished, all the lights on the Soviet phone started blinking.

"Well, I ain't see no problem," said the first caller. "I glad enough I ain't got to worry 'bout no sea urchin jooking up me foot 'pon the beach. Good riddance to them!"

"If Barbados shrinking for true," said the second, "all we gotta do is stack up on top one another like in America."

"Muddy, why you don't go and tell the white people to stop building them big hotels on the beach?"

"Mr. Pickering, how big you house is, please? Tell the truth. Don't forget I know you and you brother from short-pants days."

"Is true, Muddy family got a big-big house right 'pon the beach. Dem like they don't want no competition when the tourisses looking to rent!"

Muddy replied, "Sir, that is an old house—" But Keith shook his head. Muddy sank down in the chair.

"Mordecai, this is Mummy. Don't mind these ignorant fools. Talk yuh talk, boy! You is a prophet of Jehovah-self!"

"Mr. Pickering, I see you mother driving a Honda in town last week. She too good for the bus now? Wuh 'bout she carbon footprint? Talk 'bout *that*!"

"Mr. Everton, I want to know why you always putting these reactionaries on the air to keep down Barbados. Why you don't like to see this country progress?"

"Madam, I don't think that's fair," Keith interjected.

"You is a Guyanese or what? I hear you got Guyanese blood . . ."

"Thank you, caller. You're listening to *Open Mic*. Back after these messages."

The ON AIR sign went dark, and the two men deflated. Sabre realized she had been sitting on the edge of her seat, leaning into the tension. She felt herself deflate with them.

Could it be the last drifts of New York hot air, leaving her system?

Yes, child, nodded the casuarinas outside the window. *In this land of the serious, yes.*

Muddy had taken out a tissue and was rearranging the grime on his glasses. Keith leaned back, folding his arms above his head.

"Well," he said, "at least your mother agrees with you."

Muddy shook his head with a sneer. "That Honda was a compromise," he said. "You should see the car she wanted for her birthday. What a seventy-six-year-old woman could want with a Land Rover?"

"A prophet is not without honor," Keith remarked.

"Just now all them going feel it," said Muddy. "Something gotta give."

Vonda emerged from the producer's booth. "Survived another round, eh, Muddy?" she said, patting Muddy's shoulder. "Take it light. Main thing is to get them thinking and talking."

"Both at the same time, if you're lucky," laughed Keith. He shook Muddy's hand across the desk. "Always a pleasure, man. Keep up the good fight. Come back and see us soon."

He turned to Sabre. "And now for our soft landing," he said. "Sorry we ran a bit long, Miss Cumberbatch. I promise you'll get a warmer reception."

"Definitely," laughed Vonda. "After Muddy they don't have any fight left."

"Humph." Muddy shuffled to the door. "You wait."

"All good. I'm ready," Sabre said—to them, to Basquiat, and to the casuarina cones imprinted on her soles.

Vonda sat down next to Sabre at the mic table and began to preview the segment.

"This will be pretty straightforward," she explained, turning her laptop to show a list of questions. "What brings you to Barbados, how did you get into photography, how do you feel about the arts in Barbados, describe your creative process . . . You know. Softballs." She smiled. "Nothing you don't handle every day, I would imagine."

She looked about Sabre's age. She had a bubbly voice and a tattoo of a wing on the back of her shoulder. A woman with a serious job she loved, doing good in the world.

Vonda ceded the chair to Keith and the ON AIR light went on.

Time to restore this national treasure, girl.

~

Sabre Cumberbatch, welcome to Open Mic.
Thank you.
You are a highly blah artist whose work has blahblah in major blurblur around the world. What brings you to Barbados?
Blahblur family.
How did you bloop into photography?
Beep burp childhood blip blap.
How do you feel about the arts scene in Barbados?

~

Through the window, the casuarinas began to sway. Sabre could feel their disappointment down in her shoes. She reached into her skirt pocket and kneaded the cones into her palm. She looked into the grooves of the mic, took a breath. Felt the casuarinas inhale with her.

"I think there are more important things to talk about here today," she said, "than art."

Her throat was pounding. She took a swallow and glanced at Keith. He was pinching the bridge of his nose, and his face was frozen in a squint. For the first time, she noticed his five-o'clock shadow. His rimless glasses, the contours of his cheekbones. Hmm . . .

Come on, girl, stay focused. Push it out . . .

"For example," she continued. "The way some workers are getting . . . taken advantage of in this country. For instance."

The casuarinas nodded.

Keith looked at her, at the script (*Describe your creative blah . . .*), at Vonda in her producer's booth. At Sabre again. Something inscrutable crossed his face.

"Give us some examples of what you mean," he said at last, leaning back.

"Well . . ."

Hmm. Party, Auntie Aggie . . . OK, no need to get into all that. Anyway, this wasn't about Auntie Aggie. It wasn't! It was bigger. It was about . . . about . . .

Her mouth went silty. She swallowed again.

"Examples . . . well . . . I know there's probably a lot of oppressed workers out there, houseworkers and what have you. Why don't we open the *Open Mic* lines to them? 'Cause who am I, really? Just a concerned individual who wants to give them a voice."

"So wait. Are you saying that domestic workers face particular abuse in Barbados?"

"I . . . I'm using my platform to bring light to an issue of consequence . . ."

"But surely you have some anecdotal evidence, at least. This is a serious charge you're making."

"Well . . . Why make it about me? Why not make this a call to action, OK? Why not say, 'Come on, oppressed workers of Barbados, rise up! Don't just sit there, by yourself, all quiet! Speak up! Fight for your rights!'"

Keith cocked his head to one side staring, staring. A light flickered on the phone.

Phew.

"Welcome to *Open Mic.*"

"Yes, good afternoon, Mr. Everton," a gravelly voice said. "I agree with you that we need more facts. The young lady claims Barbados has a serious problem. I wouldn't disagree. But she can't drop a bomb like that, just so! Eh? She just now get here! She is a artist who can't talk about art, and yet she can talk 'bout maids when she ain't neither maid?"

"Your response, Miss Cumberbatch?"

"I . . . OK." *Careful.* "So . . . for example, look how some house-keepers don't even get to eat at the table with the family. They have to stay in the kitchen and eat standing up with a bowl and spoon, not even a fork and knife, OK? Like, are we on *Roots* or something? Is this the olden days? I feel like the time has come to put a stop to such things. In these modern times, we should be about equality, not about putting people in different rooms."

"Are you saying this is something you've witnessed here?" Keith asked.

"I bet it's happening right now all over Barbados, and . . . you know what? I'm gonna say it. It's abuse."

"Hold on," Keith said, fingers to his temples, squinting. "It's abuse to eat standing in the kitchen with a bowl and spoon? If that's the case, Miss Cumberbatch, there are thousands of us being abused every day. I abused myself this very morning, in fact."

"Is that a joke? I'm exposing a serious social problem here."

"My apologies. Please make your point."

"My point is, if a housekeeper is good enough to make dinner and dessert, why isn't she good enough to sit in the same room as you and eat it?"

She mashed a cone with her thumb and looked him straight in the eye like a warrior. *This ain't a joke, radio man!*

Keith stared back at her, speechless. Hmm. Probably did the same to *his* housekeeper.

"And another thing," Sabre added, before he could jump in with another lame joke. "How is it that a worker in Barbados can just get fired, like, on a whim? One second you're working your bu—your best, at an event, then you make one little spill, right, and suddenly you're being sent home without pay? You call that funny? 'Cause you know what I call it? Injustice."

Jackpot! The phone lines exploded.

"*Open Mic*, you're on the air."

"I would like to say that I agree with Miss Cumberbatch one hundred percent," a woman's voice began, enunciating every syllable. "Growing up in our house, the maids always ate separately from us, and I never could understand why. Our mother used to give all kinds of foolish reasons. Even the maids when you ask them. But Miss Cumberbatch, you are right! It is nothing but a throwback to the old British great-house days. Good for you, exposing it. We need to talk these things openly!"

"Thank you, ma'am!"

"But now, what about in your own family? I saw the article on you and your aunt, Aggie Toppin, in the paper. Did something happen at that big function? Is that what has prompted you to speak out?"

"Mmm, a fair question," Keith remarked, with what looked very much like a smirk.

The silt dried in Sabre's throat. Auntie Aggie's bleachy smile began to swim in front of her, as well as the face of her baby sis Lisette, with her ylang-ylang.

All right, come on, girl. Get this.

"Well . . . no, I'm not saying that. Don't forget I used to live here, too! I've seen things, same as you, ma'am. And now that I'm back, I just want to use my position for a purpose, to call attention to important matters to improve our society. Like the—the *scourge*, right, of oppressed workers, and civil rights. That's all."

"Thank you, caller. Next," said Keith.

The floodgates reopened.

"I ain't know if the maids getting abused in Barbados, but I could tell you who getting licks for sure: the customers! Service real, real bad in this country, boy. You go in a shop, they get on like they doin' you a favor just to say boo . . ."

"Miss Cumbatch, when yuh ain't nobody in Barbados, God help yuh."

"I hear you, caller." Well, she did! She heard him! What was that *look* on Keith's face?

"Miss Cumberbatch, what you saying might be so. But I got some good news for you. The problem you are raising is shrinking faster than Barbados if you believe Muddy Pickering. Because nowadays nobody can't afford no maid! I know very few people nowadays with one. Cost of living gone through the roof. So you sit tight, soon won't be no maids left to abuse."

"A luxury crusade, perhaps, Miss Cumberbatch?" Keith asked, turning back to the phone line before Sabre could answer. "Welcome to *Open Mic*."

"Mr. Everton, I goin' tell you the truth. I would love for somebody to abuse me right now. I serious!"

"Oh?"

"You know how long I been out of work? Eight months, Mr. Everton! Eight, Miss Cumberbatch! Abuse? Gimme them problems, hear?"

Another caller groused, "But who is this Bajan Yankee to come here and lecture us? And America so racist. Clean up your own yard first!"

"That's exactly what I'm trying to do, caller. This *is* my own yard!" Sabre was shouting now, mainlining the power of the casuarina cones through her left quad with her fist pressed down on her pocket. At that response, she thought she detected a little smile on Keith's lips.

Then, "*Open Mic.*"

"H-hello?"

"Yes, go ahead, please."

"It's true what the lady say," a woman whispered, in a barely audible voice. "My boss does mistreat me regular."

Sabre, Keith, and Vonda jerked upright.

"Speak up, please, madam, go on," coaxed Keith.

"I can't talk no louder," whispered the woman. Her accent was not quite Bajan. "I ain't want the rest hear me. Listen! A man bring me here last year say he got work for me. He tek 'way me passport and put me to live with a family. Nearly one whole year, I can't leave the house nor use the telephone. I doesn't get no pay. He say I owin' he. As God is my witness, these people like they does feed me only what the dog lef' back. Is hell I livin' in here!"

"Ma'am, tell us . . ." Keith began, but just then the ON AIR sign started flashing. Seconds to go.

"Ma'am, I'm afraid we're out of time, but please stay on the line, don't hang up . . . My thanks to Sabre Cumberbatch, Mordecai Pickering, and all of our callers today. You've been listening to *Open Mic.* Stay tuned now for the news."

Somewhere in the background, the commercials began to play. Vonda remained hunched over the phone in her producer's booth, scribbling. Keith slumped back in his seat.

Sabre could barely contain herself. She looked out at the casuarinas and felt herself swaying along with them.

"Wow. Whew!" she shouted, slapping her palms on the table. The casuarina cone she had been grinding between her thumb and middle finger went flying, narrowly missing Keith's chin.

"Did you plan this?" he asked, with rather too much attitude for a man whose show she had just saved.

But Sabre was too hyped to bite. "Destiny, man. You see that? That poor woman. Yes! *Yes!*"

"Your aunt asked us to give you a few minutes on the air to talk about *art*—"

"Are you kidding? And by the way, 'luxury crusade'? I'm exposing abuse—"

"And I don't take kindly to my show being hijacked by a—"

"We're public figures. We have a responsibi—"

"*We?*"

The word dinged off the Soviet bullet holes. She and Keith squared off.

She took him in again, irritated and titillated. The thick eyebrows, the well-defined jawline. Those fingers, interlaced on the table, long and slender, perfect down to the nail beds.

Shit. A man this fine didn't belong on the radio.

Sabre felt like laughing out loud, but the ON AIR sign lit up again, and an announcer began to read the news in the studio next door. So she grabbed the Smirnoff and put it to her lips. Keith watched with a raised brow as she drank.

"At least let me get you some chaser," he deadpanned.

"You know how we artists are. We like it raw—I mean, neat." She meant *raw*.

"Look," he said. "What happened today was a good thing, definitely. We're used to surprises around here. But you should have let us know, so we could prepare. You see it turned out to be worthwhile, even in the short time we had. But there's a lot more we could have done."

"Well . . . you're right. Also, you're welcome."

Keith leaned all the way back, studying her, stretching his long, triangular torso, forcing her to imagine the Adonis belt at the base.

"Tell me, though," he said, his voice silkening. "What got into you?"

Before she could answer, Vonda charged in.

"Girl, you got the phones *burr*-ning," she said. "Whew! We shoulda kept going, Keith. The news could always wait. This woman set off a storm."

"I did?"

Vonda pulled up a chair, and only the grinding of the casuarina cones kept Sabre's feet on the floor through what she heard next.

First of all, there was another show to be done right away, like *tomorrow*. The woman who had just called had promised to try to call again. In the meantime, she had provided Vonda with information regarding her whereabouts and was counting on Sabre—on *her!*—to follow up on her story. Others had called in, too, Vonda said, some asking for Sabre personally. She was *needed* back in the studio; she had become indispensable. And a woman from the workers' union was insisting that she call right away.

All this she took in as though atop the trees. The casuarinas nodded and nodded. Vonda squeezed her arm and went back into the booth.

Alone in the studio, Sabre and Keith looked at each other hard.

Is he thinking what I'm thinking?

Man, if that mic weren't in the way, what she wouldn't squeeze on him.

Chapter 10

For the next forty-eight hours the world wobbled on its axis, jiggling the tectonic plates under Barbados and meting out random cosmic oddities: here, a lull at the height of the workday afternoon; there, a transcendent dual orgasm; elsewhere, a thundering migraine that all the Panadol, bush tea, and craniosacral massage in the world were powerless to cure.

Those who had missed the hottest broadcast in recent memory—Agatha Toppin's Yankee niece had exposed her as a maid-beating tyrant!—made up their minds not to be cheated twice. The next afternoon became a virtual holiday. Every lick-mouth on the island, those who knew of the Toppins and the few who did not, those who faithfully followed *Open Mic* and the many who tended to ignore the radio as it hummed in the background, downed tools and prepared to focus.

Too bad! By the second show, all the gooey glop of family treason had been washed away in a torrent of tears. Callers flooded the airwaves with tales that rivaled each other in outlandishness. Were there really that many chamber pots still about the place, and did people really use them for *that*? Was the helper right to put magnesium in the milk when they fired her for getting pregnant? Some callers described the bizarre rituals they were made to endure. Some grasped at straws: "Imagine, three years I working here and they still calling me Freddy. It's Fer-dy!"

In voices brimming with fear, sorrow, or rage, the cadences of Guyana, Barbados, Saint Vincent, and assorted pinpricks up the Caribbean chain blubbered out their hearts to this new Oprah whom no one had heard of before last week. Charitable listeners noted how something in Sabre's gospel-choir "*Mm*-hmms" and "Reallys?" seemed to calm the distraught. Even the grill man himself, Keith Everton, good for bringing the heat to issues and guests alike, seemed tamed by her sincerity.

Others were unconvinced. Where was the promised dirt on Aggie Toppin? Why was Keith neglecting his duty to put on a good show, grilling Sabre like he had done yesterday, like he could be counted on to grill anyone else foolish enough to pull up to his microphone? Who was this muted traffic cop, with his "Go ahead, callers" and "We'll be right backs"? As for Sabre Cumberbatch's transformation from spitfire to saint, even the blind could see a muzzle there.

Who had shut them up?

Who else.

~

The day before, at the moment of Sabre's radio debut, Aggie had been in her car on the way back to the office after closing a monumental property-development deal. She couldn't decide which swelled her heart more: the six-figure check still cooling in her pocketbook, or her imminent enthronement as cultural royalty alongside her niece. She was so elated that when she rolled her eyes on hearing the voice of Muddy Pickering, that insufferable Chicken Little whose perpetual squawks about the environment served no purpose other than to hold back progress, she did so more out of professional reflex than genuine aggravation.

Then in one horrible instant, all the pride and anticipation overturned on her like a bucket of lava. She nearly ran off the road. Seized with shame, she jammed the gas and tore to the office. She rushed in to find the paralegal, the technician, the administrative assistant, and the receptionist all huddled around a computer listening to the broadcast, just as she had reminded them to do at least a dozen times that morning. The acid reflux rose in the back of Aggie's throat. She wanted to spit, to bark at somebody, but for once words failed her. With the eyes of her staff at half-mast, someone having discreetly turned the volume down, Aggie slunk past them and retreated behind the door of her suite.

This one was too baffling for tears or a tantrum. She pushed aside the ten thousand humiliations mounting beyond her window. What in God's good name had got into her niece? Oppression, abuse—What in blazes was she talking about? Aggie scoured the corners of her memory to put some figment of sense to it. Ever since Sabre's arrival, it had been sweetness and light in that house. Hadn't it? Smiles and celebrations and making up for lost years? Who or what could have put such ideas in her head?

Had Isilda said something?

Aggie took out her phone and called Hubert.

"*Oui*, Marie Antoinette?" he answered cheekily.

"You hear this foolishness! I tell you that maid must be done start to—"

"Nancy is here in the car with me. Nancy, don't be rude. Greet Her Majesty properly."

"Hello, Aggie," came Nancy's civil drawl. "How are you?"

"Nancy! Sorry, didn't realize . . . How are you? You listening to this *Open Mic* rubbish?"

"We heard," said Nancy placidly. Her tone made Aggie's hair feel in need of a combing. She recoiled at the thought of Nancy's icy expression.

"So your niece wants an extra place setting at the table," Hubert said.

"I don't know what possessed her. Nancy, can you imagine such a thing?"

"What, a helper at the table? Of course," said Nancy. "When Carmen comes the three days a week, we always have lunch together."

Hubert said, "Well, she can't steal the silver she needs to eat with in front of you."

"What an uncharitable thing to say," Nancy scolded.

"You and your strays. I never hear about anybody hiring a stranger from a bread line to come and work in their house."

"Hubert, you know full well she's not a stranger," Nancy retorted. "Just because somebody falls on bad times doesn't mean they lack integrity. Delphine herself vouched for the woman."

Hubert chortled. "Delphine would vouch for a sand fly if it gave her a hard-luck story."

"And thank God for that," snapped Nancy. "This country needs more like her."

"Anyhow, don't worry, this will settle," Hubert said.

"You mean me?" said Aggie.

"Don't take it on. If you don't act guilty, you're not guilty."

Aggie was tempted to lance a sharp "Is that a *fact*?" at that boil of a remark, but she decided against it. She mumbled her thanks and hung up, the image of Hubert's faded boxers wafting in the adrenaline fog of her mind.

Then it struck her. The only possible explanation: *Priscilla*.

On cue, the replay of their last real conversation, twenty years old but clear as yesterday, boomed in her head.

"Leave him, Cil," Aggie had dared to command her elder sister then.

"Leave him, and what? Go from being the hard-luck wife to the only divorcée in the family? Raise my child in a broken home and fail twice?"

"Don't worry about that for now."

"I see. Easy to say when you have a rich bull to drag around by the nose."

"Cil, it's Ronnie dragging the two of you down. You need to cut him loose. Save yourself and Sabre. Better a broken home than no home at all."

"I will be sure to ponder that on the way home from the bank, Aggie. I don't know why you love to see people on their knees. Are you or are you not going to help me keep the roof over Sabre's head?"

It had been for their good, their good and nothing else, that Aggie had withheld her checkbook that final time. Ten months later, Ronnie was dead. The funeral home had been instructed not to accept contributions from her, so Clive had had to arrange to cover the costs in his assistant's name. At the grave site Priscilla had received her condolences like a stranger, mumbling a rote response. Then, before their cheeks could dry, she and Sabre had vanished to America.

Priscilla. It had to be her. A long con.

This thawing of the ice between them, which Aggie had allowed herself to dream of, with Sabre as the precursor, had been like a mirage on the scorching Sahara sands. Her thirst for reconciliation had got the better of her. Some wounds were never meant to heal. Even murderers and thieves rejoined society once they'd done their time. But nobody could hold a grudge like her sister, and for years now, Aggie realized, her resentment must have been a simmering cauldron. Now the lid was off, and the toxic brew was threatening to flood Aggie's very sanctum.

Sister or no sister, niece or no niece, that girl had to go.

～

But in a final injury, as if to deprive Aggie of the lone morsel of pleasure she had coming, that of driving her foot up Sabre's ungrateful behind, the girl had not come home at all. Instead, about a hundred yards offshore, in a green-and-yellow fishing vessel named the *Blessed Assurance*, blanketed by stars and steered by generous currents of vodka, Sabre had spent the night literally rocking Keith's boat.

They had left the studio together and walked through the halls of the station, unable to maintain eye contact as they pretended to discuss the details of the next day's program. No sooner had they reached the parking garage, scarcely clear of the guard's beady gaze, than Keith had ambushed her up against the hood of her rental. His pelvis ground her thigh, her tongue invaded his mouth, and their hands explored each other all over. From that point on, little was said until they could express themselves freely at sea, where the turbulent pitching, screams, and moans had the fish thinking that hurricane season must have come early.

Next morning before sunrise, they had returned to shore, against the tide of boats setting out on their daily chase for flying fish as far as the waters off Tobago. They drove to Keith's house on the eastern tip of St. Peter and made love until the rising sun filtered rainbows through the crystal broadcasting award on his dresser.

It was Keith who had to suggest a change of clothes before they went back to the station. He had offered one of his T-shirts, but when he directed her to the freshly washed stack in his laundry room, she spotted under the table a pile of old burlap flour sacks labeled PURE BARBADOS ALL-PURPOSE FLOUR. Delighted, she had cut three boxy holes in one and slipped it on as a minidress.

"Surprise." She rubbed up behind him in the kitchen as he stood beating eggs.

"Mmm. I knew I saved those bags for a reason." He turned and leaned in for a long, searing kiss. "If all flour looked like you, we would spare more of it."

"But still this flour will end up around your waistline."

"Nothing pure about it."

Vonda had given them an impish look when they arrived at the studio, but she didn't comment on the dress. Instead, she bustled Sabre into a booth, and they got to work right away. They contacted an antitrafficking group to learn what to do if the mystery woman from the last show called back. When finally she did, they were able to trace the call and put her directly in touch with the antitrafficking organization and with her embassy, which brought in the police.

Sabre was on such a high from the momentum that it was only after the second show that she realized she had forgotten to check in with the family since the day before. She turned on her phone: fourteen messages. A call from Lisette came in immediately.

"Say, what the fuck! You're a real comedian!"

"You heard?"

"Mummy out for your head, girl."

"Crap. I was afraid of that."

"Ha! Not afraid enough. Should have heard her last night. Called you everything but a child of God."

"But you heard it, right? I wasn't talking about anyone specific—you know that, right? I was just—"

"Very entertaining. Best *Open Mic* ever! How you manage to find all them freaks?"

"That's not nice. We're helping people."

"So this is how you get followers in New York, rousing rabbles? Ha-haaaa!"

"You really think Auntie Aggie hates me?"

"You joking? You can't stay there again. But I guess you already figured that out. Where you were last night? By Aunt Evelyn?"

Sabre hung up and went to find Keith in his office.

"I'm sorry, sweetheart," he consoled her. "I was hoping this was a calculated risk."

"I need to explain to my aunt. She's got it completely wrong."

"Explain it to me, 'cause I still don't get it, and I've now done two shows with you."

"I just knew there were people who needed my help. I had to."

"You definitely helped the trafficking victim. The rest, we'll see. Bajans love a scandal."

"I'm sorry my aunt's upset. But honestly, this is *still* the best damn day of my life!"

"Well, you've probably made a lot more people happy than upset in the last thirty-six hours." He pursed his lips. "Now we need to think about where you're going to sleep."

"Don't you need an extra sack of flour?"

"I need it bad, bad. But I'm not set up for it. I have my kids three nights a week, and it's a whole song-and-dance with their mother about people in the house . . ." He paused. "And then, too, darling, keep in mind: Barbados is small."

"Meaning?"

He leaned back. "Meaning, in all honesty, it might not serve your cause or mine to be seen together. We would be more use to each other with a bit of distance. In public, that is."

They locked eyes for a moment. Sabre sat down.

"Wow. This is new. Most of the time people are trying to get at me. Here you are, trying to get away."

"Me? I ain't going nowhere. I'm protecting my investment. This place is small, Sabre. Don't underestimate that."

"I shoulda known. Who risks butt splinters down in a boat when there's a comfortable bed at home?"

"I wear those splinters with pride, madam. Earned every one through hard work."

"Sleep with all your guests, do you?"

"Only the ones that hijack my show and rinse out my vodka."

"Hey, I earned every drop. Through hard work."

They exchanged weak smiles.

"Don't worry. Thing now start, we going make it work. Let me find a hotel for you."

"Hotel?" Vonda poked her head through the door. "What for?"

"Aggie Toppin getting the last lash," Keith replied.

Vonda sucked her teeth. "Was afraid of that, you know," she said. "Look, Sabre, if you like, you're welcome to come and stay by us. We have the room, and I'm sure my husband wouldn't mind. Not to mention we could get some real work done."

"Oh, thanks! You sure?"

"Sure." Vonda smirked. "Unless Keith has a better idea?"

Minutes later when she finally listened to her voice mails, there were thirteen from Lisette—and one from Aunt Evelyn:

"Dear heart, from the time that program cut off yesterday I make up the spare room. I tell Ken, 'Say ain't going get away with this, not in that house!' I tell he, 'The face like the mother but the mouth like the father!' Wulossey! Stay the course, girl! Your bed here waiting for you, come anytime!"

~

Face like the mother, mouth like the father!

The phrase looped in Sabre's head as she drove back to the house. Two roofs, Vonda's and Aunt Evelyn's, to replace the one she was losing. Was that her father's doing? Another of his grand gestures, like the ones he used to pull to dazzle a trampled heart, stuff it with glitter confetti, make it forget?

She caught his deep-dimpled smile in the waves breaking near the roadside, the same smile he would flash amid the boxes and bags and rolled-up rugs whenever they were about to leave the place they had most recently called home. They would cross a new threshold, and he would sweep her, squealing, up onto his shoulders to carry her through the door. And she would grip his cheeks and try to sink her fingers into his dimples to steady herself.

Those dimples, so deep as to seem bottomless, got deeper the harder he laughed. But at the bottom of their squishy depths, her fingers would always come up against the hard enamel of teeth.

She would dig in as best she could. Sometimes, the place they entered was truly new. But often, it was the familiar refuge of Auntie Aggie and Uncle Clive's. Moving into and out of the Toppin house was part of the Cumberbatch legacy.

Swaying and smiling, she trained her gaze on the pavement as the waves receded from the roadside, leaving behind a sickle of wet sand and foam.

~

Out on the back veranda, Isilda heard the car approach. She lifted her head from Ian's chest to listen. The roughness of the engine told her it wasn't a Toppin car.

"Look Miss Hit-and-Run coming," she sneered. "Can't hide forever."

"Man, I tell you, I learn some things on that program today," Ian said. "People getting treat so in Barbados? I thought them things did over and done with. I sure that is how them girls does end up selling themselves down by the racetrack. Wonder if any of these Guyanese fellas I working with involved."

"That is what you here studying? You like you can't see what going on right in front you two eyes."

"How you mean?"

"Lord Christ, I gotta map out every blessed-well thing for this man," she muttered, buttoning the top of her dress. "Let we see now."

She met Sabre in the foyer at the foot of the stairs. "So you reach back."

"Isilda! Are you OK?"

"Why you trying to complicate my life?"

"Isilda . . ."

"Don't 'Isilda' me. If you make me lose this job, I goin' . . . I goin' . . ."

"Oh, my God. Did Auntie Aggie say something to you?"

"Not yet, but it coming, mark it."

Sabre sank down on the lowest step. "Well. She's already throwing me out."

"What!" Isilda buckled against the wall. "And you is blood! Oh Lord, I weak . . ."

"Honestly, it's kind of an overreaction," said Sabre, shaking her head. "It's not like we called her by name."

"That woman don't play! You ain't know they does call she 'the Terror'?"

"The Terror?" Sabre looked up at her. "So did you know those women at the party? The ones she didn't pay?"

"Who? No."

"Hmm. Still . . ." Sabre rested her head in her hand, massaging her scalp. "I mean, yes, she is my aunt and everything, and I adore her. But somebody has to stand up for what's right. Wrong is wrong, you know?"

"That is what you risking my job for? Them girls must be done make back that money ten times since."

"Risking your job?" Sabre looked up. "Isilda, I'm trying to save you! To inspire you and people like you and those workers who are being oppressed! Don't you get that? It's time for you to start making your footsteps heard, Isilda."

"Wuh you talking 'bout at all?" Isilda felt her nerves pique.

"A right to make noise when you walk. Don't you deserve that? I know you agree with me, Isilda. If only you felt free to express it."

"Agree with what?" Isilda scowled. "Jesus-peace, the girl gone mad."

"I saw the look on your face that night, when Auntie Aggie was going off on those women. Did you listen to *Open Mic*? Did you hear how many people called in today? It was amazing. So you see? She's not the only 'terror.' People are being oppressed all over this country."

"Wuh fuh do, life rough," Isilda snorted. "I get unfair nuff times, too. That is why I makin' sure I ain't gotta go hunting for work again."

"Ah, so that's it? I got mine, so too bad for everybody else?" Sabre asked, leaning forward. "That's such a New York attitude. What if I'd done that, hmm? I could have, you know. I could've stayed on that crazy New York ride, being a good blimp, swallowing hot air every day, just floating above it all like a mascot at the Macy's parade. But you know what, Isilda? It leaves you empty inside. In here." She brought a fist to her chest. "Trust me. You don't want to go down that road. Being here, being real, helping people like you? Yeah. This is what it's all about, sis."

Isilda stared at this grasshopper of a girl, with her twinkly face and her hands balled up under her chin, who had probably never had to bear anything heavier than that coconut head. Wearing a flour sack and all,

Father in Heaven, the very kind of thing she was working her fingers to the quick to keep from going back to. She thought of Ma, and her six-year-old granddaughter Nekisha, and of her no-good son Lamar.

"See, Isilda, I'm here to help you find your voice," Sabre was saying. "To fight for your right to . . . to sit at that beautiful table over there! 'Cause I know you deserve it. But do *you* know?" She leaned in and cocked her chin at Isilda like a pistol. "Let me help you claim it. Let me liberate you, Isilda."

"*Liberate* me!"

Something in the way Sabre pronounced her name, in the slip of her American accent, spiked Isilda's blood pressure. She took a step forward.

"Look, listen to me," she said. "Please to just make sure Miss Toppin know I ain't had nothing to do with this nonsense, hear? I ain't complaining, I ain't talking out nobody business 'pon the radio, I ain't want no liberating, I ain't want to sit at no table and keep no noise. I here to work and keep peace. Understand? Make sure you get that in she head or not I goin' put some blows in yours."

Sabre recoiled. Isilda started toward the kitchen. Then she turned again.

"You aunt did real excited when you was coming. Couldn't talk 'bout nothing else. She does got nuff things 'pon she mind and she does got she ways. But one thing I could tell you for sure: she does hold you special."

~

Isilda had taken off by the time Aggie returned to find Sabre's car parked in the driveway. The sight of it made her migraine pound all the harder.

An epic, skull-splitting tirade was surely in order, but Aggie wasn't sure she had the energy for that. As she sat behind the wheel sifting alternatives, the patio door opened and out marched the twins, each wheeling a suitcase, with Sabre following behind. Sabre rushed over as soon as she saw the car.

"Auntie Aggie! Good. Let me explain."

Aggie looked straight ahead. "All right," she said coolly.

The cool seemed to throw Sabre off. "I only meant . . ." she began. "When I . . ."

As she fumbled, Aggie picked up some sort of feed-bag dress in her peripheral vision. She shook her head in disgust. What was wrong with this child? Was she truly as scatterbrained as her father?

"OK, so Isilda was not involved," she got out at last. "OK? She was totally not involved. But it's just that . . . first of all, Auntie Aggie, I'm grateful to you for the party and everything. This is not personal, I swear. But you know, when you dismissed those workers, and . . . and Isilda's always so quiet, and . . . people are scared of you, Auntie Aggie. And I know you're not doing it on purpose, but . . . I just feel . . . well, I need to use my voice for real issues, you know? You understand, right?"

The headache surged. Aggie bit her lip, but the tears began to well. Sabre dropped forward and attempted to hug her through the open window.

"Auntie Aggie, please don't cry!"

"This is your mother," Aggie fumed. "Entirely your mother. Her stamp all over it."

"What? No! My mother? Look, Auntie Aggie . . . I came here to find something, and now you've helped me find it. I have a purpose now: to help people fight oppression in this country. That's all I want to do. Auntie Aggie, please, it's not about you at all . . . In fact, I totally defended you! Did you hear me yesterday? Wasn't that an amazing show?"

"Please take your hands off me."

Sabre pulled back. "Auntie Aggie, I did everything I could to protect you. Please believe me. I love you."

"You don't know the meaning of the word."

"That's not true! I do! Plus, it's OK now, I promise! That part about you, it's already over. People aren't even talking about it anymore. We're saving people, Auntie Aggie, we saved a woman from trafficking today! Just like *you*, the way you help people as a lawyer. We're giving them power and defending their rights!" She paused. "I mean, maybe . . . maybe you could even . . . be part of the solution? You know . . . be nicer to people, let Isilda sit at the table and stuff? I'm sure it would mean a lot to her. Even if she's too scared to ask."

Aggie sat rigid as stone.

"As long as I live, I will never understand why you have done this to me," she said. "I am at pains to put one modicum of sense to the rubbish you are talking. You have humiliated me, Sabre Cumberbatch, after everything I have done for you. For no reason at all. Your father, your mother, you . . . I'm done. Don't say another word. Just please get out of my house. Get out and don't come back."

Chapter 11

Thus began Sabre's season as a hatchback nomad, adrift in the Bajan wild, albeit with two spacious bedrooms, one in the countryside and one with an en suite bathroom close to town, plus half of Keith's bed and the run of the *Blessed Assurance*, at her disposal for as long as she chose to roam.

The island for her seemed to be always about packing and leaving, of seeking refuge and of finding it. But this time, there was nobility and purpose to it. The exile from Auntie Aggie's, as she saw it, had been a sort of sacrifice on her own terms. Never had she felt more rooted than she did now, in this rootlessness.

She spent the first night at Vonda's. Vonda's husband, Eric, a development economist with the United Nations, made squash stew and flying fish, and then the three of them sat on the patio amid the aloe and broad-leaf thyme, talking strategy.

"We know Barbados is a hub for trafficking people into forced labor," Vonda said. "That caller was the tip of the iceberg."

"See?" Sabre shook her head. "I knew it. I could just smell it."

"Yeah, well, smelling is all you can do when you don't have bodies and statistics," Vonda said. "I used to be a regional journalist before joining the station. Caribbean people don't like to talk about these things because they're bad for tourism. We need to seize momentum and get this onto the regional agenda."

"All the Caribbean countries have signed the UN resolution against trafficking," said Eric. "It's the most lucrative illegal business in the world after the drug trade. But because most of the victims are women, the governments don't make it a priority."

"Typical," said Sabre.

"Well, that's part of the reason. The other part is that it's been mostly invisible," Vonda said. "But now," she added, patting Sabre's hand, "you and your camera can help expose it."

"I'm on it. Let's go rescue folks and bust some oppressor ass."

They laughed.

"You guys, I can just feel it. Can't you? This is what I was meant to be doing. Not getting atted by some stupid influencer, know what I mean?"

"If a post can bring exposure to the issue, so much the better," said Eric.

"Yeah, no, totally. I'm just saying. This is some seriously deep stuff."

"Good. Well, let's do a bit of digging tomorrow and find out which groups are actively working on trafficking issues. We can join forces and put together a coalition."

"Yeah! And I can do posters, radio spots, whatever."

"You are so committed," Vonda marveled, smiling. "I wish all celebrities had your drive."

"Celebrity? Please, Vonda, park that talk in New York. Just think of me the way I think of myself. As a servant of the people."

But a few mornings later, facing another day in Vonda's empty house, Keith preoccupied with the kids and no coalition to jump into, she decided to take her camera and go out in search of some actual servants. Servants she might persuade to serve as the face of the hidden oppressed.

She got into her car, started the engine, and then paused. She stared at the GPS. Where did one go to find the hidden oppressed?

She began to cruise the streets, turning at random, watching people go about their days. People waiting for buses and boarding them, people sweeping the pavilions beside the beach, selling snacks, or hunching over sewing machines in a luggage repair shop. People pumping gas, entering banks, parallel parking. Packing groceries into a car trunk. Directing traffic.

Sunlight filled the spaces beneath the trees, spreading its glow across the serene orderliness. Everyone and everything seemed to have its place beneath the cloudless sky, to be moving to a common clock-work rhythm.

It was all highly inconvenient. She phoned Lisette.

"Why is everybody here so freaking happy?"

"Excuse me?"

"Where's the misery? Where are all those people who called in to the show?"

"Chile, people who have time to be on your little program are too idle to go outside."

"I swear, this place is like a Disney version of itself."

"So let me hear you right. You're mad that we're not all out here sulking like angsty New Yorkers?"

"Who said anything about mad? I'm just trying to find people to help."

"I know exactly where you can find a disturbed woman with too much time on her hands. Already a proven hazard to herself."

"Ha ha. Did Auntie Aggie get my email?"

"Email? Girl, what part of *persona non carry-yuh-ass* do you not understand?"

"I feel awful."

"Bullshit. You love it. You're like a cross between Oprah and Joan of Arc. Look, Mummy's a drama queen, you know that. This is just grist for her mill. She'll get over it."

"The racetrack!"

"What?"

"That's where the prostitutes hang out, isn't it? Maybe I can go there and shoot."

"You can go there and *get* shot. Stay in your lane, Joan of Oprah. That's my advice."

"Now who's the drama queen?"

"Hey, listen. Since you're so anxious to hobnob with horses, why don't you come to the polo club with me and the girls this Saturday? We have a box. Unlimited drinks, and the players are hotter than those jockeys at the racetrack. The average jockey only comes up to your waist. Although, come to think of it, that might work out quite nicely for you . . ."

"Lisette. Are you serious? I'm trying to be about a cause, and you're inviting me to sip cocktails at a polo club?"

"Sor-ree. Go light your own stake, then. Call me when you get thirsty."

"Actually, you know what? There is something you can do for me. I need a number."

~

Isilda was home experimenting with pureed sugar-apple pulp as a base for cream pies. It was a Saturday morning, the end of another tense week at work, during which she had labored harder than ever to avoid Mrs. Toppin as she moped about the house. She was in test-kitchen mode, her happy place, stirring clockwise while wining counterclockwise to a dancehall tune, when a call came through, interrupting the music from the Bluetooth speaker.

"Hello?" she called, hoping the intrusion registered in her voice. Who was still making phone calls in this day and age, and on a Saturday morning to boot?

"Isilda?"

That Yankee voice. She rolled her eyes.

"It's Sabre. Do you have a minute?"

"I don't remember sharing out this number."

"Sorry, I know. I got it from Lisette."

Isilda pursed her lips. Lisette had never called her for anything, much to her appreciation. "It is Saturday, please," she said tersely.

"I just wanted to check in. Are you OK? Are things good with Auntie Aggie?"

Isilda could not resist a bitter laugh.

"Looking for fresh meat for yuh program, nuh? Well, I ain't sellin'. And you better not be recording me, neither, 'cause I would clap you in court so fast—"

"No, no, nothing like that," Sabre cut in. "I swear. I was worried about you, that's all."

"The time to worry about me was before you open yuh trap last week."

"Can I make it up to you, then? I have an idea."

At that moment, Isilda's six-year-old granddaughter Nekisha entered the kitchen.

"Gran-Gran, may I have a taste, please?" the little girl asked, pointing to the puree.

"Not yet. Eat your breakfast first," Isilda told her.

"Isilda! You're a *grandmother*?" Sabre's astonished voice came through the speakers.

"Who's that?" asked Nekisha, surprised.

"Mind your business."

"Hi, sweetie!" Sabre called, in a singsong voice. "What's your name?"

"Nekisha," the child giggled.

"Nekisha, hi! I'm Sabre. Would you like to be in a photo shoot with your grandma?"

"A what?" Isilda exclaimed, shooing her granddaughter toward the dining room.

"Ah, I thought that would get your attention," said Sabre. "Just hear me out. So, you know I'm a photographer, right . . ."

"How I would know that, and wuh de France it got to do with me."

"Well . . . people know. Anyway, I want to photograph you. But only in a way that's authentic and honors your dignity. I want to show you in your space. It could be at home, in your favorite park, with Nekisha, or wherever you like. The idea is to show the workers of Barbados how to reclaim their power, make themselves seen and heard. You know? And you would get to be the symbol of that in posters all over the island. What do you think?"

Isilda popped two slices of whole-wheat bread in the toaster and shook her head. What really could be the matter with this girl?

"I'd do it for free, of course," came Sabre's voice through the speaker. "It would be my pleasure. We could get the best makeup artist you have here—not that you need one! Nothing too stylized; we'd keep it simple. Salt-of-the-earth style, you know. To symbolize the raw untapped strength of the marginalized in their . . ."

The more she went on, dribbling her torrent of rubbish, the more convinced Isilda became that the hours Sabre had spent standing in direct sunlight out in the Toppins' garden must have frizzled her brain. Perhaps it was a good thing she had moved out of the mansion after all. No good could come of proximity to her.

"Isilda? Still there?"

The toast popped up. Isilda considered hanging up. Or telling Sabre exactly where she could stick her camera. Instead, she said, "No pictures, no thank you. And please to lose this number."

To her indignation, the woman had the nerve to holler, as the speaker was being switched back to music, "Well, if you change your mind . . ."

~

Undeterred by this setback, Sabre continued to hunt until she found what she meant to find. Three weeks later, by the time Eric had arranged for her to attend a meeting with the UN and a local antitrafficking group, she had amassed a collection of images large enough to need editing.

She was sitting in Vonda's back garden with her laptop, absorbed in this task and drinking a Banks beer, when her agent popped up on FaceTime. In her distraction, she took the call.

"Hey, Katya."

"Favorite girl! You make me suffer, eh? How are you?"

"Busy. How are you?"

"Delighted, how I am doing. I approve of your new career."

"My what?"

"Your Barbados radio show, darling. Fabulous. I listen while I am on treadmill, you say your big surprise, wow! Wow-wow! Sabre, I am so blown, I swear to you, I fly right off machine into the lap of my husband!"

"Oh no!"

"Oh yes. Oh yes, yes, yes! Sabre. Do you know what this means? It means you are now, officially, *international* rebel! Eh? You are wild in New York, you are wild in Barbados, you are wild in paper, you are wild on the radio! It's perfect!"

"Yay," she replied, half-listening. "Perfect."

"Yes! So listen, darling. Our friends, Topsheet, they are aware of your Barbados doings, and they are mad more than ever to work with you. They—"

"Katya! We talked about this."

"Sabre, *dorogaya*, hear me out. It is a different idea. Listen. They want to do a video, eh? Very edgy, very wild. You will play revolutionary, kind of sexy Robin Hood, in the best taste. You will ride horse through the desert with sheet on your head like a turban. You enter a village where everyone is bored. You take off the turban, you spread it in town square—pow! It is movie screen for entertainment. Everyone is happy! Then you see little child who is cold, you go into your bag—pow! You pull blanket and wrap in baby. Then there is a woman sitting on ground—pow! You take sheet and make hammock for her to relax.

Then you ride to house and jump into bed with sexy boots on. You are: Topsheet Rebel! I love!"

There was a stilted silence on both ends of the line.

"Sabre?"

"Do you know what I'm doing right now, Katya?"

"Tell me. Pinching yourself."

"I am preparing for a meeting with the *United. Nations.* About human trafficking. Do you know what that is? Real, substantial stuff. OK? Helping real villagers."

"Ah, a new market! We get finders' fee. Wonderful."

"Goodbye, Katya."

"Sabre, I'm kidding! I tell Topsheet you think. Ciao, rebel girl."

∼

The following evening, Sabre entered a conference room at the local United Nations office, her neck tingling with significance.

One day, years from now—she hesitated to speculate how many, but hopefully not too, too many—the UN visitor pass she had just placed around her neck might turn out to be some sort of artifact. Today felt auspicious, in a never-wash-your-neck-again way. Someday, perhaps at some future auction, somebody bidding on this visitor pass might reflect on her name and the photo printed upon it, recall the significance of this date in Barbadian history, and agree.

In New York, the UN building was basically a tourist trap. Tricked out like a carnival ride, the flags and the obnoxious lines. Always showing off. Trust Barbados to keep it sensible.

A sensible office with seven sensible people around a sensible conference table. Eric, Vonda, a woman from the UN, a man and a woman from the antitrafficking group, a union woman, and Sabre. Sensible room-temperature water, sensible UN paper to write on. Everybody sitting straight and strong, even though the meeting was taking place after business hours. No slouching. Putting the *ass* in gravitas.

Eric called the meeting to order. There was a fleeting round of introductions, impressive for the way everyone stuck to the script: name and title only, no bloviating. Then it was straight down to business.

The business part lost her almost as soon as it began. They were talking about UN resolutions and about implementing outcomes, or *out*plementing incomes, of a high-level . . . something? Sabre's notes looked to her like gobbledygook on the page. Meanwhile, everybody else was duly nodding and jotting, except for the union woman, who was checking her phone.

"We see this as an opportunity to enhance engagement with stakeholders at national and regional levels," the antitrafficking guy was saying. "The results survey for the prior reporting period suggests inadequate issue recognition among civil-society partners."

"Have all the implementing agencies now matrixed antitrafficking indicators into their results frameworks?" the UN woman asked, looking at her papers.

"They were supposed to, in order to secure the first round of disbursement," replied the antitrafficking guy.

"Supposed to and did are two different things," said the UN woman. "I checked the compliance dashboard this afternoon. Look at this." She projected a chart onto the conference room screen, full of tiny lettering in blocks of red and yellow and green. It might as well have been a Lego sculpture or a round of Tetris.

"You NGOs promise the moon and stars," the UN woman continued, "and then we're the ones having to skin cuffins explaining to the donors when the deliverables don't get met."

"That's not fair," the antitrafficking guy countered. "We can't be held responsible for what other groups do. You can look at the framework for our organization and clearly see that our mechanisms are robust."

"All right, look, this isn't the time or place," Eric cut in, with the first fully comprehensible sentence Sabre had heard since the meeting began. "The dashboard is the dashboard. The point is we need to get the implementing agencies onside. Capacity needs to be scaled up on the ground to facilitate our pressuring CARICOM to strengthen the legislation. And if we can't show that, then we stand a real risk of losing the Dutch in the next funding cycle."

"Dutch!" Sabre exclaimed, grabbing onto the word like a branch in a flood. "Yeah, I work with them, too. Man, they're everywhere, right?"

"Yes, the Dutch government is a major donor to women's empowerment programs," said Vonda.

"Perfect," gushed Sabre. "I know what they like—trust me, they will not leave me alone! In fact, I've been doing a little homework of my own. I think they might really go for it. Tell me what you guys think."

Before they could go back to playing Tetris, she connected her laptop to the projector and cued up the first image. It was of a white man lying by a pool in a backyard, and a Black man, barefoot and holding a tray, putting a glass down next to him. It had not been an easy shot to get. It had taken forever to find that neighborhood, and if her life depended on it, she couldn't find her way there again. The houses had been big, spread out, colonial-looking mansions. She'd had to park on the street and walk from house to house, looking for people doing things outside. This particular shot had required her to take her longest lens and stick it through a hedge *plus* a fence. On top of that, she'd had to focus, which of course was off-brand for her. Then she'd edited it in black and white to make it look depressed and, for the same reason, chosen not to crop out the bushes in the foreground. She needed the UN to see the commitment, the activism.

"Now look at this," she narrated. "Dude's chilling, not a care in the world, right, and meanwhile this poor servant has to . . . deliver his deliverables without even a decent pair of shoes. Look how sad he is! And look at the shirt—here, let me zoom in on the holes. See that? Probably the only one he owns."

The meeting went quiet. Drinking it in.

"Where is this from?" the antitrafficking woman asked.

"From right here in Barbados," Sabre replied emphatically.

"Yes, but where?"

"That looks like somebody's house," Vonda said, squinting at the shot. "There's a swing set in the background."

"Exactly. Spoiling their little rug rats but can't spring for a pair of sandals for their staff."

"A lot of people don't wear shoes in the house," shrugged the UN woman.

"I know I don't," said the antitrafficking guy.

Feeling them straying from the point, Sabre hurriedly moved on to the next shot. This one was of a guy halfway up a tree, hacking away at a branch with a machete. Also barefoot and wearing a raggedy shirt, but she decided to let that go and lead with something else.

"Again. Blatant disregard for this gentleman's well-being. Forced to use primitive tools, no gloves, no goggles, no safety brace. Working in danger. If that's not exploitation, I don't know what is."

"Seems to be just pruning a branch," the antitrafficking guy remarked. "You say you got these where?"

"Sabre, were you breaking into people's backyards?" asked Eric, alarmed.

"No! I mean, not per se . . . Look, how else are we going to find victims? Sit around and wait for them to call the show? We gotta be bold here, guys."

"You're right," said the union woman, smiling. It was her first comment all evening.

"That may be, but I don't know that these pictures get us there," said the antitrafficking woman. "First, we don't have any idea about their actual circumstances. Second, they didn't know they were being photographed, so there could be privacy issues there. And third, even if we got past those two hurdles, they're still the wrong—"

"Gender," everybody intoned in unison, chorus-style.

Sabre swallowed her dismay. "Fine," she said, hoping it came out more eager than irked. "Then I'll try to find some oppressed women."

"The thing is, Sabre," said Eric gently, "we may be getting ahead of ourselves. What we need to do first is formulate an option assessment, aligned with the policy guidelines embedded in the resolution. Then we can pull together a working group to draft some proposed legislative text—"

"Right," agreed the UN woman. "And it would have to be quick, like in the next three to six months—"

"*Months?*" Sabre exclaimed. The others shot her puzzled stares.

"Sure," said Eric. "So we can list it in the next round of donor reports as an achieved result."

"But—"

"Or as *many* achieved results," said the UN woman. "Don't forget, this is gender, so that's women—*bam*. Depending on who the victims are, it could be kids, so that's education and child welfare—*bam-bam*. Plus labor rights, reproductive rights, and who knows what else—*bam-bam-bam-bam*. We could kill a lot of birds with this stone."

At this, everyone exchanged satisfied nods around the table.

The antitrafficking woman turned to Sabre. "And you can get us some good shots for the report, right? Especially the cover. Got to be a woman. Something grimy and decrepit. You could donate that, right?" She smiled.

After another few minutes of gobbledygook, the meeting adjourned.

Sabre avoided eye contact as she unhooked her laptop from the projector. What had just happened? She felt reduced, useless. The only result she wanted to achieve right now was to leave. While Vonda and Eric chatted with the others, she slipped out the door.

As she hurried across the car park, she heard someone calling her name. She turned to see the union woman running up to her.

"Them so don't get it," the woman began, gesturing toward the building. "Missing the forest for the trees."

"Oh, my God, right? I thought I was the only one!"

"Bureaucrats," said the woman, snarling the word like an epithet. "Everything is a damn report. That man in your picture, he could fall out that tree and land on their heads and they would need a fact-finding committee to tell them what happened."

"I know!"

"And all the time, people suffering in this country," continued the woman. "Local, foreigner, man, woman, it ain't rocket science. What's this 'gender-bam'? So disrespectful." She shook her head and sucked her teeth. She was older, heavyset, and she radiated fire.

"What's your name?" Sabre asked. "The intros were going kind of fast in there."

"Jessica," replied the woman. "I'm the union liaison, so they invite me to these things when they feel like it. They're wasting you."

She looked evenly at Sabre as she said it. Her gaze lifted Sabre's spirit.

"Your vision is too big for this lot," she went on. "They want reports, and you want results. You looking to get people out from under, and they fooling with dashboards. Y'all ain't speaking the same language."

"We're not. We're absolutely not."

The two women locked eyes. Sabre's flimsy UN visitor pass flapped in the breeze. She pulled it off her neck before it could chafe.

Chapter 12

Quick while the kerfuffle was still nice and warm, an announcement went out from the national union for a special public meeting to discuss what they were terming the Cumberbatch Initiative, featuring an in-person appearance by its originator, international activist and artist Sabre Cumberbatch.

That was the first surprise. The second, for Ian, was that Isilda wanted to attend.

"How come?" he asked, keeping a safe distance across the fence as she beat out a Persian rug hanging from the laundry line.

"How you mean 'How come'? You ain't know you is to keep your friends close and your enemies closer?"

"Enemy? That's harsh, when you weigh it up," he ventured, watching to see if the rug would be made to suffer for his effrontery. "I mean, she kinda impulsive and whatnot. But the things she talking make sense."

"Good. Well marry she, then."

"Come on."

"Look how much confusion she cause in this house. And now tekkin' she show 'pon de road. She goin' soon got everybody head turn. I goin' be there to mark she close."

They agreed that Ian would come to pick up Isilda two hours before the meeting. This built in the time he would undoubtedly have to wait for her to finish getting ready, since he had long observed how she routinely added five to fifteen minutes to her arrival time at work. Extrapolating from there, he estimated at least one outfit change, possibly including hairstyle, which would conservatively add a further fifteen to twenty minutes. Fortunately, Isilda's place was nineteen minutes from the union hall in light traffic, leaving ample time to find a good parking spot and comfortably select their seats in the auditorium.

No aspect of Ian's life was haphazard. Each morning he got up before sunrise to do calisthenics in his small backyard, its coral rock garden framing a cart-wheel centerpiece that he had painted himself. Then he read a passage of scripture from one of the world's great religions, which rotated daily on an app on his phone. After that he led his elderly neighbors on a morning walk around the district. Breakfast was on the light side: fruit—whatever was in season, plus a banana—followed by a bake with sardines and a cup of Ovaltine. In the evenings, he prepared a dinner of mostly vegetables purchased at the market from vendors he knew and trusted. Sometimes he made his five-star meal: raw christophene salad with gooseberries, grated sweet potato with ginger and coconut milk, and a piece of grilled marlin. When it was especially good, he took some over to the neighbors. Then, in his special reading chair, by the light of his special reading lamp, he read one of the two books he assigned himself each month, cruised his favorite sites, then swallowed a concoction of fish oils and honey and tucked himself into bed underneath an ever-expanding firmament of images of handsome, well-turned-out men that he had printed from Pinterest boards and tacked onto his wall.

Saturday afternoons he played cricket or football with the neighborhood sports club, and Sundays were always reserved for his parents, whose yard he swept clean with a broom of coconut fronds while his mother made dinner, ignoring all his dietary prescriptions.

Quiet and regimented, Ian managed to alienate people while at the same time earning their respect. He had few friends, kept mostly to himself, and yet, at just thirty-one years old, constantly found himself thrust to the fore. Treasurer of the local sports club. President of the neighborhood improvement association. Lead tenor in the Christmas chorale. Chief mason on the job. And for the past two years, shop steward for the collective of stoneworkers and skilled craftspeople at Gibbons Amalgamated.

He took out a dark grey dress shirt and instinctively passed the iron over it, even though, like every garment in his closet, it was already press-perfect. He needed to think.

A special union meeting for the Cumberbatch Initiative. He didn't know when last he had seen Jessica Payne and the other bigwigs so pleased. Usually it was their role to scowl and protest. But no, right there in today's paper, another picture of Jessica, Sabre, and Ophelia Walcott, the union's general secretary, their three grins so broad you couldn't make out where one set of teeth ended and another began. The headline read CUMBERBATCH: STAND UP AND BE COUNTED!

And standing up they were, he had to admit. These days, no public forum—whether *Open Mic*, Letters to the Editor, even Dear Darlene, the romance columnist—was without an oppressed houseworker ready to testify. Some of the stories seemed to repeat, but no one seemed to mind. They could scarcely be more repetitive than Jessica and Ophelia, who took every opportunity to remind Bajans that such misfortune never fell upon those who stood under the union's mighty umbrella.

This Cumberbatch Initiative had to be the best thing the union had stumbled upon in years. It was no secret that union power had been fading. There were diehards like Ian, who could personally attest to the value of specialized training and collective bargaining agreements, and then there was just about everyone else he knew—the un-, under-, and overemployed—for whom the value of a union in this rough-and-tumble market was harder to see. Like the kerchief he liked to carry in his breast pocket, the idea had gone out of style. The union's glory days, days of the hundreds-strong cane cutters and assembly-line workers fitting shortwave radios, had passed. Nowadays people were scattered, three or four apiece, to office complexes, small businesses, and freelance gigs, their collective leverage slight enough to be toyed with. Judging by the tales of suffering, people were feeling the pain of vulnerability and isolation.

But now, thanks to the Cumberbatch Initiative, these workers and the union might finally see their way to brighter days.

～

Ian had timed it perfectly. Isilda was tastefully dressed in her second outfit choice: black jeans, sage-green top, and a caterpillary pair of eyelashes. As they settled into their seats near the back of the assembly hall, they noticed a few familiar faces in the crowd.

The place was a good two-thirds full, a strong haul for a special meeting. A buzz of anticipation filled the air. Many had come for the pure spectacle of it, to watch and listen in silence—maybe, in typical Bajan style, to hold forth cantankerously later, in the car park outside. Some, like Ian, were there in official capacities as stewards or rapporteurs.

Isilda was there to witness her fellow citizens turning into idiots under Sabre's spell.

"But check how this girl really come down here to disturb we peace, doh," Isilda grumbled, looking around. "Got everybody looking for something to complain about."

"You know I'm a union man," Ian said. "I glad to see people interested."

"Interested in bacchanal," Isilda replied.

It had been nearly a month since the fabled *Open Mic* episode, and still, Ian noticed, Isilda seemed to be having trouble settling her spirit. Somehow in all this, Sabre seemed to have replaced Mrs. Toppin as the primary source of her aggravation. "This girl love the limelight more than she own family," she would start, if she happened to see Sabre's picture in the papers. "I glad enough I ain't got them headaches."

The tension between Isilda and Mrs. Toppin appeared to have cooled. Lately Isilda had been referring to her as Aggie more often, and she told all the ways Mrs. Toppin was being made to suffer Sabre's slight and how unhappy her life had become, in spite of everything. In fact, Isilda seemed to be developing a soft spot for the woman.

With Mrs. Toppin working from home these days, his afternoon sessions with Isilda had come to an end. Ian had to admit it had been no great loss. The time apart had caused him to see Isilda for what she really was, which was more of a work friend. He enjoyed being a sounding board as she went on about life and work, about Ma and Nekisha and no-good Lamar, her son. She seemed short of people to open up to. Meanwhile, she neither knew nor asked a single thing about his life, and Ian found he liked it that way.

~

The stage lights went up, and the troika walked in: Jessica, Sabre, and Ophelia. At the appearance of Sabre, the first live sighting for many, some of the newcomers applauded.

"You, look she dey," a woman sitting behind Isilda said to her companion.

"She real bony for true, doh," the companion said.

"Bony, yes, but the mouth fat."

"Hee-hee! Yuh en lie. You hear how she ups and move out the aunt house 'cause dem did too hoity-toity for she?"

"Chile, yes. They say she livin' with the everyday people up St. Joseph side."

"That's we girl. One o' we."

It took everything in Isilda's power not to turn in her seat and set this pair of babblers straight. Glancing around, she was unsurprised to find that the two women looked to be in their thirties. Younger than her, yes, but still of an age to know a mouse from a mongoose. Isilda scowled and felt for the Panadol in her handbag. Tonight was bound to be full of fools like these.

The general fidgeting subsided, and Ophelia took the podium.

"Comrades," she began. "Sisters- and brothers-in-arms. Welcome . . . to the dawning . . . of Barbados's renaissance! As I look out at the faces here tonight, I see . . . many things. Anger. Frustration. Indignation. Pain! But also . . . resilience. Determination. Resourcefulness. Strength. Hope! And this gathering reminds me, dear comrades, brothers- and sisters-in-arms, of the mighty *uprising* that gave birth to this great institution, the National Labor Union of Barbados, some *sixty-seven* years ago! Now, comrades, allow me to look back briefly over some of the major *victories* that we have achieved *together* . . ."

"But wait, dis a history class or wuh," grumbled one of the women behind Isilda.

"She gettin' on like she in Parliament. Stop the big talk and let the program start," said the other. "Is Cumberbatch we come to see."

Isilda scanned the room as the general secretary dragged on. Ophelia had reached the major victories of the 1980s when Isilda spotted the live stream feed on a monitor at the engineering booth, directly ahead of where she was sitting. A big green REGISTER button was flashing on the screen. At tables around the perimeter of the hall, union staff placed cups of pencils and stacked registration forms.

Clearly the union was milking this Cumberbatch nonsense for every rancid drop.

Ophelia finally ceded the floor, and now it was Jessica speaking. This was how the pair worked, as Ian had explained on the drive over. Ophelia might be good for grand speeches or closing negotiations, but when a crowd was there to be raised, Jessica was the woman.

"We are here to fight for you," Jessica said. "You are the reason we exist. When you in a job, and people want to feel they could treat you any old how—I don't know, maybe you ain't went to the right school, maybe you ain't know the right body, maybe you skin too dark, you head too scruffy—and they look at you and want to get on like they higher up and better off? Who goin' put them in they place? Eh?"

"Slavery done!" muttered a man in the audience.

"Done, comrade! But certain persons in Barbados like they ain't get the news. Want you work for nothing, like you ain't got to eat and put shoe 'pon you child foot just like them. Want to insult your intelligence. Your hard work. Want to reap all the spoils and pelt you one-side like cane trash. Want to get on like this country build itself! But I put it to you, comrades, this country ain't build itself! It is the workers of Barbados, people like you, brother, and you, sister, and me, that make this country the envy of the Caribbean! It's we sweat that water the soil that make this country grow!"

"Is them shite that fertilize it, Jessie!"

The crowd snickered.

Jessica put on her thousand-yard stare and drew herself up like Moses on the mount. "Laugh!" she cried. "Laugh. Go on! But while you laughing, comrades, remember this. Tonight-self when you home sleeping in you bed, huggin' up you darling and feeling sweet, a next boatload of people going be touching Bajan soil. They going camp out in a container. They going eat SodaBix and drink from the standpipe. They going sleep on the iron floor with thirty or forty other people, do they business there, everything. And then early o'clock tomorrow morning, they going turn up where you working, or where you looking to find work, and they going offer to do your job for next to nothing. They going can't even speak English all that good. And"—here she paused, leaned over the lectern, and peered at the audience over her heavy-framed glasses—"my brethren and my sistren, when these foreigners turn up at your job, and offer to work almost for free, who you feel your boss going listen to? You, or the stranger? You child belly rumbling, or the money jingling down in they pocket?" Her gaze swept the crowd. "You see, you ain't got to know English so good, 'cause that ain't the language they does be speaking 'bout here at all . . ."

"We is Bajans, got to speak Bajan!" someone called out.

"Eh? But what I hearing at all? All who really and truly feel that Bajan, or even English, is the language of business in Barbados, raise your hand."

All hands stayed put.

"Oh. Thought I did wastin' my breath," Jessica continued. "Comrades, wake up for me please, I begging yuh. These people, the big-time high rollers and shot callers in Barbados, that want to get you and the foreigner racing one another to the bottom, is only one language they speaking! Sons and daughters of this soil, somebody tell me what it name, do!"

"Cash dollars!"

"Brek fuh yuhself!"

"All-is-mine!"

"White power!"

"*Greeeed!*" Jessica bellowed. "Nothing but pure, fluent Greed-ese they speaking, comrades! Them ain't care where you born or who deserve to eat in this country! Greed-ese is all them know! But I put it to you, brethren and sistren, somebody got to make them remember Just-ese! And Equalit-ese! And Fair-Wage-For-Fair-Work-ese! Them want to feel that these languages dead like Latin in Barbados, but comrades, we got to make them speak we language again!"

"Dead like Latin!" yelled one of the women behind Isilda, fully missing the point.

The crowd applauded furiously. Isilda looked at Sabre on the podium. She was perched on the edge of her seat, nodding and smiling with her elbows on her knees, like she had been on the steps in the parlor the day Mrs. Toppin had turfed her out, the day she had tried to convince Isilda that up was down and a decent job in a peaceful house was something to be "liberated" from.

Sabre was rocking, hands ready to clap as soon as Jessica finished a sentence. She was gussied up in the national colors like a government building on Independence Day, in a wide blue-and-gold sash and a blousy black top over white trousers.

"The government ain't making them speak Equalit-ese, sistren and brethren! Them ain't know nothing 'bout Just-ese! They letting them do as they like! When last you minister do anything for you? Eh? When last you see he to talk to? Who in here can tell me a time that the minister for their district stand up for them over the big dollars?"

"In Barbados?" shouted someone in the audience. "Mekkin' sport, girl."

"Well, all right, then," said Jessica. "Now. Just in case you feel that this is the, I don't know, the vaporings of a madwoman . . ."

"Talk yuh talk, Jessie, we hearin' you!" somebody shouted.

"Well I glad to know that, comrades. But I want you to understand this thing *serious*, you know. Serious! It ain't just you in here that hearing what going on in this country. It ain't just we so, we loyal sons and daughters all, that smelling a foul smell in Barbados. Comrades, I put it to you that the stench of injustice and exploitation in this country has reached as far as New York City in the United States of America!"

"Up there stink, too!" boomed a voice in the crowd.

The pair behind Isilda chortled. Even Isilda had to laugh at that one.

"I don't say not, brother. But imagine how, from all the way up in America, one of our own smelling the stench and hearing the cries of the people," said Jessica. "This daughter of the soil"—turning toward Sabre—"Comrade Cumberbatch."

"'Bout time," Isilda heard one of the women behind her say as the crowd whooped.

"I missing the last bus for she, yuh," said the other. "It better be worth it."

"Trust me, it goin' be worth it."

Jessica continued. "An internationally famous photographer, brothers and sisters, a person who could easily turn her back, bathe up in her accolades, and ignore our suffering. Instead, she has heeded the call of her people to come and shed light on the state of our workforce. Barely back on the island for the first time in twenty years—twenty years, imagine!—and the stench of oppression done cuff her in her face. Comrades, I put it to you, Comrade Cumberbatch could have spray some sweet-smelling air freshener and gone back to taking her pictures. But instead, what did she do?"

"She fight 'the Terror' with terror!" someone called out. The crowd laughed. Sabre shook her head and wagged a finger with a little smile.

Isilda sucked her teeth. "The gall," she muttered, louder than she had meant to.

"Wuh you say?" said one of the women behind her.

Isilda turned and glared. "I say is the blind leading the blind," she said and turned her back.

"Miss lady, wuh wrong wid you?" said one.

"Everything all right here?" asked Ian.

"Dotish people ain't know what they talkin' 'bout," muttered Isilda, her volume deliberate this time.

"My good man, carry she home, do," said one of the women. "You woman face push up the whole night."

"She could wells go home and stop bringing down we vibe," the other agreed.

"Shh! Less noise," scolded someone nearby.

Onstage, Jessica and Sabre were still laughing at the joke.

"Well," Jessica said, "all I know is, our comrade here is troubled by what she seeing, and hearing, and *smelling*, enough to sound the alarm. And that alarm, brothers and sisters, is why we are here tonight. If you agree with what we saying, if you can't take the stench no more, then comrades, daughters and sons of this great land, I urge you to join this movement. Don't feel that because it's only you one working somewhere that you don't have no rights. You are not alone! We are with you! So fill in the form that the ushers are handing out. Take some for your friends, too! Those of you watching online, click the registration button and join us! Join so we can fight together. Leh we make them speak we language! And if you really ready to fight, we have a dues button online and a table at the back, there by the doors, where our comrades are waiting to receive your contribution. And now, Comrade Cumberbatch, the floor is yours. God bless you all, and God bless Barbados!"

The crowd took to its feet in applause. Sabre leaped up and went to hug Jessica, but the older woman caught her by the shoulder and engaged her in a bone-rattling handshake instead, ushering Sabre to the lectern as the volume of cheers rose even more.

"We joining up or what?" Isilda heard one of the women ask.

"You got a pen? I ain't study to bring one," said the other.

With a line forming at the dues table in the back, the nattering died down, and everyone trained their attention on Sabre's beaming face above the lectern.

"Wow!" Sabre began. "Well. This is certainly a night to remember, isn't it? Please, another round of applause for Jessica Payne!"

The crowd obliged.

"That's right! A woman of the people, ladi—er, brothers and sisters—a woman of the people. Now, you know I am new here . . ."

"You is one o' we now, man!" someone sang out. Isilda rolled her eyes.

"Oh, thank you, sir! Comrade! This means so much to me, you have no idea. I feel like we are, you know, an engine, driving Barbados out of the past and into a new day . . . of equality . . . for all!"

Everybody clapped on cue like a troupe of circus seals. Isilda popped a Panadol and swallowed it dry.

"Yes! Well, one thing I have to say, this is definitely not a 'Cumberbatch Initiative.' This is an initiative of the people! Of all of us together! And so I would like to turn it over to you, comrades, and hear your thoughts. What's on your mind, how do you think we can move forward? Ushers, do we have microphones? Yes. Anybody."

The place was humming like a beehive, but nobody was stood up. Typical! Just like Sabre to tear open a hole and expect other people to fill it. Nerve upon nerve, this girl had.

At last, a middle-aged man stood up. "Maybe you could tell us something about the labor movements in the States, or in New York?"

"Hmm! Thank you, comrade! Let's see . . . You know, in New York it's very, very different. People are more aggressive. I mean, New Yorkers have attitude! If they don't like something, they let you know. They rise up! Just like we're rising up here tonight!"

"But what about the workers in the sweatshops and so on? And the subway drivers and teachers that always in the news?"

Exactly! What about them, Miss Movement? Isilda chuckled to herself. She wished she had brought some popcorn.

"Yes, well, the unions . . . the subway union, for instance, you know it's a lot of Caribbean people like us. Did you know that? Yes! And the sweatshops, right, sure. Super oppressive. A lot of women, like, immigrant women . . . Actually, I think a lot of stuff is made in China now? And you know what? They need to fight for their rights, too! Yeah, absolutely."

Pffft! A perfect fart of a response. Isilda began to feel tipsy.

The hum grew louder. A large woman with intricate cornrows took a mic.

"Comrade Cumberbatch, how do you propose to organize domestic workers spread out in different homes and whatnot? Obviously it can't be the same as having a group of workers assembled in one workplace."

For the first time, Isilda thought she saw Sabre's smile twitch.

"Well, thank you, comrade," she said. "Excellent question! What do you suggest?"

What did *she* suggest? Isilda shook her head. Wasn't it Sabre herself who had come humbugging her, a domestic worker in a home? Now, all of a sudden, out of ideas?

"What do *I* suggest?" asked the woman, perplexed.

"Sure," replied Sabre. "I mean, this is a dialogue, right? We're all equal. Who has a good idea? Anyone?"

The cornrowed woman looked for somebody to hand the mic off to.

"Come on!" Sabre chirped. "Speak up, somebody!"

Ophelia took over the lectern briefly to say that collective agreements were unlikely for domestic workers, but that the union could still intervene in certain disputes.

"See?" Sabre chimed in. "There you go. Next!"

"Are you in a union?" someone shouted from the back, without a microphone.

"Me? Well . . . well, no, but . . ."

"Ever been in one?"

The dues line froze.

"Good. Look bacchanal," Isilda crowed to Ian.

"I . . . well, I work . . . for myself, I guess, but as an art—"

"Oh! So you is management, then!"

Sabre, smile still pasted on her face, turned to her comrades onstage, but Jessica had already bounded to her side.

"Comrades, let us not lose focus," she said. "Keep it straight. Comrade Cumberbatch is not management, and she is not labor. She may not be an expert in organized action. But to my mind, she is something even more honorable: a concerned defender of this country, who has found the courage—at great personal sacrifice, some of you would have heard—to speak out on issues that affect all of us. Why should we stoop to attack the messenger when the message is so vital to us all?"

Light applause came from the middle of the room. Jessica sat down, and Sabre amped her smile back up.

"These are fair questions, for sure," she said, in a sugar-water voice. "But guys, this is about you, not me! This is your night. Just like tomorrow will be your new day!"

A young woman rose from the center of the floor.

"Miss Cum'batch—"

"Comrade!" someone growled.

"Sorry! Miss Comrade, I just want to tank you for all wuh you doin' to help the wukkas in pee-pull house. Since you come on the radio, it have plenty wukkas now who knowin' they rights an' who ain't friken again. We know we can come to you, Miss Jessica, an' you, Miss Comrade!"

Something about the woman's voice, with its small-island accent, sounded familiar to Isilda. As she tried to place it, someone in the audience shouted, "But wait, she ain't no Bajan!"

"Come on now!" Sabre urged. "This movement is for everybody."

"Lewwe see she papers, then!"

"Comrades, please!" Sabre shouted, rapping the lectern. "Unity, remember!"

The young woman gripped the microphone with both hands. "Miss Comrade, it's me!" she cried out. "Remember? I is the one who did wukkin' you auntie pah-tee! You was stannin' up side-o' she, remember?"

Of course. Rice and peas. It was the rice-and-peas attendant from the party!

The tipsiness drained from Isilda's head. Sabre's smile dimmed.

"Miss Comrade, if you see me hey stannin' up in front all these people, it's you an' the Almighty I must thank for that! After we hear you 'pon radio, me an' the otha wukkas, we confront we boss 'bout we pay. We say we goin' 'pon radio with Miss Comrade if he don't seckle we contract. Same day he come back wid we money! Lord bless you, Miss Comrade!"

"Oh. OK great!" Sabre exclaimed, bursting into applause so loud that the audience felt obliged to follow. Jessica and Ophelia nodded approvingly.

"An' Miss Comrade," the rice-and-peas attendant went on, "is not only you ah thankin', eh? I have to thank Miss 'Silda, too, 'cause she real help me get tru that night wukkin for you auntie. Oh gosh, I was so friken! But Miss 'Silda did real nice to me."

"Who?" Sabre leaned in.

Isilda's veins turned to ice.

"We gotta go," she hissed at Ian. She leaped to her feet and grabbed her handbag. "Now."

"Lady, sit down, you ain't mek outta glass," complained one of the women behind.

The rice-and-peas attendant shouted, "Miss 'Silda—see she dey!" and pointed to the back of the hall.

Everyone turned to look. Isilda felt her stomach drop.

"For real? Isilda's here?" Sabre whooped. She shaded her eyes against the stage lights and peered in Isilda's direction. Isilda's feet froze.

"Isilda, wow! You came," exclaimed Sabre, bringing her palms to her chest.

"You know she?" gasped the woman behind Isilda. "You is somebody to Cumberbatch?"

"Not at all. I ain't nobody at all," snapped Isilda.

But it was already untrue. People were staring and whispering, which meant, thanks to her stupid decision to attend this meeting, that she was now, at the very least, not nobody. How dare they deprive her of the right. How dare Sabre Cumberbatch and the rice-and-peas attendant, of all people, get together to strip her in public.

An usher was coming up the aisle with a microphone. Microphone for what?

Her legs rediscovered their purpose. "You coming?" she hurled over her shoulder at Ian, who in confusion was still rooted to his seat.

"Isilda," she heard Sabre say from the stage, "would you like to share a few words about your journey?"

Isilda slid through the door just as the usher reached her row.

～

Ian leaped up and snatched the microphone, startling everyone around him.

"Comrades! I really have to say," he began in a booming voice, and without the slightest idea what he really had to say, "that this story we now heard is . . . something that should make everybody feel real proud. As a shop steward myself, I feel good to see all of us doing our part to protect workers and stand up to mistreatment. You don't have to be a shop steward to take a stand. Look at this young woman! The more we hear stories like this, the more powerful we should feel. So thank you, Comrade Cumberbatch!"

"Hear, hear!" shouted a man behind Ian.

The three on the podium basked in the ripple of applause that followed. The rice-and-peas attendant handed off her mic and retreated into obscurity. Sabre went to say something, but suddenly Ian felt anxious about whatever next could be coming out of her mouth.

"And Comrade Cumberbatch," he plowed on, "hearing this comrade speak reminds me of another important issue that you have raised. I know a lot of us would have heard it on the radio: this whole business about human trafficking. It's a serious problem, and all of us should be concerned! Speak to us on that, please."

"Ah, good point, my man, excellent point," called the man behind Ian.

Ian turned to find his supporter in the row behind him, next to the two women. He was a young man, handsome, with a twinkling grin. He raised a fist in solidarity.

"Should be you on that stage, boy," he said to Ian.

The women chuckled. A warmth flooded Ian's torso, making him feel exposed. He turned back to the podium.

Jessica and Ophelia began to protest that this meeting was supposed to be about union affairs. But Sabre went rogue.

"Yes! Thank you for raising that, comrade. So, as you know, there's this issue with people being brought into the country as forced workers . . ."

"Slavery!" a woman shouted out.

"Exactly! Now a second ago when our sister was speaking, people were being mean. But brothers and sisters, is that what we need now? Suppose she was one of those forced workers—sorry, ma'am, I know you aren't, right?—but just suppose. Is she our enemy? Is she the one we should attack? Or should we attack, you know, the system?"

"True!" somebody brayed.

"It's the system, you guys," Sabre said. "I'm telling you, even when it seems like it's working for you, you gotta watch out. I may be standing in the spotlight today. But I know what it's like to be in a different kind of spotlight. Not the kind you want on you. I know what it's like to have to live with that spotlight whether you want to or not."

Her hand went up and absently began to stroke her bald scalp. There were a few snickers, but Ian could sense that Sabre was beginning to float away.

"We don't get to choose how we come into the world, or the things that happen to us. But we can respond. Anybody who puts you down, you know, makes fun of you, makes you eat alone in the kitchen, underpays you, whatever, is against you." She floated back to Earth. "Anybody who tries to stop that, who respects you and sees the real you, no matter where they're from or how they look or sound or what they do is *for* you. Right? So come on, people. We got work to do. We gotta come up with a better system. And we gotta do it together!"

She came to such a sudden crescendo that the audience missed its cue to applaud. After a beat, people began to clap. But under his relief at having diverted attention from Isilda, who was probably boiling with rage as she waited by the car, Ian couldn't make it add up.

What could a world-famous artist really know about being oppressed? It reminded him of the dress rehearsals for the Christmas chorale, that sense of being both inside and outside himself at the same time, performing while gauging the performance.

The audience had broken into song and was on its feet, led by a man in the crowd who evidently had come determined to be moved to song, as he had brought a guitar. The women on the podium joined hands and did their best to recall the lyrics of the song he was playing, a classic calypso about Caribbean integration. Ian used to hear his parents sing it as a child, so he joined in, yet he found it hard to put his whole heart into it.

We tek one trip across the sea,
Down in the ship of indignity.
And it no matter where we land,
We share one spirit, one command:

Of our ancestors, be the pride,
Vanity, selfishness, cast aside.
No one can rise if another fall,
Only in unity we stand tall.

Chapter 13

To see them filing out of the assembly hall that sultry April night—
women and men of a certain or near-certain age, singing, whistling,
swaying, drumming fingers against thighs, laughing, chatting away, lin-
gering in the car park to reason and ruminate, now and then somebody
chortling or throwing keys high into the air to emphasize a point—
you could be forgiven for thinking that you were in the afterglow of
a revival. To see them gather under the mahogany trees, disperse and
regroup here and there across the grass, then filter off few by few to
join the queue of cars snaking out of union headquarters, the scores of
headlights infiltrating the night like an army of the newly enlightened,
you would not be hard put to predict an outcome typical of revivals,
with most who had caught the spirit tonight squarely back on course for
damnation tomorrow. To see the dues collectors backstage in the empty
hall, counting the night's take by the light of the combined gleam in
the eyes of Jessica and Ophelia, their star attraction having floated off
like a balloon on a string, you couldn't help but recall the evangelists
on Sunday-morning TV, spreading promises of divine bounty as broad
as the jeweled watches bogging down their wrists.

It was April, dry season. Is that why no one noticed the first drops
of the tropical storm?

Two days after the meeting, an irate woman barged into the nave
of St. James Parish Church, where the son of the Minister of Health
was marrying the daughter of a soft-drink bottler. The soloist had just

finished warbling the "Ave Maria," and the vows were about to begin, when people in the back were startled to see a middle-aged woman stride in carrying a bundle in her arms. She marched to the foot of the sanctuary steps and, turning her back on the wedding party, announced in a clear voice that she had not been invited to Angus Rowe's wedding "after I been washin' he frowsy socks for near-most thirty years." She reminded Angus and his bride that she had been working for the family longer than either of them had been alive, and that if anybody should be at a Rowe wedding, it was her. Then she turned to the parents. "So I good enough to wash pretty clothes, but I ain't good enough to wear them?" she cried. "Well tek these here and rot in them!" And she spilled the bundle on the church floor—shirts, nighties, briefs, brassieres, crusty sheets—and stormed out before anyone could stop her.

The morning after this, chaos broke out at a senior citizens' home when a groundsman accused one of the residents of feeling up his dreadlocks as he crouched to weed the hedges along the path where she was being taken out in her wheelchair. According to the nurse on duty, the old white woman, her eyesight failing, had reached out a liver-spotted hand and plunged it into the groundsman's thicket of hair, saying, "But Esther, wuh kinda bush this is?" The groundsman lashed out with his trowel, tipping the woman from her chair and scarring the nurse's leg. In the torrent of insults and recriminations that followed, the groundsman was heard to exclaim, minutes before the police turned up: "Wunna better start respeckin' Black people 'bout hey! Wunna forget this country belong to we!"

Two weeks later, eleven housekeepers walked out of the Brinkley Brook Estates en masse. They had become friendly with one another during their commute to and from work, via the densely shrubbed, butterfly-festooned, guard-patrolled pedestrian entrance to the gated complex at the top of Foal Hill. On one of their chats down to the bus stop, they discovered that there was a $180 spread in weekly wages among them. So the next day they got together and drafted a letter, which each housekeeper was to address to her boss. In it, they demanded not only an immediate raise above even the highest earnings, but also a list of intangibles like "dignity," "equality," and "respect." Then they went on strike.

After a few days of striking, one of the women went up to Brinkley Brook to see what was happening. She arrived to see faces she did not recognize filing through the trellis of pink, yellow, and white bougainvillea. That was when the guard gave her the score: four of her colleagues had torn up their letters and returned to work the next day; two had managed to negotiate raises; one had been turned down but was on the job anyway; and the rest, including her, had been permanently barred from the community.

The woman turned to the union for help but, having never joined up, was told by one of Jessica's deputies that there was nothing they could do, and that she would be well advised to sign up now and avoid such incidents in the future. When she reminded the deputy of all that had been said at the union's special meeting, the deputy snapped, "So why you ain't join when you had the chance?" and hung up.

Incensed, the woman went straight to the most hardcore union man she knew: her neighbor's brother-in-law, shop steward for the Collective of Hospitality Workers of the five-star Maiden Bay Hotel. In short order he organized a massive "Solidarity Day" with the maintenance and housekeeping staff of Barbados's eight largest hotels.

Solidarity Day turned into a sit-in lasting three days, bringing the hotels to heel and driving hordes of tourists to the guesthouses and boutique hotels, or onto early flights home. At the end of it all, the hotel staff returned to their jobs, and the woman was quietly taken on as an assistant in the Maiden Bay nursery.

Dust began to kick up everywhere. People seemed to be on every side of the issue at once, only never at the same time as whomever they happened to be talking to. Some admired the grit of the hotel workers yet balked at their irresponsibility, to say nothing of the foolhardiness of the Brinkley Brook Eleven, risking bread and butter to grab with hands that were already full. Taxi drivers, never happy to see a slowdown, were glad to herd disgruntled tourists to and fro at a premium. Small hoteliers were thrilled to see visitors beating paths to their doors, yet they worried what seeds of revolt could be sprouting in the minds of their own staff. The civic-minded were full of cautions about the ills of these gated communities, with their weird, Christmas-card-sounding names, where foreigners holed up to do as they liked, but equally grim were the hazards of basing a whole economy on the whims of holidaymakers. Union types were quick to condemn the rudeness—alleged, mind—of that deputy who had mishandled the woman's call, but crowed over the groundswell of "people power" that had brought big business to its knees and shown the world what could happen when you mess with a Bajan.

On and on it raged. Still, for the great majority whose lives had nothing to do with the tourist industry, who had been in no position to employ a housekeeper for at least a generation, who in fact were barely a generation removed from being housekeepers themselves, the whole episode, beyond its entertainment value, was a bit of a head scratcher. All this shoeshine over domestics and their eggshell "rights." Wasn't this country rough and tough for everyone, whether you wore an apron or not? What made them so special?

And what had become of their leader these days? How was it that she seemed to be everywhere and yet nowhere to be found?

That was what the offending groundsman wanted to know. All day he railed to his cellmates, to his court-appointed lawyer, and—at his arraignment, a spectacle in its own right—to the judge that only Sabre Cumberbatch could help him. He also felt sure that, as a famous zillionaire from America who believed in uplifting the small man, she would not hesitate to post bail for him and possibly even throw the old woman a few coppers, if that was what it took to get apologies out of white people. He was so insistent that his beleaguered lawyer eventually made the effort to track Sabre down.

～

Sabre had stopped taking calls. Starting with Katya's.

What choice had Katya left her? The woman had become a nonstop Topsheet barker. *Do this Topsheet video and make us rich. They get that you're not interested, and they love that about you. Good news, the offer still stands. They're willing to shoot in the Caribbean. To push the launch to October.*

Topsheet expected her to pause a social movement midbirth to ride horses in a turban. To save pretend people from their pretend problems, while real people were looking to her to save them. People who had no interest in the Style section.

No wonder Basquiat was famously testy with clients who disrespected his vision. Never in a million years, for a billion dollars, would Basquiat have agreed to put his face on, like, a Basqui-hat.

Of course, the way her movement was growing, Sabre felt there was a strong possibility she'd end up on a T-shirt one day. Like Che Guevara. But that was different.

Visionary to visionary, she understood Che, too. Something had made him go cruising those villages on his motorcycle, just like something had compelled her to return home to give a voice to the people. Destiny chooses you. If somebody had told her that one day she, Bald Pigeon of Bed-Stuy, would bring liberation to the oppressed of Barbados, she'd have thought they were crazy. She'd have balked. So instead of whispering it in her ear, destiny planted the mission in her gut.

Everything was clear now. Her purpose. The reason she had been born.

Maybe that was Basquiat's mistake. What did he have to believe in? All he had was art, nothing bigger. Even when his world started closing in and he tried to escape, the best he could come up with was a vacation in Hawaii. Where was the bigness in that? Where was the revolution? Hell, he probably *did* wear a Basqui-hat while he basked on the beach.

In New York, when people recognized her on the street, they whispered and pointed, sometimes taking pictures or video. But in Barbados, people called out to her by name. Here, for instance, on Keith's boat, where she was spending more time these days, just to float and clear her head, the fishermen waved and said, "All right, Say, do ya thing!"

She loved it when they called her Say. Other calls, though, were starting to wear heavy.

How many Cumberbatch Initiative rallies were they up to now with the union? Five, six? A lot for a place this size. It was like being a politician on the campaign trail.

She still couldn't fathom that Jessica was a grandmother of two. The woman was a human pogo stick! Meanwhile, Sabre found the rallies draining, and even though her name was right there in the movement's title, the constant publicity was something of a personal sacrifice.

At least the sacrifice wasn't in vain. Everywhere the two of them went, she and Jessica, people were hearing the call and rising up to fight oppression. Staging sit-ins, protesting unfair conditions, renegotiating contracts, joining the union, speaking out.

That guy, though. The gardener from the nursing home, whose lawyer kept calling?

She'd had no idea what to do there. No guidance from Jessica, either. Sabre had had to press her for a response, and when one finally came, it was not what she had expected:

"Sabre, not every tomcat that come mewling is to feed."

Jessica had shrugged and changed the subject, willfully ignoring Sabre's gaping surprise, the dismissiveness doubling the insult.

In that moment, Sabre had looked at the older woman, calmly talking logistics as she scrolled through a spreadsheet of planned appearances, and recognized for the first time her own mother.

Caustic, unyielding, pragmatic to a blistering fault.

~

Sabre thought about the gardener. There was no question he had messed up, overreacted in a flash, but that overreaction had come from somewhere. It had had a base, a burrow, a lair. It must have been there all along, coiled up inside him, waiting for the right trigger to unleash it. What must that have been like? Was he a person living in the light, or in the darkness? Had it been his choice?

Did it matter that the woman he attacked was white? Bajan whites were furtive figures in her childhood memories. Like some invisible element in the atmosphere, they were present all the time, but out of sight, unless some chemical reaction caused them to appear. They were as Bajan as anyone else, but other than Lisette's boyfriend, Sabre hadn't come across many. They had been absent altogether from the union rallies.

So had the gardener popped off because the woman was white? Because he was a gardener? Because he was tired of living life underground? Because she had touched his hair? Surely white people in Barbados knew better than that.

Come to think of it, what was his name?

She couldn't remember. See? She was part of the problem. She couldn't let it go. She had to feed the tomcat.

Though she had stopped accepting calls, she made an exception and called the gardener's lawyer back. The lawyer immediately requested that she post bail, pay off the victim, and cover the gardener's legal fees, all with the slightly irritated air of one who had been kept waiting. She managed to hang up without making any promises.

She had a better idea. Something more valuable than money.

People who live underground didn't need cash. They needed somebody to tell them they're worthy. To inspire them to rise up and claim space without landing in jail. To liberate them.

They needed the Cumberbatch Initiative.

So she found out where his family lived and set off to uplift them.

~

The gardener's name was Ras Aman Abebe. When Sabre had asked if he was Ethiopian, his lawyer replied, *As are we all.*

Ras Aman came from a Rastafarian community called the Uprising House of Akan, which was geographically apt. From a place way up in the eastern highlands, she had to park at the base of a hill and then hike up a steep, winding footpath to reach the gates of the commune.

She walked through the open gateway into a peaceful garden. Beyond it was a large field planted with vegetables. The plant beds rippled out around an open-sided octagonal wooden structure painted in red, gold, and green. The place had a spectacular view of the Atlantic.

Before long, she saw a man and a woman approaching. It occurred to her then that she hadn't prepared any remarks.

A union rally this was not to be, which was probably a good thing.

"Greetings, sistren," said the woman. "Welcome to the Uprising House of Akan. We ask respectfully that you cover yourself before proceeding." Smiling, she handed Sabre a dark green wrap.

Sabre hesitated, unsure which part of her look was causing the greatest offense: her head, her tank top, or her shorts. The woman herself held no clues. Despite the blazing heat, she was draped in flowing black muslin from tip to toe.

Sabre opened the wrap and placed it over her shoulders. The fabric cascaded down to her calves.

"Sorry about that," she began. "My name is Sabre Cumberbatch."

"Yes, we recognize you," the man said. "Greetings in the name of Jah."

They spoke in low, patient tones.

"Thank you. I wanted to speak to you about Mr. Abebe. To visit with his people and offer my support."

"We see it," the man said. "Come, follow this way."

They led her to the center of the octagon and offered her a cup of water. The woman went off to round up some community members. Eventually two men and a woman appeared, their ages hard to place, all bearing the calm, grizzled energy of people who grow wise from living off the land. They nodded greetings and arranged themselves in a semicircle around Sabre. The main man motioned for her to begin.

"Comrades . . ."

He stopped her right there.

"Sistren," he said, "Rasta don't really deal in the isms and schisms."

"Pardon?"

"The comrade rhetoric is against Rasta ideology, you see it? I and I walk upright in the ways of Jah."

"Ah, right. Well, would you be more comfortable with 'brothers and sisters'?"

"Proceed," the man replied.

"OK. Brothers and sisters, I just came to let you know that I am with you. What happened to your brother is truly sad, and I know people might say he overreacted and whatnot, but still, I can tell, he was coming from a place of deep oppression, which is so unfair. Now, you probably aren't online that much, but maybe you've heard of the Cumberbatch Initiative? Well, I'm Sabre Cumberbatch, the activist who started it, and I'm here to say that it's time for everybody to rise up and demand respect, and when we say everybody, we mean it, no matter where you're from or where you live, or . . . you know, your ideology or anything like that. So yeah. I'm here for you, and this Cumberbatch movement is uprising like your house here, with the amazing wrap-around views, and rest assured, I'm not going to let Ras Aman or anybody here get left behind. I'm here to boost you up! OK? So, let's go!"

Straight off the dome. She had to hand it to herself sometimes.

Had to, indeed, because nobody else was. Did Rasta ideology forbid applause? Her audience continued to sit and stare. Finally, the leader stood up.

"Peace and blessings upon the sistren for coming forward, still. The sistren is seeking to boost up the House of Akan. Sistren, how do you intend to do this?"

"Well, by . . . by coming here, in person. By showing the brothers and sisters that I see you, and I care."

"We respect that," the leader said. "We take that to heart. But a righteous heart cannot rise up on an empty belly."

The light seemed to change its angle across the calm, grizzled faces. Sabre sighed. "I understand. Is his family around? Maybe I can give them a little something?"

"All of us live in communion, sistren. One family in inity."

"Right."

"Sistren, you can see we are a proud and upright people. We work the land, and the land provides. We have liberated ourselves from the bondage of Babylon. We don't bend back for no man. We welcome all sons and daughters of Zion. We take to heart the respect you bring forward. Respect for Rastafari is respect for the teachings of the ever-living Jah."

"Yep."

As the leader was speaking, she reached for her wallet in the back pocket of her shorts, relieved to find that no one was fainting away at the sight of her exposed knee. She removed a fifty-dollar bill. Then another. Then a twenty . . .

"I'm not sure how much . . ." she said, suspecting that no guidance was forthcoming. "We know the movement is not about money, but if it can help . . ."

"It is a necessary iniquity," agreed the leader. "Righteousness is a matter of respect. We children of Zion must rise up and claim it."

"Yes. That's why I've come to rise with you. Please."

She wasn't sure how to feel as she handed over the money. These were poor Bajans, she reasoned hastily with herself, not vain New Yorkers or the out-of-touch Dutch. Poor with an ocean view, acres of farmland, and potatoes for days, yes, but still. It was money she could afford and was happy to pay, to help Ras Aman and the Uprising House of Akan to . . . well, rise. To uncoil and stand tall, in power and visibility.

Fair enough, she concluded.

The leader was posing expectantly, the bills resting on his still-open palm. It was getting awkward. Everybody seemed to be observing some hidden protocol.

She pulled out her last fifty dollars and put away the wallet. "And . . . a little something for this beautiful scarf, right?" she said, hoping to help them all save face.

There was a pause. The leader closed his hand at last.

"Respect. Blessings for the journey, my sister," he said. "Go forward in peace."

The gathering rose, each one giving her a little bow with hand to heart before leaving. The man and woman walked Sabre back to the gate.

"Please visit us again," said the woman. Sweetly she slipped the scarf from Sabre's shoulders. "We'll hold this aside for you until next time."

$\sim$

Which of them is even related to Ras Aman? Sabre wondered as she stomped downhill.

Another car was parked behind hers. A man was getting out as she approached.

"Is that Sabre Cumberbatch? Well, well, well," he greeted her. "Shane. Remember me?"

He seemed warm, not transactional. Sabre lowered her guard. "Sorry, remind me?"

"Lisette's friend? I was at the welcome party for you." He gathered his Shirley Temple locks and piled them on his head. "Remember now? I had an updo that night."

"Oh yeah! How are you? Do you *live* here?"

"Just visiting," he said. "I like to come and reason with the community."

"I see. Well, I hope you brought your wallet."

He laughed. "My sociology professor lives here. All types of people, actually: teachers, artists, farmers, scientists, mystics. It's good vibes. Quality weed, too. What brings you here?"

"That is a damn good question. Do you know a guy named Ras Aman Abebe? That gardener who went to jail for attacking a woman in a nursing home?"

Shane shrugged and shook his head. Sabre was surprised. The story had been all over the papers, the call-in shows, the news blogs.

"You come to a Rasta commune in shorts?" he laughed. "They fine you for that."

"Yeah, lesson learned."

"I've been seeing you everywhere," he said, leaning against his car door. "Got the whole island hot and bothered."

"Ha. Well, it's not really me. It's the movement, taking off."

"Of course it's you," he said. "We had an incident at our firm just last week. The cleaners and cafeteria staff called a half-day meeting with the architects about a 'Cumberbatch upgrade.' Their actual words. Your name."

"Really?"

"Don't act surprised," Shane teased. "The people behind you, the union under you, who else they following?"

"Hey, I wasn't there," replied Sabre, laughing. "Anyway, how'd it go? What did your colleagues get?"

"Well, *that*, first of all—to be referred to from now on as our 'colleagues,'" said Shane, crooking his fingers into air quotes. "And, you know, pay bump, promotion plan, profit-sharing—or, really, a *promise to consider profit-sharing in the future*. Stuff like that."

"Awesome. Sounds like a win to me."

Shane raised a skeptical brow. "I guess." He nodded toward the hill with a grin. "You looking to Cumberbatch the Akan now?"

"Ha! I wish. I got nowhere with this bunch at all," she replied. "It's like we were having two different conversations. They didn't even care that I came all the way out here to be with them."

"These people? Too much talk and you lose them," said Shane. "You have to sit down and reason, or just keep quiet and do what you came to do. Sometimes a lot of talking isn't good. You lose the spirit connection."

"Spirit connection was close to zero. I should have shut up. Maybe not come at all."

"Rhetoric and fellowship ain't always friends," he said. "Drains the vibe."

"You sound like one of them."

"Serious thing. When you stand over people and talk and talk, like you and your crew at those rallies, sometimes a connection can't form. The connective tissue is love and fun and vibes, not one-way lecturing. If you just sit and breathe air together, I find it's a better way to fellowship."

A chilly current came in off the sea, cutting through the heat.

"Fellowship is an exchange," Shane said. "You have to listen as much as you talk."

"Trying to tell me I've been talking too much?"

He chuckled. "Not necessarily. Maybe just vibe out a little more. Feel people out, create more joy. Here, give me your number. Next time we'll visit together, and I promise they'll show their fun side."

They exchanged numbers, then Shane waved goodbye and started up the path to the compound. Sabre watched him climb, step by serene step, almost envious of the better experience he was about to have.

She looked up at the sky as another gust blew in and a big raindrop landed with a plop in the middle of her forehead.

$\sim$

There is a plop on deck and the boat dances on the waves, rocking to and fro. She gets up to check.

A flying fish is flopping about the bow, its blue-and-silver scales iridescent in the moonlight. It stops on its side, still. One eye bulges in her direction as it gasps.

"Fly, flying fish," she commands.

"The net is getting tangled," it replies.

"Fly," she insists. "I want to see."

The fish spreads its wings, leaps up from the deck, and makes an arc over the side of the boat. It comes up again on the other side and lands in its original position. Its eye glows.

"What you ain't fish for you catching, and what you fish for you throwing back."

"No riddles, please. It's been a stressful day."

"The net is tangled."

"How come you didn't have a boat? Seems like an easy way to make money."

"Things slip through your grasp. It takes time to learn how to hold them properly."

"Remember when you taught me to swim?"

"I remember. Saturday mornings. You, your mother, and me."

"You taught me to ride waves and tread water."

"We would take you out where you couldn't stand up. You were a strong little girl. Fearless. Our true child."

"Daddy, I miss you so much. I never swim in New York. The water is cold and nasty."

"Keep or throw back. Come, now."

The glowing eye begins to bulge.

"I'm tired. I want to go back on land. Let's play on the beach. Play under casuarina trees. Daddy, make a swing for me. Push me. Catch me when I jump, and let's fall down laughing."

"Fix the net. Fish and catch, Basqui-hat Ras-quiat."

"Daddy, let's just go back to the root, when things were happy."

"FIX YOUR NET!"

The fish begins to puff and swell. Its eye flares at her, red and angry. Another fish flies over the side of the boat and lands on the bow, plop. Then another, then another and another, all flailing, gasping, their glutinous eyes glowing a violent red as they pile and loom. They fill the deck by the hundreds, one-eyed monsters straining the boat, cramming her up against the hull, suffocating her with their eyes.

Chapter 14

The Bajan labor force was in Cumberbatch mode. Among those whose uniforms rendered them invisible, those whose tools drowned out their voices, and those so deprived as to only dream of such erasure, the prospect of a better life within reach had taken root. Some, in silence, nourished the seeds sprouting in their hearts. Some whispered to each other in break rooms and back alleys. But others spoke with full voice, discovering as they did so that whether the words they spoke formed a question, a statement, or a demand, what reached their employers' ears was a threat. A threat that, on its own, was often enough to forge a path—or, for some, a shortcut—to change.

It was only when the top hotels saw their profits hemorrhaging and came shaking their fists at the National Tourism Association that the grin disappeared from Lisette's face. She'd been enjoying this maelstrom created by her cousin, whose exile from the Toppin household had served only to amplify her presence among them. Watching her mother strain these national developments through the pinhole lens of her own reputation, reduced to seeking solace in Isilda's company as the rest of the family shrugged off her doomsaying, had been more fun than Lisette liked to admit.

But at a tense emergency meeting of Assistant VPs, Lisette at last felt the bracing winds of hostility she'd been longing to inspire in her colleagues from the beginning. No more backslaps: people's end-of-year bonuses were on the line! Lisette realized that overnight, everyone in that office would forget her many innovations—well, one, really, but an effective one: posting fake reviews on travel sites to big-up their client hotels and bad-mouth the competition. They spent whole days on it, she and the rest of the team. It was what she did when not clacking through hotel lobbies in her patent-leather Louboutins. If Sabre's antics were going to cost her the little edge she had worked so hard to eke out, it was time to shut her down.

With a sense of purpose, Lisette set off to play her ace: an in-person appeal to Sabre at her latest hideout, the original Ifill homestead in Comfort Seat, deep in the countryside, where Aunt Evelyn and Uncle Kenroy still lived.

There were people she knew of, clients of the clients who kept her in patent-leather Louboutins, who paid good money to spend nights in this Bajan countryside, even wrecked their behinds in the back of a Jeep combing the desolate outscapes on self-styled "safaris." And Lisette, pitchwoman that she was, had no idea why. Why leave the rolling hills of England and come to Barbados just to watch cane field dump into cane field? Why forgo rhinos and big cats in Africa for these indifferent blackbelly sheep?

Just look at the scenery. Gas station. Cricket pitch. Chattel house. Roundabout. Cane field. Sugar factory. Potato patch. Gully. Housing development. Church. Church. Gas station. Gated complex. School. Church. Gated complex. Pasture. Cow, goats, sheep. Roundabout. Gas station. Tractor dealer. Chattel house, chattel house, gas station . . .

At least there were more gas stations now. And some presentable mansions to balance out the slapped-together wooden shacks that they were professionally obliged to pretend were quaint. She hadn't been out this way in a while. And she wouldn't be out here now, if not for Sabre, the eternal lightning rod. How did she manage to put a whole country under her spell? Seriously, how did she do it?

Just like when they were kids. One bale of cloth, two identical dresses, three compliments for Sabre to her every one. Piano recital, ages eight and nine: hers a perfect *Moonlight Sonata*, respectfully received;

Sabre's a stumbling, two-fingered "John Belly Mama" that turned Miss Gooding's drawing room into a karaoke salon, with the neighbors and even the people from the bus stop across the road singing and clapping at the window. Who even noticed when Lisette won first prize? Who, besides that photographer from the paper who, when she really put two and two together, could even have been on her mother's payroll?

Was it Sabre's look? Please. I mean, yes, she was pretty enough if you liked that type. One pretty face, one bald head canceled out another. Besides, Lisette had those genes, too, and nobody was going around skinning people out of wheelchairs in her name. Talent, whatever—99 percent of those in her thrall had probably never seen her artwork. And all this maid-power claptrap she was talking made no sense. Just another hazard of overexposure to American histrionics.

Look, the truth was that Sabre could be reciting the side of a Chefette snack box and people would still be all ears. It was something about her. Charisma, maybe.

Or was it because she had stayed so slim?

Alone in her car, Lisette instinctively checked around as if she were in a dressing room at the mall. Then she exhaled, releasing her stomach *alllll* the way out, something she didn't do even in her sleep. Her belly unfurled in a joyous tsunami and engulfed the bottom of the steering wheel. She pushed the seat back as far as she could without taking her feet off the pedals, which wasn't that far at all, only enough for the belly-jelly to flop down onto her lap.

There it was. Might as well be pregnant. A boy, too, they say boys carry low. In fact, if she ever had to take a bus again, she could definitely get away with her old trick from Montreal days, puffing out her stomach to get a seat. Back then it didn't bother her as much—she'd always been smooth and round, like a young calabash—but now, things were different. Too often she caught herself gawking at the scale, cursing the injustice of the fact that the human head weighs twelve pounds. Twelve whole extra pounds.

One or two cane fields onward, she ended up stuck behind a trundling bulldozer. The logo on the fender said GIBBONS. Then she remembered: her boyfriend, Damian, lived somewhere out here with his family, not far from one of the various businesses bearing their name. Lisette had never been to Damian's place, nor been introduced to any of his relatives, for that matter.

On a whim she followed the bulldozer as it turned down a long, narrow, stony road lined with industrial compounds. The area was quiet, but there was a distinct sense of busyness surging from the walls. She peered through the gates of each compound as she crawled past, trying to guess which of these faceless monoliths was the first thing Damian saw when he looked out his window on mornings. Was it Gibbons Construction? Gibbons Realty? Gibbons Landscaping? Organics? Poultry? Dairy? Manufacturing? Imports?

She pulled over and called him up.

"Yo."

"Where you are?"

"Home scratching my balls, nuh."

"Oh good. I'm out by you."

"Yeah? How come?"

"Long story. Where exactly are you?"

"Umm . . . why?"

"How you mean why?"

"You here for truth?"

"Boy, why you stalling? You and your hand want some privacy?"

Damian snickered. "Nah, man, I . . . I ready to leave here shortly, that's all."

"Well, where is 'here'? Look, put your balls on the phone. I know for a fact they can't keep anything from me."

"OK, where are *you*?"

"I ain't know, Gibbons something."

"All right. Let me meet you on the road."

"But . . ."

He hung up. Lisette sucked herself in another inch and tried to smother with belly fat whatever was starting to well up in her stomach. She pivoted the rearview mirror and began to compose her hair into an effortless tousle. From the corner, she saw two workmen emerge from the gates of Gibbons Organics. She rolled down her window.

"Excuse me! Can you tell me where the Gibbons residence is, please?"

Down at the far end of Gibbons Amalgamated, the grass deepened from yellow to yellowish green. An empty paddock began near the roadside and spread back, flanked on one side by a concrete wall and by a rough hedge on the other. Two horses grazed near a white stile at the bottom, heads down, rear ends to the road. Then the yellowish green turned to green, road and hedge curved, and finally Lisette came to a long, ivy-covered wall with a gated driveway at its center, presided over by two columns of the bearded fig trees—*Los Barbados*—that had given the island its name.

She pulled up to the iron gate. The industrial buzz faded in the still air. The driveway sloped away beyond the fig trees and disappeared behind what had to be the greatest great house she had ever seen. Three stories, thick and solid as coral could get, crumbling like a wizened queen; crimson-shuttered windows, each row squatter than the one below, devouring light but reflecting none; a terraced turret rising like the Bastille through the center with a balcony on each floor; a wide, shaded veranda encircling the structure. All this over a vast, scrubby lawn, with a lily pond under a cluster of mahogany trees to one side.

Lisette was out of the car now, her face pressed through the iron bars. The ivy on the wall wheezed an electronic wheeze. "May I help?" it asked in a pickled voice.

She popped her cheeks back through the bars. "Is . . . er, Damian there, please?" she said, not sure which leaf to talk to.

The ivy wheezed again, longer this time. "Who is the person?"

"Lisette. Toppin?"

Another wheeze, then a click. Then nothing.

"Hello?"

Silence. A kiskadee in the trees broke the late-afternoon stillness. Lisette watched a ladybird scale a leaf, certain she could hear its six footsteps. Beyond the gates the house stubbornly withheld any sign of life against the flat, hazy sky.

"Hello?"

This time her stomach threatened to betray her. She headed for her car, sucking in her belly hard. At that moment her phone buzzed: Damian. She rejected the call.

Two seconds later, the roar of an engine. She turned and saw Damian's car coming up the driveway. With a gonglike clang, the gates parted. Lisette lost no time in choosing a shade of indignation. She flung open her car door and put one foot inside, a pose of flight, buying him time to intercept her dramatic exit. Quick, before he pulled up beside her, she tucked some flyaway hair behind the ear that would be receiving his entreaties, exposing the pretty diamond drop earring, perfecting the profile.

Damian's head appeared over the top of his car, grinning like a scraggly Cheshire cat. "Hard-ears, girl."

He came and stood in front of her. Lisette froze in her pose.

"What I tell you just now?"

"Move from in front me."

"I tell you I leffin' here *now*." He moved in closer, trying to catch her gaze. He tickled softly under her chin. "Come, nuh."

"Damian, I can't come by you?" From the corner of her eye, she noticed his nose redden beneath the freckles.

"So where you think you is, then?"

"Damian. Why can't I come by you?"

"All right. You want to come by me? Well go 'long then," he sneered. "Look, the gate open. Go 'long! Who stopping you?"

For the first time she saw real annoyance in him. She gazed through the open gate across the lawn all the way to the distant steps of the veranda. A horse neighed. From a pulverized stomach, she found the strength to say, "I find this whole thing looking a way."

"What way, Lizzie? I tell you, you free to go in as you like. I gotta go. I working evening shift, and I late already. I can't stay up here all day trying to convince you."

She locked eyes with him, then looked down his usual uniform: old T-shirt, old shorts, beach sandals. "Going to work? In them shoes?"

"Work boots in the car. We ain't fancy executives like you, you know. Pretty girl." He leaned in slowly and kissed her lower lip. "Mizzie Lizzie, my miserable monkey girl."

"Shut up." She kissed him back.

"All the way out here for me? Cuddear. You want to go in for real?"

"And you leaving?"

"Don't mind. Granny there. Right there in the window. She don't talk, but she does listen. You all would hit it off perfect."

"Ha, ha." She clamped her lips down on his nose. "Well, for your information, I'm on the evening shift, too. This is business."

"Oh?"

"Going to see my mad cousin that wreaking havoc and looking to spoil my good name."

"Who?"

Lisette stared at him. "You don't read the news? A meteor could hit Barbados and if it don't dent your car, you wouldn't know."

"I is a workin' man, I ain't studyin' no paper. Mean your cousin from America? The bald-head girl?"

"Sabre. I can't believe you don't know. Guess that's a good sign, Gibbons must be cool."

"Gibbons cool, man," parroted Damian, moving in for another kiss. Just then a black Jeep with tinted windows appeared from behind the house and started up the driveway. Damian straightened up and took a step back.

"Come, babe, we blocking the road," he said. He jumped back into his car and pulled it to the side. Lisette followed. The black Jeep came out of the gate and sped off in a cloud of dust.

From her car Lisette watched Damian's gaze follow the Jeep. "Who was that?"

"My uncle."

"He lives here, too?"

"In and out." Damian turned back to her with a smile. "Anyway. Where were we?"

"Out." She grinned and stuck out her tongue.

"Aww. Not for long. Later, baby. Keep it hot."

"Uh-huh."

He followed her to the end of the road, where she swung right, he swung left.

~

There are places in the world that can cease to exist on a mapmaker's whim. Places deemed too small, superfluous, might not make it onto a map at all, or might have to settle for faint letters above some ignoble dot. Others might be swallowed whole by a neighbor, shoved in a corner for only the most avid explorer to find. Montserrat, Andorra, Djibouti . . . all expendable as dandruff. It is a question of scale.

At 166 square miles, Barbados knows well the soft end of the cartographer's pencil. On any world map the island is as likely as not to be drowned in the Caribbean Sea or washed over by the Atlantic, or a crude arrow somewhere between Cuba and Venezuela will point to near emptiness and half-heartedly remind you that it's there. Indignant Bajan schoolchildren scratch the missing Barbados onto any globe found lacking, yet the problem persists: sometimes it appears, and sometimes it vanishes.

Comfort Seat is one of the forgotten places on the forgettable Bajan map. To get there from anywhere, travel the new highway northeast, then strike onto the old highway. When the old highway narrows to a single lane, look for a flock of goats grazing on your left, and turn right. You then follow the modern road, a pothole-riven donkey track that seems to wind mainly out of boredom. Track this across the pasture, through the cane fields, around a sharp bend, and when the patchy gravel starts to slope upward, you know that you have arrived.

The first sign of civilization is the rum shop on the edge of the hill. Nothing like the slick chrome-and-candle bars beckoning the beautiful people in town, nor the carefully shabby wooden shacks luring foreigners with names like De Seamen's Sinkhole. This rum shop has no name. No name, and since 1963 no doors, either, because that was when it first occurred to Mrs. Skeete that doors might be bad for business. Whenever she has had enough for the night, she simply hands off to the most reliable barfly and heads to bed. The system works, and no one questions it.

A blanket of dust drapes the assortment on the sagging shelves behind the counter: pepper sauce and rubbing alcohol, bran bread and mosquito coils, white rum and Cream of Wheat. The local notary, Fitzpatrick, who uses the shop as his office, can always be found there marinating in whisky when needed to scrawl his name to a job seeker's Certificate of Good Moral Character. "Righty-o," he might add, his fee passing directly from candidate to notary to shopkeeper. "Go out an' mek yuhself nuseful to de worle."

When a hard rain begins, the regulars leave off solving the world's troubles at the tops of their lungs and fall quiet. They tip forward, settle into their sandals, and turn in the worm-ravaged stools, their faces trained on the raindrops as if God were delivering a sermon. But those moments are rare. Most of the time, they hold forth on how the West Indies can win the next World Cup, who really built Stonehenge, whether Chinese imperialism will be worse than American, and why the city nurses did not get their raise. Epiphany after epiphany for an inattentive world forever on the verge of erasing them.

Dusk was creeping over the horizon by the time Lisette came up the hill into Comfort Seat. She sped past the rum shop tooting and waving, a move calculated to feign affection while fending off the long-winded. She swung into Aunt Evelyn's driveway obliquely opposite and bounded through the open side door.

"Hellooo?"

Right away she rammed her hip into a sideboard full of family pictures, a jab so painful it almost felt as if the sideboard had rammed into her. The photos rattled, and scores of Ifill eyes glared up at her, some smiling, most not. Rubbing her bruise, she glared back.

There was her grandfather Conrad, first as a velvet-suited boy standing with his parents and siblings, then on his wedding day with Flora, then surrounded by his daughters, her mother, Aggie, on Flora's knee. Aunt Madge, the eldest, on the day she left for England. Then in nurse's uniform at the Leeds hospital, a thick bun on each side of her horn-rimmed glasses. With a husband and two children whom Lisette had never met. A framed copy of her funeral program. Aunt Evelyn and Uncle Kenroy at their wedding. Their daughter Rowena at her graduation from University of Reading. Rowena with Ghanaian husband Nigel and four children at home in Kumasi. The lovely Aunt Priscilla at her engagement dinner. Lisette and Sabre as little girls, grinning gaps for front teeth. And her own mother, Aggie. With Lisette's father on their wedding day. At Lisette's christening, standing apart from the group in a peach pillbox hat. Pregnant with the twins. The family at the foot of the pyramids. Her mother in cap and gown at her own law school graduation. Herself in cap and gown at McGill.

"Anybody home?"

Not a sound. Lisette limped through the parlor. Like many Bajan homes, this one had expanded with the family's fortunes over the years, so that the footprint of the house was all that remained of the place where her mother had been raised. The old wooden structure had long been walled over. Glass panes had replaced the louvers in the windows; linoleum and tile covered the floorboards; and behind the three bedrooms, Uncle Kenroy had tacked on two indoor bathrooms, a sewing room for Aunt Evelyn, a large storage area, and a patio overlooking the grounds. The pigpen was gone, but the fowl pen remained, and beyond this, part of the land that had kept the Ifill swans in three square meals a day had been taken over by rose and aloe shrubs.

But for all these changes, the house seemed to Lisette old beyond its years. It was more than having grown up under its constant show-and-tell, where the elements of every childhood anecdote, every antediluvian tale, survived in the form of a tree, a button, a nick in the back step, or some other artifact they could still point to. It was more than this. The entire space held the distinct aura of a relic. It smelled of camphor and old-people's ointments, of concoctions probably still sitting in unlabeled jars in that shop across the street. The furniture was all so heavy—not heavy like the antiques at home, but in a sort of dark, mossy, stubborn way. She never saw chairs like these anywhere else: ground level, with tall backs, long high arms, and seats that sloped up to the bend of the knee, the cushions musty with lemon oil. And when you finally stepped outside for some air, nothing in the dense crop of bush, the sway of the breadfruit trees, the cows' lumbering gait, nor the tomblike silence bearing down on all of these could prove that you were still part of the twenty-first century. It all felt, tasted, smelled like *then*. Forever unmoored from *now*.

Suddenly Lisette decided she hated it here. She felt detained against her will. Inside, all there had been to breathe were stale, acrid vapors. Now, on the back patio, the darkening silence threatened to suffocate her with its heaviness. She could not stand another minute.

She turned and charged back through the house. She was about to get into her car and speed away when the unmistakable squawk of a drunken Cathy came ripping through the air, apparently from the bowels of the rum shop. Lisette wheeled around, weighing the urge to investigate against the risk of being taken hostage by the regulars. As she stood there puzzling, rubbing her hip and vaguely lamenting her lot, Mrs. Skeete's head appeared through the open doorway.

"Hey! You there? Come through, darlin'!" she sang out, her shiny black pageboy wig shifting as she tilted her head. "The rest in the back."

Inside the entryway Fitzpatrick's well-grooved stool sat deserted. Limping in, Lisette discovered that the whole place was empty: only the flies circling the fossilized cheese sandwiches in the display case had received her wave. She followed Mrs. Skeete past where the linoleum changed from brown to beige, down a corridor that led beyond the store, past the beaded curtains of the bedrooms. She could hear far-off voices growing louder, people laughing. Cathy again. Cathy for sure.

Mrs. Skeete went down three steps and unlatched a wooden door. Lisette stepped through and found herself on a landing above a recessed backyard thrumming with people. There were tufts of grass poking up through cracks in the concrete, and front-house human was mingling freely with backyard beast. Lisette's eyes swept the scene and found her uncle, sitting on a rock and sharing a plastic pail of ice with Fitzpatrick. Fitzpatrick was pantomiming a story in his typical style. Lisette could catch only the last part: "An' man, I gi' he one lick 'cross 'e head wid a Tiger Malt bottle so—*bragadax!*"

Those who had been listening burst into guffaws. Standing above them in bewilderment, Lisette picked off the culprits one by one, all of whom, it now dawned on her, had lately become quite scarce. Cathy. Simone. Victoria, jiggling somebody's barefoot child on her lap, this same woman who was always declaring herself allergic to children. Paloma, stroking a reluctant turkey while stripping her raspy voice rawer with whatever was in that flask in her hand. Shane in his eternal linen drapery, his locks bunched up in a white rag with the word REVOLUTIONERY hand-printed in black on the side. The whole merry gang—led, but of course, by the Bald-Pated Piper herself, Sabre.

Lisette felt a curdling in her throat: "What the . . ."

But somebody cranked up a Charley Pride tune from the '70s, and all the old regulars started swaying and singing along.

Uncle Kenroy noticed her on the landing. "Lizzie!" he brayed. "Come dance wid yuh uncle, girl!"

At the mention of her name, some of Lisette's friends looked up. Cathy squealed.

"'Bout time. Join de lime," slurred Simone, beckoning with a bone in her greasy hand. She turned her head and expertly lobbed a piece of gristle out the side of her mouth. A waiting cat caught the projectile in midair. Between Simone's knees and the knees of some man Lisette did not know balanced a tray of roast pork.

Lisette realized she was shaking. Quaking from the belly. Cathy and Sabre approached as if in slow motion. Cathy looked drunk and sheepish, and Sabre had on a smile like Mother Teresa about to recite one of her edifying parables.

"Wuh going on here?" Lisette sputtered.

Cathy rushed to the base of the landing and threw her arms around Lisette's ankles. "Oh, Liz!" she giggled, resting her head on her feet.

"What the fuck, Cathy? You . . . you don't even *like* country music!"

Cathy looked at Sabre, who was making her way up the steps. "See?" she groaned. "I knew she wouldn't get it."

"Get what! And as for *you* . . ." Lisette turned to her cousin. "This is what it's come to? Stealing my friends now?"

Sabre's Mother Teresa smile softened sickeningly. "Never, cuz. Never." She moved to hug Lisette.

"Don't touch me." Lisette jerked backward, almost kicking Cathy in the teeth. "What y'all doing here? It ain't my birthday, so it sure as hell can't be no surprise party."

Sabre sighed. "I was afraid this would happen," she said. "We didn't know which way to go. We went back and forth: Should we invite you and piss you off, or not invite you and piss you off?"

"Who is 'we'? Invite me to what?"

"The *moooovement*," Cathy intoned, spinning.

"Cuz," Sabre said. "Look, I know Auntie Aggie isn't feeling me right now. I didn't want to get you caught in the middle . . ."

"Bullshit. And sneaking around behind my back?"

"Honey, we're not sneaking, we're protecting!" wailed Cathy, swaying to the music. "You can't be a revolutionary like us, we overstand! It's not your fault you're a comp . . . How you say it? A *comperdor!*"

"What the hell nonsense you talking, girl?"

"Liz, look," Sabre said, easing a hand around her cousin's shoulder. "It's so simple, you're gonna laugh. So a few weeks ago I ran into Shane, and he invited me to come hang out—"

"You always busy, Liz!" Cathy said. "We called you, but you never—"

"So I suggested that they come up here for a change—"

"Oh my God your auntie is so main character—"

"And then we started chatting with some neighbors—"

"Fitzpatrick is a whole freakin' mood—"

"And then next day, Cathy came back with Simone, and it just—"

"Couldn't keep it to myself—"

"Took off from there." Sabre searched Lisette's face. "See? We weren't trying to leave you out. We just didn't think you'd want to be here, with everything going on."

Lisette looked from Cathy to Sabre and back, then over the twenty-odd minglers who seemed barely to have registered her appearance.

"So what is it, then?" she asked dejectedly. "Some kind of club, or—"

"It's *solidariteeee*, sister-en!" cried Cathy, pulling herself clumsily onto the landing next to Lisette. "Solidarity wid de wukkin' man, woman, an' choile! Why you tink none of we ain't went work today? We nah sell out!"

"Wait, you mean the Brinkley Brook thing? That Solidarity Day whatever? But that's over!"

"Not Brinkley. I tellin' you, Liz, it's a *move*-ment!" Cathy giggled. "They getting ready to shut down the place again, bacchanal in they backside! Right, Sabre?"

"What?"

"Well, that's the rumor," Sabre said, eyes twinkling. "With all these equality enforcement groups springing up, the word is something big's about to go down."

"Equality enforcement groups?"

"I know, too long for the T-shirts," said Cathy. "And Shane still claim he going have them ready by next week. Now tell me how!"

"T-shirts." Lisette turned to Sabre. "Let me guess. With a picture of your face on the front, and 'Cumberbatch Initiative' on the back?"

Sabre and Cathy laughed uneasily.

"Or I know. See if this'll fit: 'I came back to Barbados for the first time in twenty years, tore up the country, embarrassed my family, stole my cousin's friends, destroyed her career, ruined people's lives, and all I got was this lousy T-shirt.'"

The Mother Teresa drained from Sabre's face. "Liz . . ."

"Better yet, how about: 'I was a little dry-foot girl whose daddy couldn't pay his debts and drank to his grave, and everything I owned my mummy had to beg my auntie for, and then my mummy couldn't take the shame, so we ran away to America, and all my hair fell out like a chemo patient and I got famous, and now I want to come back here sponging off people, and biting the hands that fed me and forgetting that just the other day I was a piece of nothing.' How about that?"

Was she shouting? She must have been shouting. The backyard was still. The music had died down. Every head was turned. Even the animals were staring.

Lisette watched Sabre's body sink like an anatomy-class skeleton. Sabre's eyes probed hers, looking for safe harbor. But an unrecognizable force had welled up in her.

"I came here to ask you to ease up on the talk, for my sake," Lisette said, surprised at the steadiness of her own voice. "But now I don't give a shit. Just stay away from me, Sabre. I don't want to see you or any of these starfuckers again."

"Sellout!" Shane called at her back. But she was already halfway to the brown linoleum. She limped across the street to her car, her jiggling belly settled at last.

Chapter 15

Contrary to known laws of nature, Aggie had taken to skulking about
like one of the green monkeys she liked to clap off the boughs of the
mango tree early on mornings. But whereas the monkeys always reappeared in their numbers the next day to jeer and toss mango seeds onto
the lawn, Aggie seemed to be in a state of unchecked retreat.

Polo season had come and gone without a single sighting of a horse-
blinding necklace in the Toppin box. In vain did spectators turn their
binoculars on Aggie's seat from one Saturday to the next: there it sat,
gloomily collecting sawdust from the passing hooves. At the Pickwick
Bazaar, an exclusive weekend market held on the grounds of a plantation, where socialites and influencers could swing their straw baskets
like the pretend islanders they followed on Instagram, vendors gave
up and marked back down the items they had set aside for her. And
at the Toppin Law Chambers, the senior paralegal Tunde found himself abruptly promoted to junior associate, a rise in rank to match the
number of headaches he now had to field on behalf of his absent boss.

Aggie's initial response to all this unwanted attention had been
to try to give off an air of unruffled dignity, knowing how it tended
to ennoble one's suffering. In practical terms this had called for wearing large, dark sunglasses in public and striding through places with
a stronger than usual sense of purpose. Still, the whispers that shad-
owed her—at first in the atmosphere, then gradually, then constantly,
in her head—gnawed away at her resolve, and each time she recalled

the goodwill she had squandered on Sabre, it made her want to scream her innocence to the world. Which would only make her look more guilty, of course.

So she resolved to work from home, in the dim, book-lined, deep-carpeted library that had been designed to acclimate her children to the atmosphere of an elite university abroad. But having spent little time there herself over the years, she soon discovered that the place felt like a dungeon. No wonder the boys refused to do their homework anywhere but sprawled out in the parlor, and Clive took all his work calls from the balcony of the master bedroom. Aggie decided that if she was going to be made to suffer false accusations and a wrongful conviction, she deserved the white-collar experience at least.

She took to setting up in the formal dining room, where she could luxuriate in the peace and beauty of the garden view. She enjoyed being alone in the house, save for Isilda across the way in the kitchen.

It was not that Aggie had forgotten the open file Isilda still had on her. But whatever she was planning to do with it, if anything, was taking its time, and had been overtaken by more public disasters. In the meantime, Aggie had been finding every reason to top up Isilda's hand: to acknowledge the thoroughness with which she had beaten out the rugs in the entryway, for example; or in thanks for the exquisite sugarless desserts Isilda would concoct from pure imagination. The bonuses were a win-win, as good for Isilda's pocket as for Aggie's nerves. Irony of ironies, given the topsy-turvy state of her life just then, Isilda's steady, silent presence was among Aggie's rare sources of comfort.

Then one afternoon, Lisette came storming through the kitchen door, past Isilda at the counter peeling cassava for pone—which she was planning to sweeten with overripe dunks and a drop of stevia—past Aggie at the dining table, and out onto the main patio overlooking the garden. She flung herself into a chair, threw down her bag and phone, kicked off one shoe, pried off the other, tossed it halfway down the patio steps, and slouched into the chair with an exasperated grunt.

"Fucking bitch," Aggie and Isilda both heard her say.

The phrase hung in the air like incense. It wafted over the three women, each pausing to inhale its pungency, to suck into her breastbone the fresh fuel for embers that had been glowing red-hot inside.

Isilda exhaled: *Malicious harpy. Causing ruckus and harassing peaceful people.*

Aggie exhaled: *Unmannerly ingrate. Backbiting benevolence like a rabid mutt.*

Lisette exhaled: *Fucking bitch.*

Without a word, Isilda poured three glasses of golden-apple juice, and they spent the rest of that afternoon together, and many more over the next few weeks, in quiet retreat from the hostile world.

Over time, as the three of them came and went, worked and rested, the starch in their silences softened into familiarity, the awkwardness into compassion. They synchronized their movements and formed their own little ecosystem, a mossy refuge undefiled by unnecessary talk.

Underneath the moss, though, Aggie still bristled at the indignity of it all. How could this extraordinary life of hers have curled into itself so easily? Where were the multitudes she had counted as friends? Their calls—when they called—were full of cheap, flaccid sympathy. It was as if, all this time, they had not been so much embracing her as encircling her, like a coliseum of muted spectators who had paid dear and waited long for the bloodletting to begin.

Even her own family members had failed her, truth be told. Clive merely rubbed her shoulder with the empathy of a scarecrow when she expressed her grievances (not even both together, like a proper massage!). And the boys delighted in repeating whatever nonsense the children at school had to say about their family. Instead of wilting in shame, they had hammed it up as second-generation bullies until the story had died down.

Thank goodness Lisette had come around, or at least eased up on the insolence that had become her preferred mode of engagement. On the days when Lisette worked from home, it felt good to spend time together, the pair of them close enough to hear each other tapping away on their laptops, although Aggie could not help but notice that Lisette seemed to spend a great deal of time bitterly perusing her former friends' social media. Sometimes she would forget to turn down the volume, and suddenly the sanctity of their space would be invaded by a snippet of the tomfoolery from which she had been excluded, usually with Sabre front and center.

This stunt of Sabre's was spinning off into ungovernable realms. Judging by the stories in circulation, the equality-enforcement people were proving to be a gang of squabbling loons who couldn't even agree on whose equality to enforce. The most visible cohort, the one headed by Sabre, seemed to be mainly good for roaming the countryside in a pack, invading rum shops and sports clubs in matching yellow T-shirts, and loudly befriending the localest locals. They handed out shirts, gave a rambling talk about rights and unity, and then bought a round—or, if they were not in a place where rounds could be bought, produced a bottle and passed it or, if they were not in a place where bottles could be passed, tried to get people singing and dancing or kicking a football about.

The whole pantomime should barely have registered on the national barometer. But something in the shape of it seemed set to linger. Every sensible person could agree that this equality-enforcement business was nonsense. Yet nobody was looking away.

Part of the problem was that there was nowhere left to look. When the nursing home groundsman got sent to jail for a year, his family complained that the sentence was harsh because he was poor and Black. People of good sense were quick to ridicule that idea, but by then the assertion had become such a familiar refrain that it seemed all along to have been part of the general background hum of life, waiting to be set to words. Now each settled score—whether in the schoolyard, in the workplace, or in the diatribes of every other petty criminal hauled into court—added to the chorus.

On such matters the yellow shirts, consumed with befriending and proselytizing, tended not to weigh in. No counterbalance to the heavy hand of Justice DaCosta, whose purse-lipped, bespectacled headshot darkened the court pages at least once a week.

The sight of Hubert's picture became Aggie's subconscious trigger to close the paper and engage in a bit of palate-cleansing chitchat. She glanced over her shoulder at Isilda, who was cleaning flying fish at the kitchen sink.

"What a world, what a world," she threw out.

"Mmm," replied Isilda.

It was after two. Lisette had gone into the office for the day. Aggie looked out over the grounds, lush and fragrant from an afternoon sunshower. The still-hazy sky gave the pool a milky glimmer. The flowers keened with fresh droplets. Bastet scampered across the lawn with something in his mouth. Aggie's mind ran to flamingo beak.

"How is your little one?" she asked Isilda.

This was what Aggie had taken to calling Nekisha, Isilda's granddaughter. Just a few weeks ago, Isilda would have read it that Aggie couldn't remember whether the entity in question was boy, girl, or pigeon. But these afternoons of quiet communion had changed things.

"Good, good," Isilda replied. She took a sip of water. "As good as you could be with that wutless boy for a father."

Isilda liked to tack this coda onto any reference to her son Lamar, however oblique. But this was the first time she had ever let it slip in front of Aggie. Neither woman noticed.

They drifted off, each on her own accustomed cloud.

"Men don't be no use to you," Isilda murmured, her eyes traveling through the kitchen window, grazing the biceps of the workers on the building site next door. "No use at all. Bare headache and pressure in you system."

"Mmm," replied Aggie.

"That one. Know he got a child home to provide for. Child mother in the ground. Every next day, poor girl at the clinic. Not a good cent in he pocket. You feel he would get up and look for something to do?" She sucked her teeth. "Up and down behind them vagabonds. I does don't even want to know. Once he don't bring no confusion home at me."

"Mmm." Aggie stared out to the sea.

Isilda took another long sip and gazed through the window to the empty lot beyond. "Not a thing new under the sun. He father ain't no different. My mother warn me, 'Don't mind them taxi drivers. Bare woman and talk.' Time you hear the shout, child come, and he ups and gone."

Dispassionate as the evening news. Aggie turned to look. Isilda stood in profile. She had put her glass down and was now calmly scaling the fish with a knife. Her shoulders were relaxed. The part of her face that Aggie could see, lit up by sunlight streaming through the window, was downright beatific.

"I tell you," she offered, watching Isilda's fingers fly. "These men, eh? You never know."

The fish went limp. Aggie glanced up at Isilda's face, but just then Isilda raised her arm and wiped her forehead on her sleeve. She resettled her stance, pushed forward her hips, straightened her back. Then she flipped the fish over and continued to scale it with vigor.

"Sometimes you does know," Aggie thought she heard her say, under the scraping of the knife. "And when you know, you must thank the Lord for he mercies and don't be tempting trouble." She plunked the fish with a splash into a waiting bowl of lime juice and salt water.

What? Even from that distance, Aggie could have sworn she felt some lime-salt droplets land on her face. She flinched.

Was she being insulted in her own home? Was that some sort of threat?

If only Lisette had been around to help her distinguish something from nothing.

As she sat gaping, the phone struck up "Für Elise." Tunde, the junior associate, on time for once with the afternoon update. Grateful for the distraction, Aggie assumed her power pose.

"Yes, Tunde," she barked. "And speak up."

She got up from her laptop and strode along the terrace. The news was good. Better than good: a big new deal with an old client. A group of partners—friends, really—whom she knew and could still trust, selling a massive plot of land to the government. The kind of straightforward matter she could handle in her sleep, and with the kind of fee that could sweeten her dreams for a long, long time.

She hung up triumphantly, and a familiar, long-dormant surge flooded her groin.

She turned to Isilda's back. "Nearly finished there?" she trilled. "Don't worry with the other dishes—I feel like cooking tonight. Please, allow me to drop you home."

~

The traffic in Isilda's head always became more frenzied the closer she got to home. From the moment the bus hit the roundabout and offered the first glimpse of the top of her gap, she would look up from her notebook, her chest would tighten, and her lovely mouth would begin to form its preemptive scowl. She would close the pages into which she had been pouring her ideas for a sugar substitute. And when she stepped off the bus, her heart would sink with the step, down into her stomach, vexed and resigned at the same time, even before she knew for sure what there was to be vexed or resigned about.

Isilda was usually too absorbed to notice these changes. All during the walk from the bus stop to the house she shared with Ma, Nekisha, and—when he felt like it—Lamar, the bleak contents of the files she kept in her head would lunge and leer.

Ma's diabetes: How many biscuits had she had today? Was she going to have to go through the house counting wrappers in the rubbish bins? Had the people from the ministry managed to drain the stagnant water outside Nekisha's window? The stench was getting as bad as the mosquitoes, and they couldn't afford another asthma attack. Praise God, Nekisha was safely almost through the school year. So bright. Always the bright ones who had to suffer. That child was the only good Lamar had done in this world. The only thing that kept him from being the complete good-for-nothing he meant to become.

But on top of this, for the whole ride home today, she had to put up with Aggie, who out of nowhere had suddenly got into one of her high-pitched moods. Changing the radio station every minute and belting out the wrong lyrics to Rihanna songs every Bajan knew by heart.

"We found love in a O-A-SIS!"

A decent man at home and still Aggie was complaining. "You never know." What did she know about never knowing?

Isilda tried to remember the last time she'd had a half-decent man sniffing behind her. Well, all right: there was Ian. But that had died of natural causes, even before that ill-fated union rally. Nowadays she was content to wave at him across the way if he happened to look up from his work, which somehow seemed to be increasing as the building neared completion.

When had she last felt excited? Chased? Minded? Who was there to rub her shoulder, like Mr. Toppin did whenever he passed close to his wife? To kiss her forehead, smooth her nerves with scotch and chocolate? But Aggie never touched the stuff. Starving at the feast, and with the gall to pretend it was famine.

Exactly when were the meek supposed to inherit the earth?

They circled the roundabout, and Isilda took in the typical scene. The clump of aimless boys, her son Lamar among them, some draped against bicycles, some slouched over the drainage wall where their legs had dangled another day away, making the stray dogs and chickens foraging around them look purposeful by comparison.

At the top of the gap, she gave Aggie a terse thank-you, scuttled out of the car, and set off on the long walk to the bottom. As had long become her custom, though not as long as her present mood might have tempted her to imagine, she stomped past her son and the rest of the drain-wall crew without so much as a word or glance in their direction. She did not see Lamar send a hurried signal across the way, nor a sprightly woman on the opposite side ease on her flip-flops and bound down the steps of her veranda. She kept to her pace, her mind whirring with annoyance at Aggie's ingratitude.

"Sildy! You deaf?"

The woman came running up alongside her. It was her neighbor, Delphine.

"I did calling your name so long! You pass me like a full bus, girl."

Delphine propped a wiry hand on Isilda's shoulder and bent to straighten the strap on her flip-flop. Isilda looked down at the top of her head, the thick silver hair neatly parted into two cornrows.

How old was Delphine? Seventy? A hundred and five? She was at least as old as the gap itself, for which the pink-and-red walls of her house served as the main landmark. Instead of retiring quietly from teaching physical education, she was now the gap's gatekeeper, town crier, bailiff, counselor, nurse, janitor, and—thanks to the sweep of trophies she took each year at the senior games—its resident celebrity.

Like many of her generation, Delphine's husband had gone to work in Curaçao in the '70s and never returned. But unlike some of her generation, Delphine had taken splendidly to his absence. Into her life had poured a parade of cuffed and collared men besotted by her wit, laughter, and gleaming shoulders and of wellborn women captivated by the confidence, discretion, and ease with which she seemed to belong anywhere. Every evening Delphine had a different meeting to chair, a different visitor swirling falernum and coconut water, a different reliable source breaking next week's headlines under their breath as she sat cross-legged and rapt on a plump ottoman.

Although Delphine had no children, all the residents of the gap were her adopted sons and daughters. Yanked from her thoughts by Delphine's grip, Isilda felt annoyed at herself for being incapable of dismissing the older woman when she felt like it.

"Sorry 'bout that," she mumbled, her eyes pulling homeward down the gap. "Head busy, you know how."

"That is Aggie Toppin who drop you off just now?"

Isilda didn't bother to answer. Such questions had become non-questions. The effort it had taken, since the incident, to stifle gossip and snuff out lies made her cagey about her private business.

"Listen," Delphine went on. "I want you talk to she. Things brewing 'bout here. Serious, serious things. We got to get a lawyer."

She seemed to savor the look on Isilda's face for a moment, misreading irritation for intrigue.

"Fix that face. It too pretty to put so. Now listen." She lowered her voice almost to a whisper and pulled Isilda along. "You hear 'bout this new stadium going up? Good. Well, I hear from a fella where they planning to put it. Where you think, girl?" Delphine's eyes flashed, and she stamped a slipper on the stony ground. "Right 'pon this soil here so-so!"

"Oh?" said Isilda, half-listening. She could tell this was not going to be brief. Nor light: Delphine tended to take in more than she let out, and what she let out tended to come true.

"Sildy, you hearing me? Here-so! You understand what that mean? All o' we going get move off we land. Every man jack gotta shift. The gov'ment tekkin' we land, girl! And dem ain't buying nor borrowing it neither!"

"Wait . . . what?" Isilda caught herself. "They can't do that."

"How you mean?" Delphine sucked her teeth and pulled Isilda's arm closer. "Look. They got something name 'compulsory acquisition.' If you is the gov'ment and something want building, you could go at anybody and tek up dem land to build 'pon. Sometimes dey does pay and sometimes not. Dem ain't easy, hear?"

"But . . . but they can't just turn you out so. They must got someplace to put you."

"Good. I like how you thinking," said Delphine. "That is why I want you talk to Aggie Toppin. To help we defend weself, mek sure we get all wuh we got coming. Good?"

Isilda felt her heart sink. She avoided Delphine's piercing gaze. "Aggie? Wha . . . How we going afford that now?"

Delphine gave a little sigh, her eyes still fixed on Isilda. "Well, chile," she said, "when it's home and hearth . . ."

"'Home and hearth'?" Isilda sucked her teeth. "You see this place good? I would be glad enough to leff 'bout here, tell the truth. Wherever they planning to put we can't be no worse."

"Oh? You sure 'bout that?" Delphine retorted. "You sure they planning to put we anyplace at all? So why they ain't tell we nothing up to now? Why I got to be whispering something that done plan already? Why they ain't even bother to *ask* we nothing? Why nobody ain't talking 'bout compensation?"

"I ain't studying all that," grumbled Isilda, regretting once again that Delphine had picked this evening to intercept her.

"And why they ain't saying nothing 'bout equality enforcement, Sildy? Doan mind these foolbert youngsters touring 'bout. Look, a chance right here for the politicians to prove that poor people in Barbados ain't got to be sucking salt from cradle to gra—"

"That again? This equality foolishness does get me sick!" Isilda fumed. "I got time for that? Before people try and do what they gotta do, running 'bout crying for inequality. Me? I got to put bread on me table. I got to keep that wutless boy from sending all o' we under the earth before we ready. Equality? That is for them that want something to worry 'bout!"

They had stopped walking a few paces from Isilda's house near the bottom of the gap. The smell of stagnant water and weed wafted from the far side. Beyond the house lay a gully thick with mango, breadfruit, and coconut trees that only the monkeys raided with any regularity, scrambling over the refrigerators, tires, roofing, and garbage that the residents discarded there. Isilda bored her gaze into the dense green.

"Well, my girl, I going tell you this," said Delphine. Isilda tried not to notice how Delphine's arms had folded into her waist, tried not to feel Delphine's eyes searing into her cheekbone.

"I been 'bout here since before you come along. Is me that help put you and you mother in this house when you did still in primary school.

Good? Good. Now, personally speaking, the Almighty never bless me to know nobody who ain't got no worries. But believe you me, soon from now all o' we 'bout here going got nuff more to worry 'bout. We accustom helping one another. Even these young fellas on the corner does pull when they got to pull. All o' we got to stick together, or not we could wells lay down and leddem do as they like with the little that we got."

Through the open window of the house, they could hear floor-boards creaking and straining. Ma, probably en route to her latest stash of biscuits, which the postman continued to smuggle in for her despite Isilda's threats.

"Sildy, people ain't blind," Delphine pressed. "Everybody see how good Miss Toppin treating you ever since she family talk out she business 'pon the radio. You ain't got to tell we nuffin. We know she got favors for you. Talk to she, tell she wuh going on. Lewwe pull together and see how we could fight this thing. Good?"

Another nonquestion. Isilda felt torn between saying too much or nothing at all. She did not face Delphine. "All right."

"My girl." Delphine stroked her arm. "I waiting. Keep it quiet for now, though, good?" She began to move off. "And tell Cora put down dem biscuits. Tell she put on a short pants and come walking—I passing for she ha-past five tomorrow morning!"

Delphine's laughter ricocheted in Isilda's head as she watched her bound back up the gap. Coming the opposite direction, Lamar met Delphine halfway. Isilda watched the pair as they stood for a time, talking intently, Lamar gesturing from the elbow in that slack and lanky way he did when he was agitated, which was rare, since he seemed to care for so little in this life he was clearly set on wasting. Isilda could never understand how the bond between those two continued to thrive, like a cactus in the desert, even as she and his grandmother point-edly and repeatedly condemned him to his own wicked devices. Only Delphine seemed to have it in her to deal with him and the rest of that worthless lot, day in and out, as if she saw in them some good that no one else did.

The evening program had begun. The snow-cone cart and the ice cream truck had both pulled up and were in a sound clash for customers, the snow-cone man tooting his Woody Woodpecker horn and the ice cream man piping "Home on the Range." Children had flooded the roadway. A boy was trying to drip snow-cone ice onto a dog's nose. Next to him, Isilda spotted Nekisha. She was laughing, jostling her way to the front of the ice cream line. Two women set off on a walk, sharing a set of earphones between them, their biker shorts jiggling in sync as they stepped to the rhythm. Isilda tried to guess which song they could be listening to. Then she remembered she was supposed to be miserable.

As she turned, pouting, toward the house, her eyes picked up a swaying near the top of one of the mango trees in the gully. Two monkeys sat on an upper branch, mother and baby, nibbling mangoes and tossing seeds with their backs to the road. The larger one turned and locked eyes with her. Clutching a half-eaten mango, she scooped her baby under her chest and vanished into the brush without a sound.

Chapter 16

Sabre shot upright in bed, trembling and naked. Rain was pelting the galvanized roof. She tried to remember where she was.

A room, a fan, a beamed ceiling, the glint of a bicycle spoke in a corner, and beside her, Keith.

She eased out from under the mosquito net and tiptoed to the door.

It was a one-room house, alone on a cliff on the northernmost tip of St. Lucy. The glass door was open slightly to the breeze. She stepped through the billowing curtains onto the veranda. The dawn enveloped her. A storm was heaving, gusting sheets of rain. The sky was the indigo of the sea.

Thwack! Lightning cracked, rolled into thunder.

She could make out the foam cresting the waves of the Atlantic below. She was trembling, her body pushed and pulled at the same time, as though on a wave. Only the force of the wind steeled her spine.

Another dream about her father. This time, there had been no words.

Should she visit his grave? People did that; maybe they were onto something. What were they looking for? To lock the door and throw away the key, or to keep it open with the lights burning night and day? Did they know which they wanted before they got there?

And where to find it? How long did muscle memory keep? Would her legs find their own way, tracing the path they had wobbled along twenty years ago? Under a fog of voices, whispers grazing her body, each embrace perplexing, the kisser knowable only by the reflection in her shoes. Her hand slipping in her mother's grip. Grains of soil sticking to her palm when she tried to throw a fistful into the grave. She had wanted to dust them off, because a girl in class had said that the dirt in graveyards was duppy dust—dead people's remains. But her mother's grip had held firm, so she had wiped it on her dress instead. As soon as it was over, her mother had taken that dress and the one she herself had worn and burned them in an oil drum in the yard.

Thwack! The sky lit up. The shifting wind spattered raindrops across her legs.

Had she ever seen her mother happy? Truly happy, behind the eyes, underneath the ribs?

When she was growing up, her mother was known as the Jewel. That should have been a hint. Where else does a jewel belong but in a solid setting that allows it to dazzle in comfort and stability? That supports it in a gentle grip, prongs curved around the jewel's edge, loose enough to cause no harm but never letting it fall?

The reality had been nothing like this, and had anyone stopped to check the metaphor, it would have been clear how doomed her parents were from the start. If Priscilla Ifill was a jewel, radiating light for others to absorb, Ronnie Cumberbatch was a filigree artist, weaving webs out of golden threads. His threads crisscrossed her light until it was nearly snuffed out. How had no one noticed this? No wonder everything came out of her mother filtered and refracted, and even the best moments felt tarnished.

The three of them moved five times in four years, starting when her father gambled away the deed to the house in a game of dominoes. Her mother had ranted till she was hoarse, and in hindsight it was clear that her voice had never fully come back. Even so, Sabre found delight each time they had to up stakes and shuttle off to Auntie Aggie's, where she and Lisette could play all day and tell stories all night, like real sisters, while her mother and aunt huddled at the table, nervously furrowing the labels on their tea bags.

The house they had taken in Glenmorgan Hill was across from a big tamarind tree. Each day at a certain time, a madman would come, strip off a piece of bark, rub up against the exposed trunk, and lecture passersby on the sins of the flesh. Her father nicknamed him Griney and would put them in stitches imitating him, using her mother for the tree. After Griney came a place in Serenity Lodge, where Sabre was not allowed to visit the houses of the neighborhood children but would loiter whenever she was sent to collect fish cakes from the landlady downstairs, a woman with a deep voice whose Friday fry-ups could run into Sunday. And so on, until finally they found themselves way out in Boarshore, in a chattel house like the one she was in now. There were not many children, so she would play by herself, making meals from the wild fruits that grew in the area: fat pork, cashews, sea grapes, dunks. Like the blackbelly sheep that surrounded them, she developed a tendency to roam. Back and forth, to and fro over the scrubby hills, to scrub away the loneliness and fear that began to dim her heart.

Her mother's face and her father's mouth. The jewel trapped in filigree. One shamed off the island, one shamed under it.

Thwack!

Did Lisette really mean those things she'd said?

Keith came out and pressed himself up against her.

"Hello, morning glory." He kissed the back of her neck. "Not enough pyrotechnics for you inside?"

"Just getting some air."

"Not just air. All the elements." He stroked her damp breasts. "Why you out here getting wet? We have indoor plumbing, you know. These country showers are overrated."

She turned and kissed him, burying her face in his neck. "I had a dream."

"You did? I had a dream, too. Sign of a quality mattress. Tell me about yours."

He pulled her close. Her body soldered to his warmth. Even on the vertical, their bodies fit together perfectly, lip to groin. His morning musk intoxicated her.

She slid her hands down his sculpted pelvis. "Another time."

"That bad?" He looked into her eyes. "Poor baby. Mine was odd. It was about you, actually. Help me decipher. We were lying in bed, and I was drifting off to sleep, and then your phone rang. Someone from the union. Then it rang again, and it was one of your equality enforcers. Then it rang again, and you threw it across the room—"

"Very funny. You know good and well that was no dream."

He cupped her face in his hands. "What's going on, darling? You losing stride?"

She turned against his chest and stared out at the waves fading into view with the ebbing rain. "I don't know," she sighed. "I don't know."

"You can't not know now. You got the natives restless."

"This is just . . . not how I thought it would be."

"How did you think it would be?"

"I don't know. Faster. Straighter. More . . . *supersonic*."

"It's hard to control the momentum of these things. But you've been handling it."

"I don't know about that." She snuggled her head against his chin. "All I know is, everybody wants a piece of me. Just wants and wants. It's getting to be not fun anymore. In fact, I've been wondering if it's even good for me to still be up front. Shouldn't I be stepping back, so people can run things without me? If things are moving forward on their own, what do they still need me for? My work is done."

"Well, when you get tired of the theatrics, I know Vonda's been missing you."

"Keith. Don't make me feel worse than I already do. Honestly, there just wasn't that much going on with those UN suits. Plus I haven't had time, with all the community upliftment work I've been doing."

"Ah yes. Too busy touring with the yellow-shirt posse."

"Say what you want, those guys make things happen."

"Come on. Some bored rich kids playing local, then running home to the heights and terraces? Name one thing they've achieved."

"Guess you haven't opened a paper recently."

"Have *you*? That nursing home gardener kept your name in print right up to when they clapped him in jail."

"I know, I feel bad about that, too. But what else did he want from me? I tried to go help his family at that commune, and you see how that turned out. I'm an artist, not Santa Claus or a defense lawyer." She stroked his jawline. "I'm Basquiat, remember? Not Martin Luther King."

"No, maybe not. But if all you came for was a rum-shop tour . . ."

"Keith Everton, it's your day off. No one's paying you to be annoying."

"I'll annoy you for free because *you* need to focus, Sabre. What is it that's driving you? Seriously. Let's pin it down. Is it migrant workers? Housekeepers? Human traffickers? Gardeners? Rude rich people? You need to pick an issue and stick with it. Otherwise you'll spend all your time chasing equality through every rum shop in Barbados with that pack of twits."

"In other words, your way or no way." She withdrew and went to lean over the veranda railing, suddenly feeling lightheaded.

"In other words, fire-calash, get over yourself a little bit. You really think you're the first person to try to change things on this rock? How you think I got into this business?"

"Let me guess. A love for the sound of your own voice."

"Hmm. Seems to me you can't stand the sound of yours." He came up behind her and nestled his chin in her collarbone. "Here you are, with not one, but two platforms to work from."

"The unions and Vonda?"

"You and you. You could reach people through your art, which a lot of the people following you around have yet to see, or you could reach them through your ideas. Through applied passion. Through the movement, if you want to call it that. But you can't be effective when you're all over the place like this."

They stood quietly for a moment, breathing in sync. Morning had broken through the haze, streaming sunlight over the waves, across their faces. The earth smelled sweet with rain. Sabre watched as an earthworm appeared near the base of the veranda and burrowed back into the soft, black soil. The grass sparkled like jewels. Keith's stubble began to itch her cheek.

"Fine," she said quietly. "Equality enforcers out, union in. Happy?"

He stroked her face with his beard. "Getting there. Union in . . . for what, exactly?"

"Oh, Everton. Always with the questions. This interview is over."

Chapter 17

The "for what" was already coming.

Things were not getting better. People were twitchy. The line between servers and served had become a high-voltage frontier. No one knew for sure where the checkpoints were. The sentries patrolled under cover. Each time a car pulled up to a gas pump, or a shopping cart to a register, served and server eyed each other down, trying to gauge the odds of a border skirmish.

That the served in one instance became the server in another seemed not to matter. What did seem to matter, to some sentries at least, was one's reading on the melanometer. Anybody clear or lighter, and anyone musky or darker, required special dispensation to engage with each other, a clearance provisionally granted and arbitrarily revoked. Some managed to infiltrate, usually by putting on a charm offensive verging on the sycophantic. The rest laid low or avoided mixed company.

Visitors and foreigners of all hues were generally considered neutral. Yet once the travel sites had been peppered with enough reports that Barbados was going through some sort of social reckoning from which hotels had not been spared, tourists began to siphon off elsewhere. After all, Barbados, Barbuda, Bermuda, Bahamas—beach was beach, and the passport stamps looked more or less the same.

The hotels were reeling. The big ones stopped sinking money into training staff and started sending managers to cultural-sensitivity classes instead. They shipped in a cultural-sensitivity coach from Florida, a man whose website boasted of his having once negotiated the release of some factory owners who were being held hostage by a group of workers demanding respect.

The coach flew in on a ten-day contract. On his first day, he announced that he would need some time to observe. He began by lurking near hotel service entrances and taxi stands, hovering wherever he saw employees taking their breaks, scribbling and muttering into his breast pocket. He took the next few days to conduct what he called a double-blind 360-degree feedback exercise, which obliged him to order room service with sufficient frequency to develop the kind of rapport with staff that would cause them to drop their guard and speak freely in the confidentiality of his waterfront suite. Next, to better contextualize the demographic, he asked to be escorted to a representative sampling of local neighborhoods. He traipsed the gaps and lanes, scribbling and muttering and declining offers for directions to his hotel.

Finally, with two days to go, he gathered the senior managers in a mirrored conference room and had them recite affirmations to their own reflections, to optimize the sincerity of their facial expressions. With an overhead projector, he reviewed key vernacular phrases that his research had uncovered, which he urged managers to incorporate into their conversations with staff as a bonding technique. So, for instance, instead of saying, "Did you wipe down these lounge chairs, Nelson?" management was better off saying, "Did ~~you~~ *wunna* wipe down ~~these~~ *them* (alt: *dem*) lounge chairs *they-so*, Nelson?"

Above all, he stressed the importance of memorizing a few details from each employee's personal history file, to be sprinkled casually into exchanges. Staff meetings were to begin by giving employees a chance to air their feelings, with managers calling on each speaker thus: "Nelson, please go ahead. By the way, how is *wunna lovely wife* [*Sonia*]?"

The cultural-sensitivity coach left the island and cashed his check before anybody thought to Google him properly. Midpage in a basic search was a small article revealing him to be a former US border-control officer from Pompano Beach, Florida, who had been fired after taking it upon himself to break a standoff between the Cuban American owners and the Haitian workers who had been holding them hostage at a shoe factory near his house. He and his vigilante group had stormed the factory, ambushed the "alien" Haitians, and turned them in for deportation. The article went on to describe how some of those deported had turned out to be US citizens, who eventually had to be repatriated to American soil.

Their reserves draining by the hour, the hotels decided to get creative. Surely this strange moment Barbados was experiencing was not the first of its kind? The marketing people racked their brains. These knots of race, complexion, and class were too stubborn to untangle by the next fiscal quarter. There were those in the middle trying hard to untie them, and then there were those on the ends pulling them tighter. Yet even in a pigmentocracy under crisis, life had to go on. Profits had to get turned.

Finally someone came up with a plan, inspired by the most obvious model: South Africa.

Of course. If the South Africans could pull off that elaborate Truth and Reconciliation pageant to spackle over apartheid, why couldn't Barbados put on a reconciliation event of its own?

And so it was that a consortium of hotels approached their fair-weather foes, the union leaders, with a proposal for a new joint venture: the All-Barbados Social Unity and Reconciliation Day. An extravaganza featuring top entertainment from all over the world, it would be marketed across the social spectrum, and there would be something for everyone: Caribbean soca and reggae artists, American hip-hop, jazz, pop, and gospel singers, Senegalese dancers, Ivoirian drummers, Nigerian Afrobeats stars, Zimbabwean choirs, Italian opera singers, and English orchestras, even acrobats and contortionists from Czechia. The stage was to look like a United Nations poster, and each act would give a little talk about bridging divides and coming together. The hotels would back the show, and for a sizeable donation, the unions would front it, providing the populist credibility that they alone—with their golden goose Sabre, of course—could bestow.

Most ingenious of all, it was agreed that the show would take place on Emancipation Day, the national holiday, which this year happened to fall on the day after Kadooment Day, when carnival fever was still high. Despite its lofty name, Emancipation Day usually found Bajans nursing hangovers on the beach, or home rubbing down with Benjie's Balm after a night of partying. For once it would be a day to remember.

The headlines went crazy:

WORLD'S HOTTEST ACTS TO COOL DOWN BARBADOS?

UNIONS, HOTELS KISS & MAKE UP IN UNITY PARTY

ABSURD BEDFELLOWS

Now that the media had found a new chew toy, it was of no mind to let go. Each day brought a fresh round of conjecture. Reconciliation Day would be a transformative success. A cataclysmic failure. It would upstage Crop Over. It was the perfect after-party. It was the rich trying to palm off the poor. The opposition trying to show up the government. It was guaranteed to boost the economy. Stall traffic. Wake the dead.

~

In the cool of his second-floor chambers on the outskirts of Bridgetown, Hubert DaCosta took in these latest rumblings with a commensurate case of indigestion. It was becoming his default reaction to annoyances of all kinds: repeat offenders, lawyers who stuttered, room-temperature food, and wrongheaded revisionists bent on muting the immutable.

Unity and reconciliation, his foot. Barbados was as united and reconciled as it was ever going to be.

Take this fellow in the car park below his window, washing cars under the hot sun. Was this fellow looking to unite with him? Did he want to become his best friend, and go and eat pudding and souse together on a Saturday? Did he want to take up golf and make him godfather to his firstborn?

Or did he simply want to be the one sitting in the air-conditioned office instead? Where, in his place, he was sure to rain down twenty times the contempt on the same poor from among whom he had just emerged?

And just what were they supposed to be reconciling over on this Reconciliation Day? A past in which white was master and Black was slave, a past that set your starting point on the racetrack by your proximity to either extreme?

Was he to apologize for having been born more master than slave, and spend the rest of his days atoning for it? The rest of his days leveling off with this car washer, whose bare back glistened smooth and damp and black like the tires he was slopping down with dirty bucket water?

No. Not a bit of it! No one alive today had set this course. Judge that he was, Hubert knew better than anyone that there was no decoupling the present from an ungainly past. No erasing, for instance, his own petty crook of a grandfather, bundled off to Barbados on the night boat from Venezuela under cover of a balled-up tarpaulin. Or his great-grandmother, who had made a living sprinkling chicken blood over the convulsions of believers in the basement of a Caracas brothel. You shook out where you shook out and pushed off from there. What was the point in looking back? All you did was bump into things and fall down holes.

Look at Kingsley, his younger brother, a star who had had all the makings of a scholar. No sooner had the scales fallen from his adolescent eyes, exposing him to certain truths, than he had begun to feel ashamed of his own light skin and wavy hair. Swept up in the throes of anti-imperialism, he had joined a group of schoolboys out to slough off the amniotic slime of privilege by offering themselves in servitude on a Carib reserve in Dominica. By the mismatched accounts of those who had eventually scurried back home, reclaiming the comforts of civilization with zeal, Kingsley had either been embraced as a long-lost native, with his strong resemblance to the Caribs themselves, or been driven mad from the roots and herbs that their hosts consumed in endless concoctions. In any case he had never been heard from again, nor had the scholarship that surely would have been his due been awarded to any Carib or Carib substitute.

Not to say that altruism didn't have its place. Most Saturday mornings, by the time he woke up, Nancy was already out of the house, busy doing her fundraisers or food hampers with the clucking hens in that women's club she ran with the ubiquitous Delphine. It had the dual virtue of keeping her occupied into perpetuity, since no scale of intervention would ever make the needy unneedy, and of freeing up his Saturdays to spend as he liked. Everybody happy. The true beneficiaries of charity work were the husbands left in peace to their own pleasure.

The intercom buzzed. "Counselor Toppin to see you, Your Honor."

"Send her in."

This was unusual, Aggie coming to see him without an appointment. Was she finally getting bold? On the one hand, in theory, such feistiness turned him on. On the other, in practice, it had become a bore walking her time and again through the same quandary. He wished she would either shut up and get on with it or shut up and go home. And whichever option he put to her with his usual tact was bound to yield the opposite result.

"I need your advice," she began, her eyes searching.

"On what?"

"Isilda."

"Who?"

"Who. The maid, Hubert."

"Oh. What happen? The two of you falling out? Just in time for Reconciliation Day?"

They glared at each other across the desk. Hubert felt Aggie's ire rising. And his own even higher. Here it was, another casualty of bloated bourgeois guilt. Another would-be martyr, having made the most of providence's favor, now ready to chomp down on its hand in some misbegotten pappyshow of equality. As if, like tipping a boulder into a shallow pond, to bring the high low was to bring the low high. A Pyrrhic penance.

Aggie was talking, and as she talked, she spun her wedding band around and around her finger. It occurred to Hubert that this must be how she had poor Clive wound around her finger. He chuckled inwardly.

His desire for Aggie was nothing new. He had made up his mind to have her the moment he first laid eyes on her, the moment he returned from his studies in England to find that, whereas he had dutifully selected a bride from among the serviceable and suitable, Clive had managed to unearth his own gem in a backcountry quarry. Something in the victory had seemed to upset the natural order of things between them, as it were, and Hubert had kept it in the back of his mind to right the balance someday.

Now, all things considered, he had to admit that his perseverance had been the only unqualified triumph. He was an old man and Aggie was a high-maintenance woman, always needing and seeking. Had he known better, he would have tackled her back at the height of his powers.

"Are you listening?" she was saying. "They want me to represent them. To be ready when the ministry finally moves to seize their land."

He sighed. "And?"

"Not 'and.' 'But.' But I'm already representing the group on the other side, selling the government the land that they're to be moved to."

"Right. So, conflict of interest. End of story."

She looked at him. "Is it?"

"Isn't it? You see another way?"

"I see a very disappointed woman with cards still to play."

This nonsense again? Hubert swore under his breath at the turning wedding band. "All right," he said. "Then drop those clients and represent your housekeeper instead."

"Don't be daft. You know they can't afford me. And I'm already on retainer."

He shrugged. "Well then, Counselor?"

Aggie gazed out the window. "Maybe . . . I was thinking maybe if I offered her a substantial raise?"

"Perfect. That's it. A nice solid one, so she understands what is involved."

"Yes. I've been giving her little gifts here and there, but this would be a game changer. That should take care of it, right?"

"Should. Just don't be subtle about it. Call it what it is."

"Yes. And for their case?"

"We'll find somebody for them. Not much they can do at this point."

"No, poor things."

"Good." He smiled, reached a hand across the desk. "Now come around here and feel the nice solid raise I have for *you*."

Aggie got up, straightened her skirt, and walked around to him. She bent forward and put her lips close to his.

"You filthy old goat," she muttered. "You ain't tired putting me in trouble? I gone, before I got to give your receptionist and all a raise, too."

Hubert didn't try to call her back. He just chuckled to himself and enjoyed the view as her barre-toned behind bounced out the door.

Lord knew the only thing solid under his desk right now was the bunion on his big toe.

Chapter 18

As the only member of her team who could claim to have set foot in South Africa, even if she was only nine years old at the time, Lisette successfully argued her way to the position of junior liaison for Reconciliation Day. Though the title itched like Guyanese gold, it still had some wattage. It meant that, as far as the world outside the office was concerned, this extravaganza was all hers.

Lately Lisette had been feeling her luck changing. Having disowned her entire crew after the Comfort Seat incident, she had begun to dig more thornfully into Damian's side, insisting that they spend as much of his free time together as possible. Gradually he had taken her on, to the point where they now spent every free Saturday and Sunday together at the Gibbons family beach house. To become yet more of a fixture in his life, she had even learned to surf.

Then soon enough, Cathy and the rest of the traitors had found themselves deserted like leaky sandbags. One by one they lodged complaints: *Sabre stood me up, Sabre left me on read, can you believe Sabre, how could Sabre, Sabre's such a . . .* Ha! The body count was piling up. Yet those zombies were still putting on their equality-enforcement uniforms and hunting for new spots to equalize, forever hoping their leader would reappear.

Their leader was a show pig, with more vacancy under her scalp than on top of it.

Even so. When all was said and done, was it not Sabre that she had to thank for bringing Damian closer? For her new surfer thighs? For teaching her friends a lesson—and now, for this promotion?

Lisette felt her heart soften ever so grudgingly. Some kind of how, Sabre's bungling was paying off quite nicely for her. The cruelty of her last words to Sabre began to repeat on her like the acid reflux from her disappearing belly.

Little dry-foot girl . . . daddy drank to his grave . . . hair fell out like a chemo patient . . . a piece of nothing.

So vicious. Where had they come from? Sometimes she scared herself.

It was wrong, she knew that. How Sabre had grown up wasn't her fault.

Uncle Ronnie might have been a drunk but at least he had presence. Unlike her own dad, mere quarter-drunk that he was, neither here nor there, pleased with everything however it happened to be, floating through life dispensing favors like lollipops and never demanding. Devoid of *grrr*.

Uncle Ronnie took big steps, did big things. She remembered how excited she would get whenever the Cumberbatches moved to another house. But each time, in short order, Sabre and Aunt Cil would be back at their doorstep. And whatever they borrowed her mother would insist they keep. Sabre was always squeezing into new clothes that Lisette had yet to wear, which thrilled Lisette, because it made her feel like the elder of the two. When Sabre began to go bald, after Uncle Ronnie died and Aunt Cil announced that they were moving to America, Lisette had immediately offered Sabre some of her hair. Her aunt's strained laughter at the idea had puzzled her then.

Now, as she looked back on it all, it couldn't have been fun. No wonder Sabre was unstable. Stable people didn't become artists and start cults. Every motor had disturbance at its core.

She'd been an ass, and now she owed Sabre big. She reached for the phone.

~

"Hello?"

There was a long pause.

"Hello, Aggie."

Another.

"Priscilla?"

"How are you."

In Aggie's imagining of events, the one she had rehearsed countless times, this conversation occurred in person. There were people around to serve as referees, most likely at a wake, death being about the only event that could draw her sister back to Barbados. Not that the conversation was ugly: it was a quiet debate, she and Priscilla trading assertions in low, measured tones, steeped in the blend of contempt and forbearance that passed for courtesy in such situations. There was blame enough to share around. But always, as it played out in Aggie's mind, the picture clouded over before it could resolve.

Now she felt the script evaporating in her head.

"It's good to hear you," she heard herself say. "It's been a long time."

"Trying to reach Sabre. Some of her business people need to contact her urgently. Her agent is here with me. Evelyn seemed to think you might know where she is."

"Sabre?"

The name threw her off. It struck her that she had not heard it in some time. With Isilda handsomely palmed off and the land deal absorbing her time and energy, Aggie realized that, for her at least, Sabre's circus had dwindled to a sideshow.

"No, I . . . I haven't seen her. She . . . I don't know if Evelyn told you. She's been busy. With events."

"So you don't know where she is."

"Even mail address it's OK," a voice pressed behind Priscilla.

Aggie paused. "You haven't heard from her either?"

Priscilla said nothing for a time. "OK, well," she said finally. "If you happen to see her, please let her know."

"If she is in the bad mood, I talk to her," said the agitated voice behind Priscilla.

"OK, then," Priscilla said into the phone.

"Cil?"

"Yes."

"Can we talk?"

"I have somebody here, Aggie."

The voice behind her said, "This girl, always she is running . . ."

"Is this your number? Can I call some other time?"

"Always I am running after," the voice said.

"Talk about what."

Aggie felt herself in pigtails.

"Some things," she managed to say, her voice a thin crack. "Many things."

Behind Priscilla's silence, she could hear the other voice muttering in a foreign language.

"All right," Priscilla replied. "We can talk. But not right now."

~

Less than an hour later, Aggie made out Sabre's familiar dome in the passenger seat of Lisette's approaching car.

Since the Reconciliation Day planning had begun, her relationship with Lisette had been flourishing like one of those plants that suddenly blooms after lying dormant for years. Although they had both returned to the office, their bond continued to grow stronger. Often she would come home late to find Lisette at her old spot at the dining table, hacking away on her laptop. Before she could open her mouth, Lisette would rattle off the latest plans, the words tumbling out as though from a rammed cupboard.

At the end of the report, she would pause, searching her mother's face. And Aggie would see it: a reflection, from an old mirror, of herself—young, thrusting, questing. And she would be flooded with desire to defend against whatever perils lay beyond the frame of the glass.

Out of charity she refrained from pointing out the obvious: that, whereas she herself had recovered from scandal and prevailed on her own unsinkable strength, Lisette, bless her, just happened to be profiting professionally from the recklessness of her cousin.

Her foolish, flighty cousin. All feed-bag dress and rash moves and half-wild blood. This feral creature Priscilla had foisted on the world.

She picked up her cabernet and went to the edge of the terrace, where the drizzle was tracing a frontier on the top step. Was it the wine, or the ceaseless dampness, that had her in such a humid mood? Her errant niece was approaching, finally within range to receive the contents of a glass straight in her face, just as Aggie had fantasized on so many occasions. And yet all Aggie felt to do was take the child in her arms and squeeze her *close-close-close*.

~

Isilda was in the powder room preparing to leave. It was a Friday, and for once she had plans worth an extra coat of lipstick. She was heading to the birthday party of a friend from church, whose cousin worked for the Barbados Diabetes Society. After trying Isilda's confections at their patronal festival, the friend had asked Isilda to make the birthday cake: pineapple upside-down, with no cane sugar whatsoever. Child's play. Ripe Antigua Black pineapple has a fullness to it, and if you add a little okra and apple cider vinegar to the batter, then let it soak overnight in fresh juice—*not from concentrate*—the sweetness evens out so the glucose doesn't spike so hard.

Isilda was looking forward to impressing the cousin with this cake, and with her other ideas, including the sample of homemade soursop powder she had stashed in her fancy new bag, a gift from Aggie on the day she had announced Isilda's raise.

Isilda didn't really have an endgame in mind. It wasn't like interviewing for a job or requesting a favor. She was just thrilled at the prospect of meeting another kindred soul who was doing more than complaining, denying, or cowering in fear from diabetes. She couldn't believe she hadn't thought of approaching the BDS before. Maybe she could join them, as a volunteer, if they accepted nondiabetics.

As she exited the bathroom, she overheard Aggie and Lisette chattering on the patio. A tenderness warmed her heart. The household had indeed become happier and more harmonious than Isilda had ever seen it. After all this time, those two had finally dropped their weapons and were behaving like mother and daughter. And the—

Wait. Was she hearing things? That third voice . . .

Blessed Christ. Not Beelzebub sheself back at this doorstep!

Isilda peered around the corner through to the patio. Sure enough, there was a sliver of that bony elbow, that bony backside, that overly glad laugh at God knows what.

Sabre turned and caught eyes with her. The warmth in Isilda's heart began to char.

"Isilda!"

Pretending not to hear, Isilda whipped out her new AirPods and fumbled to jam them into her ears as she hustled toward the kitchen door. But Sabre came after her.

"Isilda, wait." She caught up and blocked her path. "Hey!" she began, smiling her newspaper-headshot smile. "How are you, Isilda?"

Why did this girl insist on keeping Isilda's name in her mouth? Each time she pronounced it in that accent of hers, it was like gum snapping: *Ai-sel-DA*. The last time was at that ridiculous union meeting, which she had had to flee like a chicken evading slaughter.

Aggie and Lisette were still chatting away on the patio. Isilda recognized that if Sabre had managed to crawl back into their good graces, it would behoove her to proceed with caution.

"Good evening," she said stiffly, her eyes on the doorknob behind Sabre.

"It's great to see you. *Sooo . . . ?*" Sabre lowered her voice. "Looks like everything's worked out here?"

No thanks to you, Isilda thought. "I was just about to leave—"

"Listen," said Sabre. "I was hoping I'd run into you. I know you've been uncomfortable with some of the choices I've made—"

"My bus is coming . . ."

"Even though they were for the greater good. We each have our journeys, and it was wrong of me to pressure you before you felt called to serve, like I did . . ."

"Uh-huh. No problem." If she had to listen to *one more* syllable of this rigmarole . . .

"So, here. A peace offering."

Sabre reached into her bag and pulled out a small bottle tied with a red ribbon. Isilda read the label: Magpie Dark Cherry Puree.

"I saw this in Gourmet Grotto and thought of you," Sabre said. "Those cherries you made for me when I first arrived, and how we both love cherries. It was a perfect welcome home. Of course, this won't hold a candle to your recipe. But I thought it would make a nice gift."

Trust Sabre to not know better than to end up in Gourmet Grotto, that shiny hawker of imports that had rich people paying dear to poison themselves. Isilda turned the bottle over and checked the fine print. *Made in the Philippines,* it read. *High fructose corn syrup. Sugar. Maltodextrin.* And down the list, past a stream of unpronounceable chemicals, *morello cherries.* Whatever those were.

Sabre Cumberbatch was out to kill her, one way or another. Isilda had to cough to keep from laughing.

"Thanks," she said, as cheerfully as she could manage. "OK, then."

"Oh, and one more thing," Sabre added, moving aside slightly as Isilda started for the door. "The concert."

"Pardon?"

"Reconciliation Day. The big show? I'm putting you on the list. Backstage passes for you and anyone you like. Maybe Nekisha?"

"You remember her name?" Isilda was temporarily shocked out of her disdain.

"Of course, 'Gran-Gran,'" Sabre replied, winking. "She sounds like such a sweetie."

"That she is," Isilda replied. "Real bright, too."

"Then you gotta bring her. Does she like Peppa Pig? She's already confirmed."

Isilda picked up a hint of Bajan in the way Sabre pronounced "gotta": *gaw-uh*.

She smiled. "The Bajan accent coming back."

"Think so? I hope. That's the dream." And Sabre seemed to mean it sincerely.

"When this thing is again? The Peppa Pig?"

"Emancipation Day," Sabre replied. "Right after Kadooment."

"Kadooment, oh shoot," said Isilda. "Soon time to start baking. Every year I does set up and sell my goods along the parade route. It's my busy season."

"Mine, too," Sabre said. "In fact, this one's going to be a doozy for all of us." She nodded toward the bottle with a smile. "At least now you can cheat a little on the cherry pies."

Isilda laughed as she tucked the bottle into her bag, taking care to keep it well clear of her soursop powder.

Maybe Sabre wasn't Beelzebub. But if she thought this nastiness was getting anywhere near Isilda's top-quality baked goods, she might be Bobo the Clown.

Chapter 19

How you expect
That unity in effect
When you hands still join roun' me neck
And all yuh talk en' grow me paycheck?
No respect . . .

Judah Lioness, "Unity Ain't Free"

The first new calypso songs were hitting the airwaves, signaling the start of Crop Over, the carnival season. As usual, the lesser-known calypsonians were earliest to release their tunes, hoping for a head start at burrowing into the collective subconscious. They set the headlines to music, decrying injustice and vice in earnest stanzas over wailing horns. They put on sober faces and close-fitting, meaningful polyester, and wagged their fingers at the sparse crowds who attended their showcases. They sermonized and admonished. They sang in one key while the band played in another.

As a result, by the time Crop Over was at its peak six weeks later, most of them were history. Too much shaking of the head, too little shaking of the tail. Crop Over was a time to shake down.

It happened like this: At the start of the season, a bodyquake came over you, due south. It moved from the sensible civic buzz in your head to the jiggle around your middle, prompting you to join the seasonal exercisers on the beach shaping up to squeeze into their carnival costumes. Then the quake traveled down to your backside, as sweeter, ruder tunes came along to shake it. From there, it shook down to your knees, the quickening rhythms conspiring with liquor to make you "go down low" with no thought of how to get back up. And finally, with Crop Over fever at a pitch, the quake possessed your feet, making you jump and stomp to the beat.

Yes, Crop Over was a shakedown, a jolt of current feeding into the earth. As the current grew stronger and the spirit overtook you, every care, every constraint loosened and yielded to gravity. Critics complained that the modern-day bacchanal paid too scant an homage to its origins in plantation days, when field workers, having harvested the last of the sugarcane crop, were allowed to celebrate with a jig and a nip of rum. But when those critics shook their heads at the meaninglessness of it all, carnival glitter rained down from their temples.

~

About that glitter: it was scarlet, gold, aqua, bronze, lime, silver, violet, orange. Or was it aqua, gold, orange, lime, scarlet, silver, violet, bronze?

Ian pored over the annotated sketch of his assigned costume and studied the sample the designer had sent over. He picked up one of the bikini tops lying on the table, the cups artfully laser-cut in a strategic yin-yang design, and tried to determine the most efficient order for the bowls of glitter, beads, and sequins that he would soon be instructing his team of volunteer costume-makers to apply. Then he rearranged the embellishments in an assembly line down the table.

In Crop Over as in all things, Ian was a patriot and a purist. As a patriot, he was duty-bound to throw his weight into the country's premier cultural event. As a purist, he hewed to tradition against the widening snare of the carnival-industrial complex.

So what if most Crop Over costumes nowadays were stamped out at a factory in China, assembled in Trinidad using Brazilian embellishments, and distributed by masquerade bands that were local subsidiaries of regional corporations? All the more reason to support homegrown bands like this one, Sun People. Their costumes were handmade on-site at band headquarters—known as the band house—by volunteers who came each evening to glue and gossip in the party atmosphere.

Sun People was preoccupied with authenticity, which is to say obsessed with antiquity. When it took to the parade on Kadooment Day, it featured a live steel band up front, something most masquerade bands had long abandoned, and a traditional Bajan tuk band in the rear. Its only concessions to modern times were the skimpy costumes and a DJ truck blaring soca in the center of the band, around which the revelers tended to congregate.

And so what if the themes had become disposable excuses for people to gyrate half naked through the streets each year? All the more reason, Ian felt, to channel the spirit of the theme into each costume. He himself wasn't much of a partier and brought the same serene precision to the gluing of tassels onto a G-string as to the setting of a window or the plastering of a wall. And with this year's theme of "Harmony" coinciding with this new Reconciliation Day, there was even more cause for reflection.

Ian was relieved that the organizers had gone to pains to assure that Reconciliation Day capped off Crop Over rather than competing with it. Even so, the amount of money they were pumping into the event easily dwarfed the government's entire festival budget. Clearly the hotels were out for unity at any price. Even their little band house had received more Reconciliation Day posters than they had wall space to display them.

The posters were cluttered with names and faces of the major acts scheduled to appear. And in the lower left corner, a headshot of Sabre Cumberbatch.

He had come upon her one evening recently as he was leaving the jobsite. She was standing on the Toppins' patio in the shade of the mango tree and seemed to be in deep reflection.

Ian stopped in his tracks. Was she back to staying with the Toppins? Impossible. Surely Isilda, distant as they were these days, would have alerted him to that. On the rare occasions that he caught a glimpse of Isilda, she seemed to be doing fine. She no longer looked his way when she came out to pick limes or hang a bedspread. Perhaps he, too, had lost the habit of watching for her.

Seeing Sabre in a contemplative state was jarring. So off-brand from the walking pom-pom he had become used to seeing in the media. But here she was in real life, beyond the cameras, looking crestfallen. It just went to show how hard it was to really know a person.

Then she had looked up, and Ian had given her a polite nod. She had waved back absently. Ian could tell she didn't recognize him from the meeting.

People like him rarely registered with people like her.

Case in point: Aggie Toppin. How many times had he locked eyes with that woman during the weeks she had spent pacing the patio on her phone? At first he would avert his eyes whenever he saw her, to avoid causing residual embarrassment over the scandalous conditions under which they had met. But then he realized that Aggie had no idea who he was.

He had witnessed her lowest point. The dirt he had on her and Justice DaCosta would be nuclear in less principled hands. And yet there she was, yards away, staring right through the man holding the detonator. Such was the way of the world.

"Am I early?"

Ian started, spilling violet sequins from the bowl in his hand. A young man stood in the doorway of the band house. Seeing Ian jump, he put down his bag and bike helmet and came over to the table.

"Boy," he said quietly, sweeping the sequins into his hand in one move. "Crop Over now start and you jumping already. Save some for the road, nuh?"

Ian laughed, still a bit startled. "Just setting up. We weren't expecting people this early."

"I like being early. Get to choose the easiest job." The man grinned. He funneled the sequins back into the bowl. "Need a hand? You don't seem to know which end is up." He extended his hand. "Don't mind me, hear? Left home my manners. Kirk."

Ian smiled. "I'm—"

"Ian Boyce. I know."

The handshake was over, but Ian dimly noticed that his hand was still in Kirk's. He caught himself taking in the soft drape of Kirk's T-shirt over his chest. He pulled away.

"Do I . . . I mean, were you in the band last year?"

"Mm-hmm. But I didn't know the name then. Only that face." Kirk smirked and began to set out the glue guns. "Anyhow, I see you don't remember me. It was the meeting. At the union hall, back in April? You got up to speak, and I was sitting behind you. You had me very impressed."

"Oh," said Ian, glad for something to latch onto. "You're a union man, then?"

"No. I was just there being nosy like everybody else. And looka where we reach." He pointed his chin across the room to a Reconciliation Day poster. "Reconciliation Day renting out Emancipation Day. First they free us, and now they looking to buy us back." He sucked his teeth.

Ian was intrigued. He watched as Kirk set the glue guns in front of each chair, trigger pointed outward and to the right, glue sticks on the left, straightening each chair as he went.

"What you think?" Kirk was asking him. He made his way full circle and stopped where Ian stood before the pile of bikini tops.

The two men looked at each other. Ian froze. He picked up a top and began to fold and fold.

"Let me see that," Kirk said, easing it out of Ian's hands. "No point folding just to unfold."

Ian found his tongue. "Well, I can't see this thing working out."

"What thing?"

"This unity concert. People don't just change in a day."

"You're right," Kirk replied, unfolding the bikini top. He held one of its cups to his eye and peered at Ian through the cutout. "People are what they are. Can't force in wuh ain't there and can't force out wuh there."

Ian gaped, trying in vain to find an unattractive feature on Kirk where he could rest his eyes. A bullhorn speech began in his head: *If you think . . .*

As though hearing him, Kirk shifted his eye from the cutout yang to the solid yin. "Maybe that's just me," he said, placing the garment gently on the table and stepping around Ian. "You let me know if you agree."

Ian watched him walk away, his eyes marking Kirk's ten paces as if they were a thousand. He watched Kirk choose a workstation at the far end of the table, pull out the chair, and sit. People began to arrive, so Ian moved forward to greet them. He checked them in. He pointed out the refreshments table. He gave instructions for applying the glitter, beads, and sequins to the bikini tops. He was crisp and efficient as ever. But he felt a strange loosening inside.

Chapter 20

Reconciliation Day was to be free and open to the public, but space would be limited. Lisette, having never attended an event of this scale, let alone organized one, summoned her instinct for exclusivity to come up with a tiered ticketing system. The grounds and three-quarters of the stands would be for the general public, whose tickets would be awarded by lottery, contests, and promotions. The remaining space would be a special VIP area for artists and their entourages, as well as the privileged many—politicians, dignitaries, corporate sponsors, family and friends of the organizers—worthy of sipping the same Taittinger champagne. The VIP tickets were complimentary and as jealously guarded as the names of those lucky enough to receive them.

The show was to be held at the old stadium, site of every event requiring a massive stage, a flagpole, shelter from the elements, and an orchestra pit from which the national police band could crank out its eternal hit, the national anthem.

"The old stadium" had been known simply as "the stadium," until about eight months ago, when a diplomatic offer had come from China—which lately had been dolloping largesse *kerplunk, kerplunk* all over the Caribbean—to build a new stadium free of charge, causing Bajans suddenly to see their beloved ancient arena for the rickety eyesore it must long have been. Before the ink could dry on the

Memorandum of Understanding between the two governments, the Chinese had begun shipping in laborers, and the Ministry of Sports had begun prospecting for a location for the new building.

Which was why, further downstream, things were getting muddier. Forty-seven households in Isilda's district had received identical letters from the Ministry of Housing, announcing that their land was to be taken over by compulsory acquisition for a public works project. In a few months' time, the residents were to be compensated with relocation to "comparable quarters" in a place "yet to be determined." The letter turned its back as abruptly as it had shown its face. No number to call, no name to appeal to. Not a soul to question or cuss out or sweet-talk or bribe.

At first people were in shock, the kind of shock that comes with advance notice of doom. Then somebody stirred and tried to contact the district's Member of Parliament.

After days of unreturned calls, the MP appeared in the district one evening, his black Escalade pulling around in front of the dueling dessert trucks. Without fully getting out, he perched above the marsh on the step of his SUV and assured those who happened to be gathered nearby—mostly children licking snow-cones and ice cream—that he had this land-swap matter in hand, and that no one should worry because no trickery was going to get past him, that in fact, he had been busy negotiating a major upgrade as part of the deal, and that he would soon be in a position to guarantee them "120 percent" that the place they were moving to, and the houses to be offered in exchange, were beyond their dreams. Then, as more adults began to surge forward with questions, the MP quickly promised to be in touch and motioned to his driver to make haste.

They watched the vehicle screech off. "He tek we for idiots," said Delphine. "Next election I comin' for he."

"What we goin' do?" somebody wondered.

"If you ask me, best thing to do is bide the time," a woman said. "I know a girl that the gov'ment tek she land, turn round and set she up pretty-pretty in a big wall house, short by she job and all. I wish it did me, I woulda leff 'bout hey hard."

"Well I ain't leffin' hey, I tellin' you now," drawled another voice. It was Lamar, sprawled out along the storm drain wall with his eyes closed. "I ain't care what nobody say. I ain't leffin'. That is that."

The other guys on the wall muttered their agreement.

That the drain-wall crew was moved to express an opinion instantly heightened the sense of gravity. Temperance and patience suddenly felt like luxuries.

~

Minutes later, Isilda guessed from the authoritative knock at her door just who it was.

"This thing moving, girl. We ready?"

"I got a name for you. Come in."

Delphine stepped through the door as Isilda went for her handbag. She had been baking turnovers, and the scent of warm spiced coconut canopied the house.

"I ain't goin' lie. I thank the Lord when I see this letter," Isilda called from her bedroom. "You don't feel nothing good could come out of it?"

"Good or bad ain't the point," said Delphine. "It's how they treating us. Like sheep that they could just stake out wherever they feel like." She paused. "I surprised it ain't troubling you, though. Like you could just put down any old where."

"Not just anywhere. Somewhere nice. And new," Isilda replied, coming back into the living room.

"New, nuh? Like that valise brekking down you shoulder?" She pointed at Isilda's handbag.

"Oh!" Isilda tried to laugh, but the back of her neck warmed with shame. She hadn't been intending to show off. Again she felt that guilty feeling she had been getting lately around Delphine. She decided not to mention that the bag had been a gift from Aggie, although she could be sure that Delphine would assume as much. "You like it?"

"No wonder you don't care where you live. Your whole family could fit in there comfortable," said Delphine. "Especially since your son claim he ain't going nowhere."

"He could say what he like, either way no room ain't in here for he." She dug out a slip of paper and handed it to Delphine. "Look the person here. Miss Toppin say he is the best. Say she woulda hire him sheself."

"Good girl." Delphine tucked the slip into her pocket. "We goin' be ready for them now."

Just then Lamar barged into the house singing, *"No, no, we ain't leffin' home . . ."* He passed through to the kitchen and snatched up two of the turnovers cooling on the counter. He stuffed one into his mouth, then came and planted a sticky grated-coconut kiss on Isilda's cheek and another on Delphine's.

"The two o' wunna very offset," he threw out. "Don't fret, man, we ain't budging not a half a inch! We stoppin' right here-so. I goin' see to that personal." He crammed down the second turnover and dusted off his hands ceremoniously.

Delphine laughed and shook her head. "Sildy, Lamar like he more sure than you."

"I wonder why. Must be frighten I don't let him darken the door at my new house."

"New house, what," Lamar snorted.

"But how you so worked up, though?" Isilda shot back. "You that don't even look to feed yourself nor your child when the days come."

"I born here an' I deadin' here," said Lamar. "That is wuh I sayin'. Nobody can't pick we up and put we 'bout as they like. People got rights."

"You right, boy," said Delphine.

Isilda wasn't convinced. But she let it go.

Chapter 21

Early Sunday morning, a week before Kadooment, Lamar strained his eyes to read the time display over a sea of bobbing heads near the DJ stand and realized he should have left the fete six minutes ago. Mindful of what was at stake, he disengaged from the anonymous bottom he had been riding for the last half hour, tightened the shoulder straps of his backpack, and waded through to the exit.

Once through the gates, ears still throbbing, he wriggled off his plastic admission wristband and handed it off to the first outstretched hand near the entrance. He had to laugh at whichever fancy promoter thought they could make a profit from a twenty-four-hour fete. Really and truly, the whole setup made him proud of his people. The way the door guys would always fasten the wristband loosely, making sure that each one could be slipped on and off wrists all day. The way the bartenders would trim the ice off a drink and top you up with just a look. The fellows working these fetes and the ones trying to get in, they followed the same code.

The task at hand had him cold sober, not a drop nor a puff all night. Being sober actually made him vibe deeper. The fetes were all right this year but the vibe, the vibe felt different.

It wasn't the crowd milling around, posing and swaying, waiting to see who would fill the holes on the dance floor. That was the normal Bajan way. He hadn't even noticed it until he started going to Trinidad with his football club and saw for the first time what true feting looked like. From the door of the party, they would pull out whatever could make noise—bottle, pen, piece of iron, somebody's back—and put down a rhythm. Trinis had energy, drive. In fact, it was Trinis he had to thank for his own business-mindedness today.

Another twenty minutes to base. As a shortcut and because he liked the dark, he turned off between two palings and slid expertly down into a long, shallow gully that snaked behind the chain of houses. He landed upright on the footpath and was startled to find himself just yards away from a large monkey striding in silhouette with its tail erect.

They took each other in. Without breaking stride or hurrying, the monkey changed course and disappeared into the bush on the other side. There was a rustling of branches, a swish of tails and limbs under the wind. Lamar looked up and saw nothing but tree. Yet through the leaves he could feel an army of eyes pricking the edges of his earlobes like brambles.

～

Monkeys had overtaken roaches and mosquitoes as the number one pestilence. They raided crops, peed on verandas, frightened dogs, turned over garbage pails, and smelled. Only Lamar seemed to recognize in all this that it was people, not monkeys, who were the unwelcome gate-crashers. Before fancy houses had started sprouting up all over like boils on a bullfrog's back, man and monkey knew their places. Now the monkeys were getting turfed out. People were setting themselves up on every square inch and still found the nerve to complain when monkeys simply tried to claim a little space.

Monkeys didn't trouble him because he gave them no reason to. He had nothing for them and therefore nothing against them. Their actions were nowhere near as bad as the arrogance he saw in humans, always shuffling others' lives like a deck of cards. In fact, the more griping he heard about monkeys, the more he found himself siding with them.

This country had its head on backward. People were obsessed with law and order, so long as they made the law and the order put them first. They fixed life to suit themselves.

Outlaws were bred, not born. Barbados was churning them out like the sugar mills used to churn out bagasse. The old folks talked about the sugar days like paradise lost, when a simple man could see his way on however little he had. Lamar didn't know what they were talking about. All he knew was that today under the law, there were about five ways left to be a lawful success and five hundred to be a lawful failure. Two or three to get above the law altogether. Who couldn't get above it, nor survive under it, was forced to get around it.

This fact had hit him hard two years ago when Nekisha had come to live with them. He'd realized then that among the many things he and his late ex had neglected to address was their daughter's asthma. It wasn't the easy kind. Nekisha could land in hospital for days if she didn't have her medication. But the pharmacies kept running out, and however much he ranted, it was always wait lists and excuses.

Asking around, he had discovered how many people routinely went without medication for all kinds of things: epilepsy, allergies, blood pressure, even prostate. The problem was the supply chain. The big-dog countries were hoarding drugs, throwing money at drug manufacturers, and cutting off supply to small-fry Barbados, which was how Bajans ended up on their knees, begging mercy from people who didn't know they existed, praying graveside if the mercy didn't reach. The injustice of it had set his every corpuscle on fire.

Lamar was no big dog. But he knew a thing or two about supply chains. So he had announced to his crew, and to their suppliers in Trinidad, that the operation would be pivoting from recreationals to pharmaceuticals. The plan was to supply whatever was short—prednisone, epinephrine, naloxone, sildenafil, antibiotics.

It had taken time to establish the pipeline; longer still to build credibility among customers unused to dealing with real-real dealers. Now, eighteen months in, business had stabilized. His mother could talk all the talk about where his soul was headed, how wutless he was as a father, up to no good. One thing she could never say was that Nekisha was out of inhalers. His mother had no idea how much good he was up to. And for her sake and everyone else's, she never would.

His crew had got on board with the new venture from day one. But when it came to this land-move business, Lamar was stunned by their lack of vision. Every single one of them was already turning his mind to plan B, yapping about market share, like sheep herded in a new direction at the whim of a sheepdog.

Lamar had looked them over, disgusted. "I can't believe what I hearing. Market share? That is all wunna studying?" He scowled. "All right, tell me something. When last you see one of them big boys got to shift 'cause the government take over he land?"

"You ain't to look at it so, Lamar," said his deputy. "You got to see it practical. When I look at this here, I only seeing benefits. New house, new turf . . ."

"Benefit! Benefit of what? If the turf expanding, it should be *we* expanding it. It ain't because some rasshole fart high that the wind got to change. We got rights, we is big men."

"Businessmen, too, though," the deputy replied.

"My mother work for that lawyer every day and can't get nowhere," Lamar continued. "Always vex and frighten and ain't got nothing to show for it. Stressing sheself just to hold on. You feel Aggie Toppin does stress sheself over my mother? You feel she frighten for she? If the mood take she tomorrow, she could just tell my mother fuck off, flick she like a tick. Wunna ain't got no problem with that?"

The crew had kept up a few respectful moments of silence for the mention of somebody's mother. But in the interval, before his deputy eased the talk onto a different, smoother track, Lamar had come to see that he would have to go on tonight's mission alone.

～

His foot went down in a soggy patch, and he let go a curse. Muddy footprints were the last thing he could afford. Soon enough the rain would be back, but tonight that might not work in his favor.

He scrambled up the gully bank onto the pavement, slipped off his shoes, and found a puddle to rinse off the soles. Instinctively he decided to go the rest of the way barefoot.

This was the part of himself even his mother never got to see. The professional problem solver. People were always miscalculating his life-management skills, as they used to call it in juvenile. Always assuming he was either idle or ignorant. True, in the end, being overlooked and underestimated had its benefits, because you could stay below the radar. It was just that every damn body had something to say. Bajans loved to blab, whereas him, he didn't believe in extra talk. As his grandmother liked to say, those who didn't hear would have to feel.

Approaching the drain wall near the top of his own gap, he made out a figure crouching by a tree. He took out his phone and flashed the screen at the figure in a swiping gesture. The figure responded by copying the gesture three times, back and forth. Then it turned and disappeared down the gap.

Lamar put on his shoes, crossed the road, and proceeded to the garbage dump, tucked out of sight in a corner of the drainage embankment on the other side.

He flashed his phone again, this time to take in the heap of bags, stray rubbish, and Reconciliation Day posters. Some of the bags near the perimeter were oozing a magnificent slime, a mixture of mulch and pigwash. Yet another of his ingenious innovations, and not a simple one, either. It was all right to use the techniques they had in other districts: monitoring the goods around the clock, threatening grievous bodily harm to any trash collector who tried to collect trash or any bystander who stood by too long. But who else went to the lengths he did?

One, two, three: third slime bag from the right. He bent down, holding the phone between his teeth as a flashlight, and with a warrior's resolve stuck his bare arm straight into the filth.

He groped around confidently until his fingers felt the familiar lumps of taut bubble wrap under plastic. Reaching in with both hands, he pulled out a pair of neat parcels and put them in his backpack. As he placed the second parcel inside, a panic shot through him: suppose the backpack wasn't big enough for the extra package? He had done his homework, but the Trinis had not been specific as to size, and he had forgotten to ask. For the second time that night he cursed himself. Six minutes late leaving the party, now this sloppiness. Wars had been lost and civilizations destroyed over less.

But no time to dawdle. Back in he plunged, sure of where to feel but not of what to feel for. It wasn't long before the answer grazed his palm. He pulled it out, and every orifice on him contracted.

Yes, it was compact enough to fit into the backpack. But that alone could not explain the sensation of tingle and release that flooded his bloodstream, easing his heart while making the hairs on his slime-smeared forearms stand up at the roots. He zipped up the backpack and, clutching it to his chest as he had never in life embraced his own girl-child down the far end of the gap, stole away quicker and quieter than his very shadow.

Chapter 22

Bajan posse
Get ready!
Wave yuh flag an
Leddem see!
From Christ Church to
St. Lucy!
We jookin' fuh
Unity!

Jook-jook
Fuh unity!
Jook-jook
Fuh unity!

Corn Pone, "Jook Fuh Unity"

Isilda had a bad feeling about Kadooment Day from the moment she woke up to find her gas cut off. She had learned not to send Lamar anywhere to pay anything, and she always saw about the gas before the bill could reach the house, so she knew right away that this was no ordinary mishap. Not after setting two alarms, one for half past four and the other for quarter to five, so she could finish the turnovers and plum drops and have them cooling before starting the first batch of coconut cakes with enough time to then get down the road to join the other vendors who had been invited to sell their products at a special stall sponsored by the Barbados Diabetes Society.

Instead, it was a wasted call to the gas authority—"The management and staff take this opportunity to wish you a safe Crop Over and a happy Reconciliation Day. For urgent matters, please . . . *beeeep!*"—and then to Delphine, who had to pull all kinds of advanced maneuvers to roust her gas man from parts unknown to come with his equipment. By the time he finished, Isilda had made her peace with scuttling the coconut cakes altogether and was just scrambling to put in the plum drops when a terrific rain came and drenched the trays of turnovers she had balanced on the windowsill.

"Sildy, relax. The Lord telling you to stand home, that is all," Delphine said, watching her suck her teeth at the live TV coverage of the Kadooment Day parade. In the background, a vendor could be seen squatting under a tarpaulin. "Why hurt your head in all this rain? You will get another chance at the unity thing tomorrow. Call it a blessing."

Looking at the vendor on TV, her shower cap and apron dripping and the tarpaulin draining into her foil pans, Isilda began to reconsider her misfortune. She called and made her apologies to Theo, her new friend from the Diabetes Society.

"Don't mind. Just come tomorrow," he told her. "We'll have a stall at the Reconciliation Day event, too. And I promise to arrange some sunshine, just for you."

His friendly tone reassured Isilda. She relaxed a bit. Truthfully, the scene down at the parade was far from enticing. Even the commentators were hard up for much to comment on, other than the rain. And the revelers who straggled into view seemed to be either straining to have a good time in spite of the weather or too drunk to care.

~

Beyond the cameras, things were not as dire. Kadooment was Kadooment, as ever. Spectators of all ages jostled for space along the parade route or huddled on strangers' verandas and under strangers' umbrellas. Music blared from every open shop door. Roving vendors did brisk trade in Kadooment essentials: whistles, water, nuts, glow necklaces, and Barbadian flags. And at the top of the parade route, at an intersection of two major streets with a rum shop on each of its four corners, throngs of glittery masqueraders entangled like Christmas lights as they waited for their bands to take the road.

Besides, every other Kadooment Day brought rain. *But not this much,* Ian thought to himself as he distributed plastic ponchos to the Sun People security team from the bed of a music truck. The band was about to hit the road, and already the damp costumes of the white "Peace" section were detracting from his painstaking glitter work with unwelcome displays of nipple and back flab. He was glad to have chosen a costume from the black section, "Perseverance." Black suited him, even though it tended to attract heat. He adjusted the purple-and-gold-sequined front sheath over his crotch and tried not to look for Kirk over in the yellow section, "The Fires of Home."

But the Fire of Home found him.

"Missing me?" Kirk sidled up from behind.

"Behave. Come and make yourself useful."

"Yeah, boss." Kirk took over the pile Ian had been handling. "Hmm, these raincoats big enough for two. Lemme take one now and pray the rain don't stop."

Ian shook his head in half-mock exasperation. He reached down for the last pile of ponchos, and his disobedient eyes stole a glimpse of Kirk's yellow shorts, still uncovered by the costume sheath.

Ian was not yet prepared to admit that the cat-and-mouse between him and Kirk had become a favorite pastime, or that, since their first meeting at the band house, he had not ceased to anticipate the cold, delicious horror of this man's advances. Whenever he heard Kirk's motorbike pull up out front, he would find some activity to absorb his attention, double-checking beadwork or restocking the snack table. He could not get over Kirk's boldness, his ease inside his skin. He wondered how one came to be that way.

Ian didn't know, and he wasn't sure he wanted to learn. But Kirk was as persistent as he was proving irresistible. When he wasn't flirting absently with the other volunteers of both sexes, he was in Ian's ear dropping broad hints of emancipation, without checking whether emancipation was even Ian's thing.

~

When the rain eventually tapered to a drizzle, the parade of bands got underway at last.

"Come, Sildy, it on!" Delphine called from the living room. "Come and see what you ain't missing."

Isilda came out of the kitchen with a dish of plum drops. They watched as the bands came down, many of the revelers, having waited out the rain in one rum shop or another, now soggier inside than out.

It was the usual lineup, smaller bands going first. There was the Blue Balls Brigade, a ragtag group of very drunk, very local white revelers. Then the Holy Rollers, a Pentecostal group that stirred up controversy every year by how much or how little the members shook their backsides.

"Man, give us something to see," Delphine complained to the TV, as the band picked its way Pentecostally past the cameras.

"Must be saving energy for tomorrow," said Isilda. "Hope they saving their money, too, for these plum drops."

At that moment Lamar entered the house, looking perturbed.

"What you doing here?" he asked his mother.

"I should ask you that. Didn't expect to see you upright for the next two days." She and Delphine laughed.

"I smell gas."

"Yeah, the gas man went here to fix the canister."

"Why? I cut the line for a reason."

"Wuh? Boy, you hit your head or what? You cut off my gas and know I got things to do? What you trouble it for?"

"You don't mind that. Just now you goin' be thanking me."

"What that supposed to mean?"

"Ahh, looka prettiness now," Delphine interrupted, as the glimmering Sun People banners appeared onscreen.

"Boy, I ask you a question. What it is you up to?"

"Look, don't ask what you ain't want to know."

"Ha ha! Do bad, girl!" Delphine exclaimed at a Sun People reveler wining down to "Jook Fuh Unity." "Mind yuh kneecaps don't pop off!"

"I goin' be glad enough when we move from this place," Isilda fumed. "You best make provision for yourself, hear, 'cause I sick and tired of you . . ."

"Tell yuh already I ain't moving."

"Well good! You stay there, then."

"Wuloss! Look, Sildy, look!"

Isilda turned to see a pair of Sun People men wining down, bottoms to the camera, stacked and pumping in sync. Then they came up again, taking their time, savoring the ride, swerving side to side with the music. Other band members slowed down to watch. As they turned laughing toward the camera, the one in yellow suddenly grabbed the one in black and licked the corner of his mouth in a thick kiss. It was only when the one in black jerked backward that Isilda recognized Ian's face. He threw a startled glance at the one in yellow and then stumbled out of the frame.

"Wooey! Wulosssss!! That's right! Love is love, darlings!" Delphine's eyes streamed tears of laughter.

Lamar sucked his teeth and disappeared into his room.

Isilda stared at the spot on the screen where Ian had been, her mind mapping his imprint.

It was the most sense this day had made so far.

Chapter 23

"Thank you, Barbados!" Sabre shouted into the mic. "Thank you! Enjoy this Reconciliation Day! Goodbye!"

What had she just said up there?

Who the hell cared!

Nobody was listening—shit, she could barely hear herself. The crowd was so huge, so pumped. The energy was beyond. Words were the last thing on anyone's mind.

Reconciliation Day, baby!

She went over to Keith and Vonda in the media pen.

"You gone pro, man," Keith said. "No notes or nothing in front of all them people."

"Don't need 'em."

"Notes are for when you have serious things to say to serious people," Vonda teased, giving a half-joking side-eye.

"Vonda. Are you seriously telling me you'd rather be at a trafficking meeting right now? Where's Eric anyway? At the office typing up minutes? Dusting off a deliverable?"

Vonda shook her head and gave one of Keith's weary-donkey smiles.

"Sabre," she said, "I gotta hand it to you. If nothing else, you've made a lot of people very happy. For now, we'll just have to be satisfied with that."

"Vonda doesn't believe in reconciliation," Keith smirked.

"Stop putting words in my mouth." Vonda smacked Keith's shoulder. "Especially that one. You and your woman can gang up all you like. I just hope we can get back to business once this is over. Once this"— she flailed an arm at the crush of people swarming the stadium—"is out of everyone's system."

"Right away, comrade," mocked Sabre.

"And for your information, Eric is right up there in the stands, reconciling with the rest of them. Satisfied?"

"Oh, good. Glad one of you is having fun today!" Sabre blew her a kiss.

She felt sorry for the Vondas of the world who didn't know how to step back and enjoy success. It had to be tough staying focused on the bad when the good was this good. Even in the midst of a major victory like this, the Vondas of the world restrained themselves from indulging in joy or satisfaction. It was probably clinically diagnosable.

Meanwhile, at the other end of the spectrum was Lisette, working it backstage like she'd been born wearing that headset and clipboard. Sabre hadn't heard one catty remark about Auntie Aggie emerge from Lisette's lips since the three of them had made up. Who had time to be petty while engaged in things that matter? Even her stone-assed mother had descended from her pedestal of pride and started speaking to Auntie Aggie again.

Reconciliation begins at home.

And of this Sabre was sure: Barbados *was* home. This Barbados, this place she had fixed, was where she belonged.

Something had brought her here, to help these people. People she didn't know, who didn't know they needed her. It had been hard at times. But look at all she'd done.

From now on, no more invisible maids. No more looking down on people from the country or from a bad neighborhood.

No more Bald Pigeon of Bed-Stuy, bloated on New York's hot air. No more fraud.

No more Basquiat comparisons.

From now on, it was just her: Sabre Cumberbatch.

Activist. Liberator. Equalitarian.

"Superstar!"

A cloud of Thierry Mugler's Angel perfume engulfed her.

She turned around. Auntie Aggie and Uncle Clive were standing there, grinning. And next to them, in a rose silk poncho with her arms wide, Katya.

"Surprise, favorite girl!" She spread her poncho like batwings and came in for a hug.

"Katya!" Sabre felt a rash begin in her mind. "What are you doing here?"

Katya gave a whooping laugh. "You see, Clive and Agatha?" she said. "This girl, she thinks she is only one who is clever. She blocks the call of agent who loves her, but she forgets there is the news that is all time talking of her, of the big reconciliation show in the Barbados—oh, my darling!"

She whooped and swaddled Sabre in silk again.

"Katya, she's been stirring up trouble around here," said Auntie Aggie. "Get her straight for us, please."

"Come, we going miss Patti LaBelle," Uncle Clive said. "Katya, come and join us when you're ready. You have your ticket, right?"

As soon as they had left, Sabre turned to Katya with a serious expression.

"I really hope you're here for the show," she told her. "Because I'm not coming back to New York. And Topsheet? Definitely a no."

Katya smiled. It was a new smile, one Sabre couldn't place.

"Darling, my Sabre," said Katya, "today is not day for business. Today is day only for you. I come to Barbados to support. We enjoy now, later we discuss. Yes?"

～

Isilda watched it happen from the back of the stadium grounds.

Ma and Nekisha had already left after spending the morning backstage with Peppa Pig. Isilda had not joined them. She had been stationed at the Diabetes Society stall, watching her items fly off the counter. Even though she had jacked the prices way up when she saw how many tourists had come, tourists and Bajans alike kept coming back for more. People asked for her card—card?—and for directions to her restaurant—restaurant!—and whether she catered office parties or shipped overseas. It made her regret all the Kadooment Days she had spent idling by the roadside with nothing to sell.

So she was sheltering under one of the bars, taking in the spectacle and feeling good for herself. She was never one to curse the rain. Once you could keep dry, it actually cleaned up your mood, made you want to make lazy love, if you could find it to make. Sipping her beer, she tried to imagine who the next contender might be.

Maybe Theo? True, he worked for the diabetes people, but something told her he had a weakness for her kind of sweetness. Plus, she deserved it after Ian's dithering, which had finally and at last added up.

These young boys. She hoped he had found what he really wanted.

Shakira's performance came to an end, and a new emcee took over hosting duties: Demme Maxwell, a fixture on the local scene and one of Isilda's favorites. It was early evening, and the show was several hours in, the winds whipping rain in all directions. Stagehands in black slickers had to keep mopping the stage. Some of the crowd had left, but most were stubbornly holding on as dusk began to fall and the stadium lights came on.

"Party people!" Demme's voice boomed over the speakers. "Are you feeling the *u-ni-teee*?"

"Yes!" the crowd blubbed.

"I said, Barbados! Are you feeling *reconciiiiled*!"

"*Yeesss!*"

"Then answer muh this: How come some o' wunna dry and the rest wet?"

There was hooting and applause.

"Look! They tell me come out here and show that we Bajans could unite and reconcile with one another. But I ain't goin' lie to yuh! This unity that we got here, it looking very disunisive to me! Party people! Ah lie?"

"Woooo!"

"Now I ain't talking to wunna out there 'pon de grounds. I talking to my lords and ladies up in the high section." Demme bowed and gestured to the driest stands, directly opposite the stage. "My lords and ladies, a pleasant good evening to one and all. How are we feeling tonight?"

The crowd hooted.

"Lords and ladies, are you feeling the *u-ni-teee*?"

"Yes!" roared the crowd.

"Lords and ladies! Are you feeling *reconciiiiled*?"

"Yes!"

"Den beg yuh a scotch up in the dry stands, nuh."

The spotlights swung over the VIP section, and the crowd roared again. People in the stands laughed and waved. Some got up and beckoned, others pretended to offer up their seats.

"Ahh, that's more like it! Unity and reconciliation fuh trut'. Yuh can't just talk the talk, you know. Yuh got to mean it! *Riiiight.* Anyhow. Our next performer . . ."

The next performer was none other than Usher. To Isilda's surprise, before beginning his set, he took up Demme's call.

"Our brother is right!" he called. "Unity is action, not just words! Barbados, help your brothers and sisters! If we are all one, no rain should divide us!"

This got a loud cheer, and a significant number of umbrellas turned toward the back to see the reaction in the VIP stands.

The next act made the same plea, and so did the next two after that.

"Dem mekkin' sport," Isilda muttered. "Not after people skin cuffins to get in the VIP section. Dem must be just looking for applause."

"Hmm. Watch and see if they going do it for true," said a woman next to her.

By now several clusters of people had dashed away their umbrellas and were prancing about in the rain. There was movement in the stands, too, with those seated around the waterlogged edges converging toward the covered center seats.

Demme Maxwell returned to the stage. "Party people!" he called. "I like how you moving now. This looking more like unitation to me! Lords and ladies, I see you loving up!"

Again the lights were turned up on the VIP stands, the perimeter of which had now been invaded by people from the wetter stands. Some of the prime VIP seats had been abandoned, and as many people seemed to be trying to leave as trying to get in.

"Rain dancers! I see you loving up!"

"*Woooo!*"

The spotlights danced over the thinning crowd on the grounds. The restlessness on the edges seemed to be permeating the core, with much milling and movement. The rain, which had tapered somewhat, ebbed and gusted with the breeze.

"But listen! Some o' wunna enjoying this rain too much, yuh. Some o' wunna like yuh jooking fuh unity in truth!"

The crowd laughed. The DJ started up the hook to "Jook Fuh Unity," prompting an eruption of cheers. Some of those who had been dancing to nothing but the rum swishing in their eardrums started to bounce in unison like peas on a sifting tray.

"Jook-jook . . . fuh unity! Jook-jook . . . fuh unity! Jook-jook . . ."

The crowd began to ebb and gust like the rain. In the distance, Isilda could make out a swirl of activity near the front. The swirl came closer and gradually uncoiled into a conga line, a mass of what seemed like hundreds of wet, drunk, laughing, bellowing spectators of all ages and states of undress.

"Jook-jook . . . fuh unity! Jook-jook . . . fuh unity!"

Hands on hips and shoulders and thighs, with no apparent leader, the line jumbled along in a wide circle around the grounds.

"Jook-jook—"

Suddenly a sheet of lightning lit up the sky, followed by a clatter of thunder. The stadium lights flickered. Many in the crowd screamed and darted for shelter. Those close to the entrance of the stands started shoving through the gates. Isilda could see figures climbing over the railing, directly into the VIP section.

"Party pe—"

Another lightning jab, another thunderclap. The stadium lights dimmed with a loud hum, and the sound system buzzed to silence. The stage lights failed. Then the stadium lights. The conga line broke formation and began to push and jam through every gateway.

Somehow Isilda managed to climb over the bar counter just as the surge of people threatened to pin her against it. She watched, along with the others sheltering inside, as people bustled about, some moving calmly to shelter, some climbing onto the stage, many pushing to leave the stands, throngs shoving to get into them. In the dusk and dampness, it was hard to make out what was what and who was who. The stands were a frenzy, the jostling punctured here and there by a cry or a scream. Droves of people—mostly men, as far as she could tell—were climbing into the VIP section, provoking screams and shouts.

Then the streetlights over the stadium wall went dark, and Isilda decided enough was enough. Looking around the sodden back lot, she spotted a small opening in the cinder-block wall behind the bar, near the service trucks. Some people had already made it to their cars in the VIP lot just outside the wall, and the light from their headlights was streaming through the gap. Grasping her beer bottle for protection, she wove through the crowd clustered behind the bar, climbed over the counter on the other side, and made her way along the lit path.

She was already through the gap when a tremendous whoosh like a tidal wave caused her to jump and twist backward in midair. The bottle went flying, and she landed on her back on the bonnet of an empty car. She scrambled upright, just in time to see the VIP stand cave in. Blistering screams pealed out over the wave, a storm of shouts and creaks and rumbles more deafening than the thunder above. The stand caved, and people above began to slide down, down, down, and those on the grounds to scatter, scatter, scatter like rice grains through an hourglass.

"Lord have mercy!" somebody screamed.

Isilda felt her ears fill up hot. She blacked out.

Chapter 24

She came to with her head rolling in somebody's lap.

"Roger, she waking up," a voice above her called.

"Good," said another voice. "You all right, love? You need a doctor?"

Isilda sat up, aided by an arm tinkling with bracelets. She was riding in the back seat of a car, and a woman was rubbing her back. A man was driving.

"What happen?"

"Stadium collapse is all I know," the woman said. Her perfume smelled of chocolate and oranges. "You all right? When we reach the car, we see you catspraddle out on the bonnet, pass out. Couldn't leave you there in that madness."

"Clare, like the power gone for true," the man driving said. "See that? Not a light ain't burning on the highway."

Isilda shaded her eyes from the high beams of an oncoming car. It passed, and the highway on the opposite side receded into darkness. Looking through the rear window, she saw a line of vehicles leading away from a jumble of headlights against the stadium's hulking silhouette.

"Lord have mercy, Lord have mercy," Clare was saying. An ambulance wailed past.

Roger turned up the radio. Isilda tried to listen through ringing ears: . . . *massive collapse* . . . *Reconciliation Day festivities* . . . *performers unharmed* . . . *stampede* . . . *emergency* . . . *assess the damage* . . . *casualties* . . .

She fumbled for her phone to call Lamar. The call would not go through. Home, either.

"Is a good thing I follow my mind and left up there," Clare said. "Imagine if we had stay to hear Beres Hammond, eh, Roger? When I see that rain let up, a mind just tell me, 'Clare, come and go down the road.'"

"Is the lightning that had people," Isilda said.

"It ain't the lightning at all," said Roger, rubbing his brow in the light of a speeding fire truck. "Is that fool Demme Maxwell encouraging people in lawlessness. How you expect all them people to fit in one stand? Rain coming down and instead of he pacify the crowd, he talking bare nonsense."

"Man tell the people to reconcile . . ."

"Uh-huh. Now let them reconcile in the hospital."

"All right, relax," Clare said. "Now ain't the time for that talk." She turned to Isilda. "Darling, you had anybody up in the stands?"

"No," replied Isilda at first, thinking of Ma and Nekisha safely at home.

Then she remembered.

∼

Barbados, unplugged, was hushed and blank.

Beyond the flickering bedlam of the stadium, now ringed with emergency vehicles, a mist unfurled over the night. It spread evenly over the searing quiet of the flatness, under the feathers of the chickens sleeping in the pear trees, into the sores of the unhoused sleeping on the steps of the Treasury Building. It unfurled and settled in, a billow of moisture leavening the earth and diluting the stars, drowsy on its own lullaby.

At the hospitals, it was rankled by a concentration of panic, premonitions running amok in the void of information. People surged through the wards shouting out names, pleading with staff, pressing into action any advantage they could lay claim to. The mist enveloped the walls and bogged the teeming hallways, filling hearts and lungs already worn with exhaustion.

The night, inky black, the blackest in generations, would offer no rest. The mist keened low, heaving its lullaby, yet waves of unease continued to radiate across the land. The night troubled the mist with its tremors, rippling out from each radio report, igniting worry house to house, district to district.

Total blackout islandwide . . .

Stadium stand collapsed, three dead, dozens wounded . . .

Events appear unrelated . . .

Through rain-streaked windows, lamplit curtains crinkling the shadows inside, shards of fear pierced the mist. What must the mist have made of those spaces between the blankness, which stirred and pierced the dark like a high-frequency scream?

With the electric wires sagging dormant on their poles, the mist gave over to the tingle of the night's unfiltered current. It swirled around the coroner's van, bearing away three lifeless bodies, pronounced dead as soon as the planks, concrete, and gnarled wrought iron could be raised from their sunken chests.

~

The mist absorbed the cigarette smoke curling from the lips of Clive Toppin, alone on his master bedroom balcony that jutted over the Atlantic. It infiltrated the hairs in his ear as he stood in boxers and slippers, an arm folded across his chest, pondering the sense of it all.

Through the doorway behind him, Aggie was pacing at the foot of the bed, checking the phones by the minute, and hugging to her chest one pajamaed, perplexed twin and then another. There was no one to call, nothing to do. No point going back: according to the radio, the roads to the stadium were closed to all but outgoing traffic. Clive inhaled smoke and mist together. He dared not peer into the clouds forming in his mind, around Lisette, around Hubert and Nancy. Around Sabre. Between the crashes of unseen waves below the balcony, he tuned in to the radio and cast his lot with daylight.

But daylight was far away. Hour upon hushed hour, the mist continued to roam, grazing its underbelly on the nerves of the haunted sleepless.

Then, slowly, softly, the mist condensed into a soft rain, as though gathering its defenses against the prickly undercurrents of the night. There was no more wind to tease it into playful formations on the roadside grass. There was no play in the atmosphere at all. Like a chastened child, the mist hung its head and cried.

$\sim$

For some, half-awake in the stillness, unaware of all that had happened, having spent the day and night withdrawn from the world, the rain sounded as sweet as a chorus of wind chimes.

Ian opened his eyes to the sound, delicious and unfamiliar through his slightly open window. Above his bed, the pastiche of well-dressed and undressed men printed out from Pinterest did not twinkle as it sometimes did by the streetlight, and hazily he surmised that it must be because of the sheer red cloth he had draped over the bedside lamp sometime yesterday. But that light was out, which meant it must have either burned out or been switched off, and he could not remember switching off his bedside lamp, let alone the streetlight.

He could not remember much. The rain was like a balm for his swimming head. Lying on his side under the sheet, he turned his ear to the window, savoring the patter of drops on leather outside. It was a cozy sound, and it felt of a piece with the coziness he came to find himself wrapped in: the soft breath on his scalp, the elbow crooked under his armpit, the fingers interlaced with his in the hollow under his chin, and the chubby, languid penis dripping warm against the back of his thigh.

He took a few deep yet unobtrusive breaths under the patter. Even from his haze, he was careful not to upset the balance of things. An alarm in his head went off dimly, a half-hearted suggestion that he come to his senses.

A voice inside him answered: *I'm here.*

∿

After the rain, as the thinning mist resettled into the contours of the land, and just before the first stirrings of daybreak, there was a low, loud boom on an isolated plain. The only witnesses were the mist, four blackbelly sheep, and an idle backhoe; and mist, sheep, and backhoe alike were atomized as the earth suddenly burst into the sky and drained back into itself. Mud, rock, flesh, and metal flew high and then disappeared down a deep, gaping crater, wider at the bottom than at the top.

The people in the nearest houses, a good quarter mile away, felt the walls shake. Some peered outside, expecting to see a lightning display or a convoy of heavy-duty vehicles, maybe on their way to restore power or fix the stadium. A few people came outside and looked around, but the darkness held no clues, only a quiet so convincing as to make some wonder whether they had heard anything after all.

But the mist became engorged with dust and heat as a cloud swelled out from the crater, blanketing the area in a wave of grey. It hung thickly over the crater for a long time before drifting off, foul and inert, like carrion in a flood.

How strange a land this is, thought the mist, as it took its leave.

No mountains. Only gullies. Only craters.

How porous. How treacherously coralline.

Chapter 25

Next morning, there was one hole in the old stadium and another hole in the ground.

People moved through the dove-grey atmosphere as if through a museum diorama. Cars coasted across unlit intersections to unlit gas stations, where cardboard CASH ONLY signs gave false hope of service. Commuter vans rumbled along in silence. On the radio, the list of business closings stretched over minutes. Traffic jammed the airport and the private runway behind it.

By evening, when the newspapers reappeared, they were saying this:

> Three people were killed and scores injured when an overcrowded stand collapsed at the National Stadium during the Reconciliation Day festivities last night.

> Among the casualties were Timothy Bostic of Hopefield, St. Philip; Justice Hubert DaCosta of Port Pristine, St. Thomas; and Stacey-Ann Neuls of Kingston, Jamaica.

> Witnesses say heavy rains marred the all-star event, causing concertgoers to seek shelter in the covered stand.

> None of the performers were harmed.

And this:

The worst power outage to affect Barbados in the last decade has left the power company still searching for answers.

The 15-hour breakdown, which has affected most operations in Barbados, began last night around 10:10 p.m., and full power was not restored until 1:10 p.m. today.

The power company's chief press officer stated that the problem originated with a monkey on a 24,000-volt line, causing a fault to occur between the central station and a substation.

The primate was electrocuted.

And this:

A massive underground cave has been discovered in Wakeplaine, St. George.

The cave, which measures almost 70 metres deep and over 120 metres wide, was exposed when the ground above it caved in during last night's storm. No injuries have been reported.

The cave does not appear on official geological surveys for the area. However, residents of surrounding districts claim to have been aware of its existence.

A source from the Ministry of Housing has confirmed that the undeveloped tract was being prepared as a resettlement site for residents displaced by the new stadium complex planned for Yearwoods, St. Michael, in the early part of next year.

The exact cause of the collapse is unknown.

～

Delphine stood at the edge of the gaping pit, the yellow police tape fluttering in the breeze, flitting droplets of dirty rainwater onto her leggings. She looked across the empty field in the early light, turning her face to let the wind carry off her tears. She could not decide whether to offer up a prayer or a curse. With a deep, quivering breath, she looked again to make sure her imagination was not playing tricks.

The roof of the cave was less than two feet thick.

She could see part of the claw of the backhoe sticking out of the rubble. With the tip of her sneaker, she kicked a clump of dirt up over the edge and into the cavern.

"Looka what we come to, my God. Scruples and decency gone clear."

"It's a good thing this got exposed in time."

"Look how deep the hole is. Look how slight . . ." Delphine's voice gave way. "I am seventy-two years old next month. To live a whole life, just to get snuff out so . . . ?"

"Don't say that. You're all right. You're safe."

"Damn right I goin' be safe. We comin' for them hard now," said Delphine, wiping fresh tears. "We goin' keep so much blessed-well noise 'bout here we goin' wake Bussa self."

"That's the spirit."

"How in hell the surveyors miss a cave that size? How Town and Country didn't know about it, when so much people talk about going caving down in there years gone by? How it manage to get wipe off the map?"

"You're asking answers. I had to do some real digging to find the original land surveys. But it was just like you said. The cave was recorded until about fourteen years ago. Then once Gibbons bought the plot from the government and started selling it off, the record got changed."

"You see that? Looka, by the time we done wid dem, dem ain't goin' dare breathe 'pon we, far less try an' get we move off we land. Unless dey payin' we some warm dollars."

"It's only fair. The other side getting more than their due."

"That lawyer sitting on he hands. But we goin' got he 'pon overtime from today."

"That's right. And you know you can count on the group, right? Whatever you need, we are ready to provide."

Delphine's face relaxed. Her caramel cheeks dimpled, and she reached over and squeezed Nancy's shoulder.

"But look at you. Mourning your dear departed Hubert and still taking on other people troubles."

Nancy lowered her gaze. She looked as though she might cry.

Delphine put her arms around her. "Let it out, girl," she said. "I know it ain't easy."

She stroked Nancy's back, grateful that it was barely dawn and that they were here alone, in an isolated place. Women of Nancy DaCosta's stature rarely got to be private citizens in Barbados. There was always an audience to perform for, protocol to observe, or, in Nancy's case, talk to rise above with a practiced uptilt of the chin.

Even the way she lost Hubert had been so public. Delphine thought of the days ahead for Nancy, of the formal letters of condolence and the courtesy calls from dignitaries, and eventually, the closed-casket funeral, the order of service already prescribed by government edict regarding state burials. She hoped that Nancy would be able to find a kernel of intimacy amid the officialdom, that her friend knew she was allowed to be, under the froth, simply a person in grief.

"It isn't easy," said Nancy. "He made sure of that. Coming and going."

Delphine nodded. "We know Hubert had his ways," she said gently. "God rest his soul."

"Mmm. I've been reflecting. On his life, on his ways . . ." Nancy withdrew from Delphine's embrace. She retrieved a tissue from her pocket and stared at it for a moment. "And you know what I think, Delphine?" She lingered deliberatively on each word, as though reading a text printed on the fuzzy tissue. "I think the best way to honor my complicated husband is to take complicated things and make them simple."

"Wuh simple in this country nowadays?" Delphine replied. "Can't even count on basic decency nor respect for life."

"It's true," said Nancy. "And no matter how much you try to do, as an individual or in a group, life imposes limits on you."

"Yes."

"But, you know, in time, you learn yourself," she added quietly.

Delphine watched her lift the tissue toward her face, then replace it in her pocket, as though she had changed her mind. Nothing to wipe on a face already dry.

"You learn yourself," Nancy repeated. "And you find out you can do more than perhaps you thought possible. I am sure Hubert would appreciate that."

She dislodged a stone with her shoe. It rolled to the edge of the precipice and fell in, ricocheting off the claw of the backhoe.

Chapter 26

"Yoo-hoo! Miss Devonish!"

"Look me here, suffering!"

Delphine let herself in and headed to the back bedroom, passing the kitchen where Nekisha was grating a hill of carrot. The scent of nag champa drifted from Isilda's bedroom. When Delphine reached the door, she found Isilda hunching cross-legged on a mattress on the floor, her notebook open at her side and a large mixing bowl between her thighs. Jenny, the massage therapist that Delphine had sent over to work on Isilda's leftover back pain from the stadium incident, was crouched behind Isilda, pressing her bent knees into the small of Isilda's back. Lamar was sitting in a chair opposite his mother, surrounded by a sea of bottles and bowls and candles and incense sticks.

"Wait, wuh going on here?"

"Miss Delphine, please to tell Miss Devonish to stop working when I am trying to give a massage," Jenny said. "The treatment can't work if she working, too."

"You all right." Isilda winced over her shoulder. "You mekkin' you money but ain't want me make mines." She consulted her notebook. "Almond," she said, reaching out to Lamar. He handed her the bottle of almond essence.

"Sildy, you worse than that madwoman you does work for," Delphine said. "You mean you can't put down the mixing even for an hour?"

"And who goin' fill these orders?"

Delphine reached down for Isilda's notebook. "You and this thing," she said. "Always scribbling like a schoolgirl. You must have enough recipes in here to publish a book."

"Giving me ideas, woman. Keep talking."

"She should go on one of them cooking shows," said Jenny. "The turnovers taste real good in truth. Not like diabetic at all."

"Ah, girl, that is the secret formula," Isilda piped up, apparently forgetting to wince this time as Jenny walked her knees up along the sides of her spine. "Next cake I come up with I goin' name after you. Hibiscus."

"A Jenny-cake?" Jenny giggled.

Lamar passed the hibiscus essence. "So wait, what 'bout me? I ain't deserve one, too?" He winked at Jenny. "No Lamar-tart?"

"If you behave." Isilda shook the bottle into the bowl and stirred. "Don't mind him, hear, Jenny? He only playing sweet because you here."

"Jenny," said Lamar, "they got a time to behave and a time to misbehave. You got to know which is which."

"Quite right, darling," replied Delphine, and she and Lamar smiled at each other.

~

The massage eventually sent Isilda into a deep and much-needed sleep. Delphine paid Jenny and saw her out, then went and joined Lamar on the porch. She found him sitting astride the railing with one leg dangling on the gully side, smoking a spliff.

"Getting bold now, nuh," she muttered, jabbing a finger into his cheek. "Right under your mother nose. Mine and all."

Lamar exhaled toward the gully. His face spread into a smile.

"You don't feel I entitled to this here, Miss D?"

Their eyes locked like jigsaw pieces. She came and perched on the railing, facing him.

"They should name this gully after you," she said.

"'Cause it bushy and I does smoke bush?"

She laughed.

"'Cause you save us to see it little longer," she replied. "You save everybody about here."

The mango and breadfruit trees eavesdropped in the stillness. An overripe breadfruit lay split open on the ground a few yards off, flies circling its creamy pulp. The faint sounds of Isilda's snoring punctuated the silence.

"How much longer?" Lamar asked.

"Don't know. Not long enough, tell you that," Delphine whispered.

"Well, just tell me wuh we gotta do," Lamar murmured. "Who or what else need straightening out."

"It ain't 'bout that no more," Delphine said. "We gotta change tactics."

"Like how?"

"Shame them. Petition. Protest. Organize. Call names. Get in the news," she said. "Them greedy devils nearly send all o' we to the beyond. The ball in we court now. We got to knock it hard."

"Hard," Lamar repeated, nodding. "I know you is the one for that."

"Not me alone," Delphine smiled. "I need my deputy."

Lamar chuckled. "You mean your enforcer," he said.

She gave his shoulder a gentle slap. "Don't tell me what I mean, boy," she said. "My tongue ain't tied. Yours, neither. It's time for you to use it. Put all that passion and creativity to good use. Let the world see wuh kinda tacticians we does produce in the gully."

Lamar took a long drag on the spliff. "I hear you, but . . . upfront ain't my style," he said. "You know I is a man of undercover action."

"Action?" she replied. "What you think this is? You feel the story done once you buss open the ground? Son, it now start. Look the extremes they does got we resorting to. A *bomb*?" Delphine's voice cracked again, even in a whisper. "A bomb to make them put value to a human life? A bomb to force a conversation?"

"Serve them right," Lamar drawled. "Mess with we, you get wuh coming to you."

"Don't mind them. It's *we* that going for what we deserve," she replied. "Come on *Open Mic* with me. Lewwe represent the district and make we demands now that people paying attention."

"The radio?"

They looked at each other again.

"You's an activist now, you know," she told him. "Might as well make it official. I goin' arrange it for next week. We gotta strike while the iron hot."

Lamar scrunched his face. Somewhere inside the house, the floorboards creaked and Nekisha's laughter dimpled the air. He put out his spliff and tossed it away.

Delphine grinned. "Ah, looka the tactician," she teased softly. "Rough and tough but always two steps ahead. Don't care what nobody say. You got the makings."

He gazed at the split breadfruit for a time, his mind floating.

"You don't feel I too pretty for radio, though, Miss D?" he deadpanned.

She knew him too well. The tears welled up in her for the second time that day.

"Come and find out for yourself," she whispered.

Chapter 27

"Hurricane season," Keith said.

The words ganged up in the air, surrounded Sabre like interrogators. Their edges itched her skull. "You mean me."

Keith's hand appeared in her lap.

"Just saying it's hurricane season," he repeated.

His hand felt heavy on hers. She went clammy.

"Look at me," Keith said.

How.

They were sitting in the car outside Vonda and Eric's house, waiting out a hammering rain. It was as if the clouds were spitting. Hacking, aiming, firing their cloud spit at her.

Look at him? She couldn't look at anyone. Not even herself.

Herself least of all.

Three people were dead because of her. Three. Uncle Clive's best friend, the chief justice of Barbados, dead. She couldn't remember ever having seen her uncle cry. But at the funeral, he hadn't been able to stop. It had been live streamed. Sabre couldn't bring herself to go, and besides, her presence would have been an unwelcome distraction. But on the live stream she could see her aunt and uncle in the second row, Auntie Aggie in her dark glasses, their arms locked, heads leaning against each other. The judge's widow in front, veiled and stoic, eyes downcast. Beside her, the judge's dazed children and grandchildren, mouthing along to their hymn sheets. Everybody enduring what would never have occurred . . . but for her.

Three people, dead, because of her. Eric could have been number four. Instead, by mercy, he was home from hospital with two cracked ribs. Him, she would have to look at today.

Barbados doesn't get hurricanes. The only disaster this season was her.

Hurricane Sabre, natural disaster.

She had signed the sympathy statement from the union without reading it. Then she had thrown her phone down a storm drain. Stopped reading the paper. She was a fugitive again, like in the old darkroom days. If only she had never come up from the underground at all.

This time, she would bury herself even deeper. Somewhere in this land of caves, there had to be a hole dark enough and deep enough to contain her.

"Ready?" Keith said.

She refused his umbrella when they got out of the car. She needed to feel the cloud spit. Keith put his arm around her shoulders while they waited at the door.

She was staring at the ground when Vonda answered, barefoot, chipped polish on her chubby toes. Vonda hugged Keith without speaking.

Then the feet pointed to Sabre. She raised her eyes to Vonda's smiling face.

"You," said Vonda, folding her in.

Sabre squeezed back. "How's Eric?" she asked tremulously.

"In there, miserable as ever," replied Vonda. "Taking this patient thing too far. Come."

It had been months since she had last been inside this house. A bygone era of precarnage innocence. The house seemed peaceful now, more peaceful than the feverish incubator of revolution that she remembered.

As they approached the bedroom, she could hear the TV and Eric's voice, sounding full strength. He was in bed, talking on the phone. His face and body looked puffy in his pajamas. He waved as they entered, and when he lifted his arm, he cringed. There was a thick, tight bandage around his midsection.

Then she noticed his foot sticking out from the sheet. Also heavily bandaged.

"He hurt his foot, too?" she whispered to Vonda.

"Girl," Vonda says, "you didn't hear? Lost a toe. Lucky he didn't lose the whole foot. He goin' be in them bandages till kingdom come. Then eight weeks of physiotherapy, at least, to learn to walk again."

Sabre felt her ribs collapse. It was too much. She turned as calmly as she could and withdrew from the room. Her lungs were wrung into a knot by the time she reached the corridor. She doubled over, heaving, bawling herself dry.

"Sabre?"

Vonda came up from behind.

Sabre grabbed hold of her. "I'm so sorry. I'm so sorry!" she choked out.

"Say . . ."

"I'm a murderer! A . . . a mutilator! This is all my fault. I'm so sorry, Vonda . . . You were right, I should have listened to you all along. Look what happened! I've messed up everything! Please, please forgive me!"

She was pouring from every part of her head now, tears and snot and dribble. In the chaos of the deluge, she thought she felt Vonda stiffen. Before she could catch herself, she wiped her running nose on Vonda's sleeve.

Vonda shook her off. "Incredible," she said, disgusted.

"I know! I can't do anything right! I'm a pathetic failure!"

"*I, I, I, I* . . . Even now."

Vonda grabbed her by the hand and dragged her into the living room. She yanked her over to the glass doors on the opposite side, where the rain was pummeling the patio furniture. She turned Sabre to face her, nostrils flared like a bull ready to charge.

"You're not a pathetic failure," she said. "You're a pathetic narcissist."

"Vonda, please . . ." Sabre's ears began to clog. She staggered against the wall.

"Standing in *my* house, crying for *your*self, when *my* husband is in there trying to press on with broken ribs and a hobbled foot. I would slap you so hard right now if I wasn't positive it would only make you feel like the martyr here."

"What? No! I—"

"*I* again? Sabre, where does this stop? You realize people have literally lost limbs following you? Lost jobs, lost family? People are in jail, they're in hospital, the women you promised to rescue all them months ago, still waiting. But all you can focus on is how *sorry* you are. Do you realize? . . . I been watching you for a long time. And you know something? I have to wonder what it is you really came down here for. Because everywhere you go in this country it's a trail of destruction. And all you know how to do is feel *sorry*. Mostly for yourself . . .

"Well, listen to me, and listen good. Be all the sorry you want— your sorry can't do fuck all for anybody else. OK? You want forgiveness? Go and see the reverend. You come here for Eric, wipe that snot on your own fucking sleeve and pull your shit together. You want to make yourself useful? Then take your hand out your panties and get on with something.

"And if you can't do that, then go back where the rasshole you come from, 'cause we don't need your sorry-sorry here."

~

Sabre flew out through Vonda's front door with her face sopping wet. Keith caught up to her just before she could charge through the gates and into the street.

He asked no questions. In silence they got into the car and drove away. At the roundabout toward Keith's house, a command dislodged itself from her chest, surprising them both.

"The cemetery. Thimblestone."

Keith immediately exited the roundabout and headed for the cemetery. When they arrived, she asked to be left alone. She felt his gaze follow her as she started along the footpath, then heard his car pull off.

She had gone back where the rasshole she had come from.

Her feet did not find their way. The cortège had not imprinted onto their muscle memory. They mushed from grave to grave, many of which were marked with nothing but a hand-stenciled wooden cross, until finally she was able to make out the etching of her father's name on a granite headstone under a tree: Ronald Emerson Cumberbatch.

She sat down on the wet gravestone and slid straight off into the mud. The shock forced a hoarse cry-laugh out of her. She retrieved herself and sat again, bearing down with her bottom. The damp soaked through the thin cotton of her skirt.

Look at her. Out here crying in the rain like a '90s R&B singer. Who was it serving? Vonda was right. She pressed a finger to her nose and tried to clear one nostril, then the other.

All right. Wet, snotty, dramatic as hell, heading for a yeast infection. Now what?

She waited, sniffling, for some ancestral wisdom to gurgle up from the tomb.

Minutes passed. An hour. The rain began to ease, her bodily fluids to subside.

Now, what?

"Favorite girl."

Sabre turned around. There was Katya, standing like an apparition one grave over, gazing at her from beneath a large umbrella. She wore a transparent slicker printed with pale pink tulips. On her feet were bronze-colored rubber booties.

"Katya?"

Katya reached into her tote and produced another umbrella. "I brought for you," she said, her voice subdued. "Barbados rain, we enjoy. But too much is for health not so good."

She held the umbrella out to Sabre gingerly, like a tamer offering a carrot to a hippo. Sabre felt feral in her veins. She tried not to cry again, as Katya approached and gently sat down.

"Did Keith call you?" Sabre asked, after a time.

Katya shrugged. "We call each other."

"What does that mean?"

"Just . . . precaution, until you get a new phone. To stay connected."

Keith and Katya, connected. Joining forces to save her from her own untetheredness. How long had that been going on? Her nostrils began to reclog.

"Why don't I ever know what I'm doing, Katya? Why am I such a fuckup?"

Katya put an arm around her.

"You are not fuckup, darling. You are a runner. You run, the world chases you. You hide, I find you. Just like now. But you can stop running, Sabre, whenever you like. You can let yourself be found."

"Don't get all Russian on me now. My brain can't handle it."

Katya rested Sabre's head against her shoulder and kissed her scalp.

"It is not brain, it is instinct," said Katya. "It is fear. Like rabbit. But the running takes energy, *dorogaya*. So much energy. Think all you could do with the energy you save."

Sabre took a deep sigh, inhaling the mix of Katya's perfume with graveyard earthiness.

Katya said, "He got a good spot, your father. Under tree. The stone is right temperature. He was very much loved."

Sabre's pupils dilated.

"I want to do good, Katya. I want to use my energy right."

"Do you want to hear a good news?" Katya asked. "I don't want to upset you."

"Is it Topsheet-related?"

"Yes."

"What, are they offering more money?"

"Sabre. The most money. It's obsane." Katya's voice was choked with excitement. "And still we can negotiate. If you like, of course."

"Negotiate the money, or negotiate the concept?"

"Whatever you like," Katya replied. "They are just so delighted with you. With—with what you can do."

Sabre caught the caution in the rephrasing. She gazed down at the umbrella in Katya's lap. Blank minutes slipped by.

"You know what? Let's do it."

She felt Katya's bosom leap.

"Are you serious, my beloved?"

"Yeah." Sabre sat up, bracing her hands behind her. "Fuck yeah. Let's use this. Use them while they use us. There's stuff we can do. I just need to figure out what. And how."

But Katya was already pulling out her phone.

"Fuck yes, my Sabre," she sang, her nails attacking the screen. "Fuck yes, yes, yes, fuck yes."

~

Gourmet Grotto is closed, so she lets herself in through the mausoleum.

Canned goods, aisle 9. She finds the mackerel at the far end, opens the can at the bottom of the stack, and climbs in.

"Bumble-dolphin, you're early."

"Just taking a nap. I need to think."

"Can't fault you. You took the long way."

"Can I fault you? They say it's your blood in me."

"My blood had more fun. They used to say I had a little—"

"Blood in your rumstream. I remember. Even Mom used to laugh at that one."

"And now look me here, plugging a hole. So much holes 'bout here to plug. Holes in the stadium, holes in the gully, holes in the ground, holes in the soul. Until you end up in a hole of your own."

"Yep. Skinless and boneless, the way they like their mackerel at Gourmet Grotto."

"Bunny-bear, you got skin. Bone, too. A whole spine. Use them, hear? Don't mind me. Take your little rest, and then go out and plug all that want plugging in this place."

Chapter 28

Grantley Adams International Airport was the usual marsh of ambivalence it became whenever a large jet was due to take off. Farewell parties dragging toward check-in seemed heavier than their bags. With each step toward the departure gate, people's back feet seemed to grow more leaden. A school of plastic flying fish, suspended from the terminal ceiling, far from lifting spirits, was a jeer to those whose misfortune it was to be leaving, a foretaste of the synthetic world to which they would soon return.

The Toppin crew and company approached the departure gates.

Sabre looked at the flying fish above her head. Its splayed wings glinted in the fluorescent light.

She had barely tasted the famous national dish in her ten months here. Almost as soon as she had arrived, it had been explained to her, almost apologetically, how flying fish had grown scarce from overfishing and changes in their migratory patterns. They had wised up and escaped to the waters of other islands, where they could survive among those who did not know to eat them. What had been a Bajan staple when she was growing up was now a delicacy, accessible only to people willing to pay ten times the old price, to patrons of five-star restaurants on the west and south coasts, and of course year-round to customers of Gourmet Grotto.

Sabre had barely had any, and she wondered when she would next get the chance. She wondered when she would see this airport again, this place she had scarcely given thought to, yet which now seemed of such outsized importance, marking off the beginnings and endings of the stages of her life like a saw slicing lumber.

Depart. Arrive. Depart. Life severed up into planks, the details ground into sawdust to be scattered by the wind. How ridiculous to think that fish could fly. At least these plastic ones had chains to keep them in the air. No matter what, whenever she next came to this airport, these flying fish would still be flying: iridescent, plastic, chained beyond the reach of those who might otherwise be inclined to eat them. Preserved at their peak, unable to harm or be harmed.

A waste of an existence.

～

Katya came over to Sabre.

"What are you thinking now?" she asked. "I am curious, your ideas."

"She's craving New York," said Aggie, watching the twins play with their phones.

"No, man. Look how she eyeing up the fish. She want a fish cutter," joked Uncle Clive.

"Maybe she is counting her money, eh?" said Katya, patting her handbag. "Eight million dollars, in the bank? She is smart girl in the end. Right, my Sabre?"

"Please make sure they stick to our terms. I'm counting on you, Katya. I've never been more serious about anything in my life."

"Sabre, it's promise. As soon as Aggie and I land in New York, we work on it. Don't worry." She put an arm around Aggie's shoulder. "You have the best on your side. Aggie and Katya. Multinational tag team!"

"That's right," said Aggie emphatically.

～

Aggie liked Katya. With her negotiation prowess and her taste in pocketbooks, it was almost like looking in a mirror. Except that she, Aggie, had it been her job, might have succeeded in discouraging Sabre from sinking so much of the Topsheet money into these outlandish do-gooder projects she was staying behind to set up, egged on by her boyfriend and their band of benevolent dreamers.

A union for independent and at-will workers? A skills training center to help people "navigate the gig economy"? A "Reimagining Barbados" lecture series . . . at the fish market? What next?

Girl hadn't learned a thing. But that was for others to worry about.

Then again, worry for what? Things came and went like holograms in the dark. You could work to the bone, and it could all disappear down a hole.

Just like the land deal, which had been close enough to taste, until it wasn't.

Or Lisette's fancy promotion, whittled down to not even a job.

Or Hubert. Uncouth, vulgar, and missed. Aggie's one foray into calamitous transgression. Watching Clive and Nancy console each other at the funeral, her eyes had moistened behind her dark glasses at the thought of all she had risked.

She looked over her brood, who had come to see her off on her first solo vacation: the twins absorbed in their devices; Lisette leaning on her father's arm, eating one of Isilda's turnovers; Sabre staring into space.

Two distracted, one unemployed, one overeating, one bent on emptying her wallet down a well of ingratitude. Whatever was awaiting Aggie in New York—and she did not know for sure; it took practice, and patience, to read Priscilla—this was the prize she had to come back to. The thought tickled her throat.

~

Lisette caught her mother's cheeks tugging slightly, a bit of mist about her eye. She went over and hugged her.

Before long, they felt Sabre's arms encircling them both.

"Group hug," said Sabre softly.

"Aww," said Lisette, patting the small of Sabre's back with the tip of her phone. "Next time we do one of these, I want Aunt Cil in the huddle."

"That's my plan," said Aggie.

~

The flight was announced. Lisette waved her mother and Katya into the departure lounge. As soon as they were through the doors, she said goodbye to Sabre and hurried toward her car. She had to beat the traffic and gain the highway quickly if she wanted to make it to the beach house before dark.

Every evening at dusk, the monkeys emerged from the coconut grove in packs of six and four, settling around the yards. They commandeered the pool behind the Gibbonses' beach house. They screeched and chased each other over the chipped tile. They swung down the ladder to splash their tails in water turned brownish green with urine and neglect.

The neighbors complained, but there was nothing to be done. The nuisances would not be deterred, not by stone, bullet, or poison. Any injury seemed only to multiply their number.

Damian had once tried to charge a group of them with his car. Some of the monkeys leaped to higher ground. The rest arranged themselves in a tight line along the edge of the pool and faced him down as he screeched to a stop, inches from the water. When Lisette and Damian returned to the beach house a few days later, they found the patio steeped in a horrible stench.

That was why, daylight or dusk, Lisette did not like to go up to the beach house alone. She was afraid. But greater than her fear, gushing over it like a newly tapped reserve geysering from her marrow, was her pride.

Pride at how she had surpassed them all. Lawyer, publisher, equality enforcer, havoc wreaker, whatever.

Pride that she had made it past the monkeys, across the threshold of that rotting mahogany doorway, to a fraying cane settee in the Gibbonses' parlor, where no Black bottom had ever been.

Chapter 29

"Mmm. Not too bad," Ma said flatly, examining the little pastry between her fingers.

"Not too bad?" Isilda put her hands on her hips. "Ma, that's the best rock bun you ever taste. Admit it."

"I mean, it edible. Gimme couple more, let me make up my mind."

Isilda laughed and handed her the tray, taking one for herself.

Ma was the right test taster for these desserts. Isilda needed to reach skeptics like her. Tomorrow evening, she was scheduled to make her debut as a featured presenter at the Diabetes Society, showcasing healthy local alternatives to sugar. According to Theo, who had become her biggest fan, the next stop could be a segment on morning TV.

Isilda had laughed at that, too. Not because it was ridiculous. She laughed because the idea did not scare her.

She knew that she knew what she knew. She had notebooks filled with kitchen experiments. Her list of sources and menu of desserts were growing all the time. Even tomorrow's presentation, which she had practiced a few times in the mirror in full dress, hair, and makeup, had her more excited than anxious.

She had been laughing a lot, lately, for all kinds of reasons. The other day she had let out a good cackle when she heard Sabre Cumberbatch and her people back on the radio. It had been weeks since Sabre had been heard from publicly, so Isilda had listened to the entire *Open Mic* segment out of curiosity, waiting for signs of Sabre's typical foolery.

What she heard instead—a reasonable-sounding Sabre, eagerly sharing airtime with others to describe a promising new set of programs—was so far from her expectations that she had been tickled to tears.

Well, well, well, she'd said to herself. *Look the rough turn smooth, the bandy gone straight.* If she and Sabre were to end up sharing a stage one day—say, Isilda giving a class at this skills training center Sabre had mentioned—it would not be the strangest outcome of this obzocky year.

Leaving Ma in the kitchen, she stepped out onto the veranda.

Another Sunday morning with no rain. The seasons were changing.

The last three weeks had been easy, with Mrs. Toppin gone to America. And at least another week before she came back. So much relaxing to look forward to.

The gap was quiet. Most of her neighbors were still either in bed or in church. Who would have guessed the lot of them had nearly been driven off this land. Had the politicians had their way, the only residents left in the district would have been the monkeys in the gully. They had already come and gone for the morning, leaving no trace. Where did they disappear to when they weren't raiding the trees? One thing for sure: they would never starve.

The brush with disaster had shifted the mood in the district. Lamar and the boys—well, they were mostly still wastrels. But she could not deny that something in her son had changed. In the weeks following the exposure of the cave that had almost become their grave, he and the others had turned civic-minded.

At the top of the gap, near Delphine's house, they had cleared some bush and created a minipark, with picnic tables and a display of large boulders retrieved from the gully and painted with the likenesses of national heroes. They had posted videos about it on their phones and were getting a lot of likes. When a reporter came to interview the residents, Isilda had been surprised to see her camera-shy son standing beside Delphine as she took the stadium planners to task for trying to mow down poor people just doing their best to live. The way things had unfolded since Reconciliation Day, it was hard to see how government would dare lay a glove on them now.

At the bottom of the gap, across from Isilda's house, the boys had cleared the bush and hung a swing from the breadfruit tree. Although Lamar had not said it outright, Isilda knew—or chose to believe—that he had done this for Nekisha. Evenings and weekends now, the area was swarmed with children, climbing and swinging and running the length of the gap when the ice cream van pulled up. Little did they know the extra exercise was good for them.

At this hour, though, the swing sat empty. Isilda swallowed the last of her rock bun, mild with guava preserve. She came down from the veranda and crossed the road. She went up to the swing and examined it closely, testing the strength and the knotting of the vinyl ropes. Then she sat down on the seat.

She backed up and pushed off from her toes. The rope creaked as she swung forward. Creaked as she swung back. Creaked as she swung higher. She laughed and laughed, climbed and climbed, thinking how pretty her silvery toenails looked, glinting in the sun.

ACKNOWLEDGMENTS

This book exists thanks to the love, generosity, and support of many.

Thank you to my parents, Joan and Kortright Davis, for the love and steady encouragement.

To Jackie Brady, Marchelle Wiley, Susan John, Nsenga Farrell, Bea Dottin, Tanya Greene, Carmelo Larose, Paola Pagliani, Roger Hillas, Ally Sheedy, David Allen, Katrin Park, Rohit Wanchoo, JoAnna Pollonais, Marcus Allison, and Paul Williams for your invaluable feedback on the manuscript.

To my agents, Charlotte Sheedy and Rachel Altemose, for your vision, guidance, and steadfast faith.

To Selena James, for welcoming this book home to Little A.

To my peerless editors, Rob Sandiford and Jason Kirk, for the wordwork and wordplay.

To my Bajan crew—Gwen Brancker, Dawn Williams, Marquita Sugrim, Paul Ashby, Richard Burrowes, Diana Guy, Robert Bascom, Adam Clarke, Roger Griffith, Eleanor Dottin, and Franklin Vaughan—for indulging my fascination with all things Bajan.

To the icons Maryse Condé and the late Paule Marshall, for urging me on.

And to my country, Barbados, for roots that drink deep.

About the Author

Photo © 2023 Joey Rosado

Andie Davis's curiosity about other people's lives inspired her love for languages and her travels around the world. Born in Montserrat, Davis grew up in Barbados before moving with her family to the US, where she attended Howard University and Harvard Law School. She works as a global development advisor focused on sustainability. She lives in New York City.